VICIOUS QUEEN

PRINCES OF DEVIL'S CREEK BOOK TWO

JILLIAN FROST

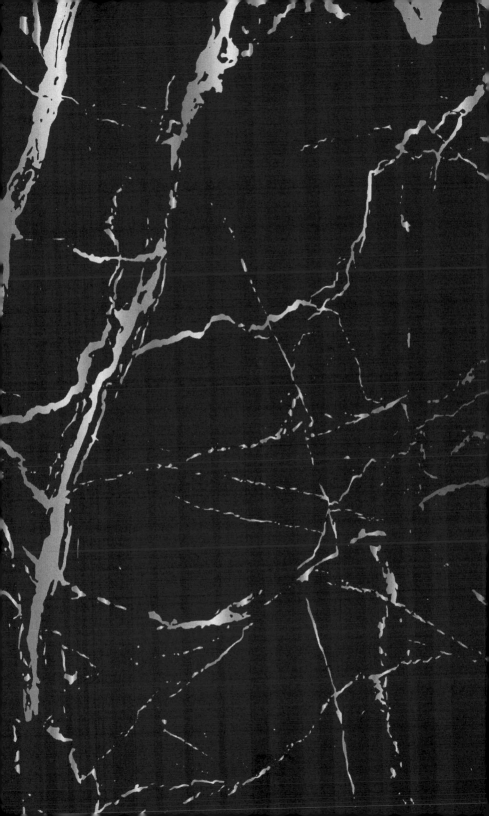

VICIOUS QUEEN

PRINCES OF DEVIL'S CREEK BOOK TWO

JILLIAN FROST

Also by Jillian Frost

Princes of Devil's Creek

Cruel Princes

Vicious Queen

Savage Knights

Battle King

Boardwalk Mafia

Boardwalk Kings

Boardwalk Queen

Boardwalk Reign

Devil's Creek Standalone Novels

The Darkest Prince

Wicked Union

For a complete list of books, visit JillianFrost.com.

R.I.P. to your panties.

VICIOUS QUEEN

PRINCES OF DEVIL'S CREEK BOOK TWO

JILLIAN FROST

Chapter One

ALEX

My stomach twisted into knots as a wave of nausea swept over me. The sickening vinegar smell burned into my nostrils, an unforgettable scent that slowly coaxed me to sleep, filling my lungs with pure agony.

Long lashes brushed my skin, a reminder I needed to stay awake. I would never get back to my handsome princes if I didn't fight the drugs in my system.

What did they do to me?

To my boyfriends?

A man lifted me off the bed and pressed my face to his chest. I tried to scream as he walked us out of the apartment and handed me to another man. Two other men walked beside us, their footsteps loud on the hardwood floor in the hallway. I couldn't see their faces, only heard them breathing deeply.

One man opened a door for us and whispered words in a foreign language. Then we descended a staircase, my captor bouncing me in his arms with each step. I tried to move, and he smashed my face into his shirt, which smelled like cigars and sweat.

I had one last hope.

Luca.

Before we left the penthouse, he was awake and calling out to his brothers, telling them to wake up. His voice sounded pained, frantic. My cruel prince hated me, but he would never let someone take me from him.

So I said a silent prayer.

That was all I could do as the man carried my limp, lifeless body downstairs. It must have been early in the morning, the lights dimmed and the house almost silent except for a few moans and screams of pleasure.

I hadn't gotten a good look at the house before going upstairs to lose my virginity to the men who'd made my life hell for years.

It still didn't seem real.

I told Bastian I thought I was falling in love with him and meant it. My feelings were growing for each of the Salvatore brothers. Even Damian, who was so beautiful but damaged, my heart ached when I looked at him.

My broken billionaire boys were slowly earning places in my heart. Breaking down my carefully constructed walls one by one. I thought about them, hoping they would find me as I fought the sleepiness washing over me. They would burn the world to find me. And after last night, we were closer than ever. We formed an unbreakable bond.

I had faith in them.

I heard a loud bang, followed by a popping sound as my eyes closed. The man stumbled, losing his grip on me, and we crashed to the floor. My back slammed into a hard surface, and blinding pain shot down my spine. My captor attempted to get up, and then I heard another two more pops.

Gunshots.

I covered my ears, my screams louder than the sound of each shot. His lifeless body slumped on top of me, the weight of him crushing my stomach. My entire body trembled, fear shaking through me. I'd never heard the bloodcurdling sound of a gun firing. A few more shots echoed off the high ceiling. The men who kidnapped me dropped to the floor with a thud beside me.

I gasped, clutching my chest, afraid to move. Curled into a ball, I lay on my side and closed my eyes.

This isn't real.

It's a dream.

A nagging pain shot through my skull, the migraine working its way to the back of my head. I needed to stay sharp and focused long enough to get out of here. But I could already see the images flashing through my mind, haunting me with memories.

The closet.

The darkness.

My screams.

"Alex," a familiar voice shouted as he pushed the man's heavy body off me. He lifted me from the floor and cradled me against his chest, his strong arms wrapped around me like a warm blanket. "Little Wellington, wake up."

Sonny Cormac.

Sonny's handsome but tired-looking face came into view. His usually styled blond hair was unruly, sticking up at the ends. Another man I couldn't see stood beside us and tucked my hair behind my ear.

"Is she dead?"

Sonny's fingers brushed my cheek in a soft, soothing motion. "No, Drake, she's breathing."

Drake Battle released a sigh of relief. "How the fuck did they let this happen? She was in the same fucking bed as them."

"I don't know." Sonny walked with me in his arms, moving upstairs to the second floor. "You're the tech genius. You tell me. What did Luca say?"

"Nothing," Drake fired back. "He hit the emergency button on his watch. It only sends out his GPS location.

There's no audio. He's lucky we found them on their way out of the house."

Sonny tightened his grip on me. "Our queen would have been long gone if we hadn't come to The Mansion last night."

"Those were Volkov's men," Drake bit out, irritation in his deep voice. "Risky move coming to a club owned by the Salvatores to steal their girl."

"They're dead now." Sonny shifted me in his arms as we reached the top floor. "Luca was right to bring her here. But if they can find us at The Mansion, it won't be long before they attack us at home."

"She almost got raped in Beacon Bay. If they had succeeded this time..." Drake expelled a breath of air. "I don't even want to think about what they would have done to her."

Sonny grunted in agreement.

My skull pounded like a rock band was playing a concert in my head. It hurt like hell to open my eyes.

As we walked down the hallway, I forced one eye open. Sonny stopped in front of the double doors that led to the penthouse apartment. Drake leaned forward to open the door for him. White smoke billowed out from the room, and they both covered their mouths and coughed.

"Fuck," Sonny groaned, choking on the awful smell. "What the fuck did they drug them with?"

Drake pressed a hand to his chest and coughed. "That taste. The smell. I think it's tear gas."

"Yeah," Sonny confirmed. "But that's not what knocked them out. Look at her. She's unconscious. The tear gas was a precaution if the drugs didn't take effect fast enough."

"Tear gas wouldn't have knocked Luca out."

"Or any of them," Sonny added. "It would have hurt like fucking hell to breathe, made them disoriented, but not enough to disarm them."

4

"Cover your mouth and nose with your shirt," Drake told him as he raised his arm to follow his advice.

"I'm going in there." Sonny lowered me into Drake's arms. "Take Alex. Find some clothes for her to wear."

Drake pressed my cheek against his bare chest. "You don't know what you're dealing with in that room. Be careful. Don't go getting any stupid ideas, Son."

"Marcello is in there," Sonny shot back, his tone dripping with anger. "I'm not letting my best friend die."

Sonny and Marcello were the same age and grew up together. They'd played on the same football team, went to the same schools, and from what I'd observed when I lived in Devil's Creek, inseparable. It was as if Sonny was his brother, his blood.

"Go ahead." Drake reached into his pocket for his cell phone. A second later, the line rang, and a male voice answered. "Cole, it's me. Send a backup team to The Mansion. We're under attack."

"On it," Cole Marshall said.

The line went dead.

Sonny entered the apartment, letting the door slam behind him. I jumped at the sound and rolled over in Drake's arms. He noticed my sudden movement, glancing down at me with surprise illuminating his handsome face. He had short, dark hair and the prettiest hazel eyes.

"Drake," I choked out, my voice hoarse.

He tilted me to the side so I could look up at him with one eye open. The pad of his thumb swept across my cheek as he smiled. "Alex."

"Just tell me they're okay," I whispered.

A worried look pulled at his handsome features, quickly replaced by a cocky smirk. "Don't worry, my queen. You can't kill the Salvatores."

I sure hoped he was right.

Chapter Two

LUCA

I woke up in a different apartment, one that was half the size of the space I shared with my brothers. Marcello slept soundly on the bed beside me, his chest rising and falling as he breathed deeply.

Someone fucking drugged us.

I sat up, confused as fuck, wondering how we ended up in this bedroom. The last I remembered, someone had taken Alex from our bed. I hit the button on my watch, and then nothing but black.

Marcello was naked the last time I saw him and now dressed in tight boxer briefs and a Yankees T-shirt that was too small for him. Someone had dressed me, too. I wore a black shirt with the MIT logo on the front and a pair of boxers that were too big.

Drake Battle's clothes.

He was a graduate of MIT and much bulkier than me. And from the look of it, Sonny shared his clothes with Marcello.

I let out a relieved breath.

The Knights found us.

"Marcello." I grabbed his shoulder, but he didn't move an inch, so I shook him again. "Time to wake up, little brother."

After several attempts, his eyes opened, and he blinked a few times to clear his vision. He glanced at me, then around the room, bewildered. I helped him sit up because he was still weak from the drugs.

"What the fuck happened?" Marcello croaked, his voice raw and scratchy. He rubbed at his tired eyes and yawned. "Where are we?"

"Someone took Alex."

His eyes widened, then he slid off the bed. I had to reach out and clutch his arm, so he didn't fall flat on his ass. He pressed his palm to the mattress to stabilize himself as his eyes met mine.

Rising to his full height, he covered his heart with his hand. "Tell me she's okay."

He knew me well. We wouldn't be here if Alex were missing. I would have dragged his unconscious ass out of this den of iniquity and slapped him around until he woke up.

I nodded. "Sonny and Drake got her."

He expelled a breath of air and sat on the bed beside me. "Where is she?"

"I don't know." I tugged on the borrowed shirt. "We're wearing Drake and Sonny's clothes. So I'm guessing they have her somewhere in this apartment."

"Was she drugged?"

I rolled my shoulders. "Don't know yet. Let's go find her."

"Where are Bash and Damian?"

"They were unconscious the last time I saw them."

Marcello rubbed his hand across his jaw and groaned. "I feel like shit." He touched the side of his head and winced. "I have the worst migraine. What the fuck did they give us?"

"Again, I don't know, Marcello." I pushed him toward the double doors. "The Knights should have some answers."

"We fucked this up," he said as I opened the door. "How did anyone find us at The Mansion?"

"It's clear we can't trust our allies." I shoved him through the entryway and into the dining room. "We need to go through the list of people who know about this place. Sick Damian on whoever played a part in taking Alex. Let him carve them up like a fucking turkey."

"Look who's finally risen from the dead," Sonny joked as he shot up from the leather sectional, dressed in a black suit.

Blond hair styled to perfection, he wore his usual pretty boy smile that stretched the corners of his mouth. He hooked his arm around Marcello and steered him into the living room. "Don't fucking scare me like that again. Fuck, Cello. I thought you were dead when I pulled you out of that bed."

Sonny Cormac and Marcello had been best friends since kindergarten. Maybe even longer than that. They were the same age, shared the same classes in school, and even played football together in high school. Marcello was closer to Sonny than any of us, but he always put his family first.

"Where is Alex?" Marcello bit out before I could ask.

Sonny pointed his finger at the back of the apartment. "She's in my room with Bash and Damian."

I followed his finger. "Is she okay?"

"Did they touch her?" Marcello said through clenched teeth.

He shook his head. "No, we found her before they left The Mansion. She's fine. Tired and probably feels like shit from the drugs and the lingering effects of the tear gas."

Marcello's eyebrows knitted as he glared at his friend. "Tear gas?"

Sonny slid his arm across Marcello's back to hold up his weak body. "Yeah, they hit you guys at all ends. My guess is they injected you with something first. Then threw a couple of flash-bang canisters to slow you down if the drugs didn't hit you right away."

"I'm glad they didn't. Alex wouldn't be here if I didn't wake up."

Marcello squeezed my shoulder. His lips parted as if he wanted to say something, but he turned his head away. He was thankful but too fucking proud to say it aloud.

"Did you secure the perimeter?" I scanned the empty room. "Where are the rest of the Knights?"

"Drake is with Cole and my brothers. We threw everyone out except for the kitchen staff. Figured we still need to eat." Sonny rolled his shoulders. "We still don't know who gave the Russians our location. The Mansion is on lockdown until further notice. Your father dispatched Alpha Command. They're arriving soon."

"My men will handle the security," Marcello interjected. "That will buy us some time to develop a new plan."

My brother had trained each man in Alpha Command. He didn't have my book smarts, Bastian's ruthless business sense, or Damian's hunting skills, but he was born to lead soldiers. Marcello wanted to attend York Military Academy instead of Astor Prep. But my father would not allow him to leave Devil's Creek. Back then, he wanted us under his authority at all times.

We walked toward the back of the apartment, with Sonny on Marcello's right and me on his left.

"I'm fine," Marcello groaned, trying to slip out of our grasp. "Stop fucking babying me."

"Shut the fuck up," I snapped. "You can barely stand."

Sonny tipped his head back and laughed. "It's okay to accept our help, Cello."

He was the only person who called my brother that. It was a stupid nickname.

We stopped at the end of the hallway.

Sonny reached for the doorknob, and I pushed out my hand. "Wait. Where is my mother's ring?"

I needed to propose to Alex.

9

We didn't have any time to waste now that our enemies had infiltrated our secret hideout. We had tons of safe houses and places off the grid, but we didn't want to travel too far from Devil's Creek with Alex's upcoming solo showing at the Blackwell Gallery. Besides, we all had companies to run. And we weren't pussies who backed down to a fight.

Sonny reached into his pocket and handed me the dark blue satin box. I cracked open the box and studied the thirty-carat round brilliant cut diamond.

The Salvatore diamond.

My mother was the last person to wear it. My great grand-father had stolen it from Italian nobility and passed it down. Pretty soon, our girl would be a Salvatore.

Alexandrea Salvatore.

I liked the sound of it.

I didn't have pockets, so I handed the ring back to Sonny to hide it from Alex as we stepped into the bedroom. Half of her body lay on top of Bastian. He had his arm around her, his fingers a few inches beneath the waistband of a pair of boxers. They were too big and probably belonged to Sonny. I hated the thought of her wearing another man's clothes.

Her blond curls covered the right side of Bastian's face. As usual, her hair was unruly and all over the place. But that was what I loved about her. She was beautiful but not perfect and didn't try to impress any of us.

It was so fucking sexy.

Damian was on her other side with his hand between her thighs. Even in sleep, it was like they both could sense her presence.

"We should let them sleep," Marcello suggested.

"No." I shook my head. "Bash and Damian are getting their lazy asses up. We can't leave The Mansion until we figure out what we're dealing with."

"It was the Russians," Sonny said in a hushed tone, careful not to wake our sleeping queen.

"We have one bargaining chip." A sinister grin curled up the corners of my mouth as I stared at my sleeping beauty. "The Knights have been keeping her safe for a long time. This might be the time to exchange Viktor Romanov's daughter. That's why the Russians are breathing down our necks. Viktor sent his goons to find the girl. He thinks he can steal Alex and force our hands."

"No," Sonny shot back. "You promised Cole that Grace would be unharmed. We all swore to protect her."

"I don't give a shit," I hissed. "My father promised Damian and Bastian revenge for their parents' deaths. We have been keeping this girl alive for over ten years for one purpose. It's not my fault Cole fell in love with his captive."

"He doesn't see it that way." Sonny crossed his arms over his chest, glaring at me. "What about Hunter and Brax? They're with her, too."

"Again, I don't fucking care." I kept my voice low, giving him a menacing look that said not to test me. "They were under strict orders not to touch that girl. She is bait. Nothing more. Even Fitzy is okay with us handing off his grand-daughter to the enemy."

Fitzgerald Archibald Adams IV was the current Grand Master of The Founders Society and Bastian's grandfather. He was the reason my father had adopted Bastian and Damian. Because of that, we thought they would spare us. That we wouldn't have to marry into a Founding Family.

But he was getting more ruthless in his old age. The old bastard was mean as fuck and richer than a god. As the head Elder, he had every politician, mobster, banker, and secret society under his command. We needed his connections to maintain our position of power.

"That's because Fitzy needs Bash more than he needs Grace," Marcello told Sonny.

"And so do we." I held Sonny's gaze, speaking with fire behind my words. "The last time I checked, I will be the next

Grand Master of The Devil's Knights. Not you, Cormac. So don't tell me what we need to do."

"Okay, that's enough." Marcello threw his arms out between us, and since we were still holding onto him, it kept me from wringing Sonny's neck.

Sonny fought with me every chance he got. The stupid Irishman never followed orders.

Marcello shook us off and staggered over to the bed. He sat on the edge of the mattress and looked up at us. "For Alex, can you two get along? I'm sick of all the bullshit."

Sonny's eyes darted to Alex, and he smiled. "Yeah, sure. For our queen, I'll do whatever's necessary."

"Nope," I retorted. "Don't tell me what to do, brother. I'm the leader of this family."

Marcello sighed. Give them another hour to sleep off the drugs. We're safe here for now."

I considered his request for a moment and then nodded. Not like I could wake up Bastian and Damian without disturbing Alex. She looked too peaceful and beautiful to touch her. But I wanted to mark her and break her some more before making her mine.

"Fine, they can sleep for one more hour. But if they're not up when I come back, I'm smacking them around."

Marcello rolled his eyes. "Dickhead."

I looked at Alex sleeping between my brothers and then left the room with Sonny and Marcello to plot our next move.

Chapter Three

ALEX

I woke up to my head pounding like a jackhammer, my skull on fire from a wicked migraine. It had been a while since I'd had one. They usually came on when something triggered my PTSD. A sound, a smell, or even a song on the radio could sometimes stir up the flashbacks that usually accompanied blinding pain.

I opened one eye and found Bastian staring at me, holding me in his strong arms. Even though he was disheveled, his dark brown hair sticking up in random places, he still looked good enough to eat. For a moment, I thought about last night. All the ways he touched me, tasted me. Fucked me so good I passed out from the pleasure.

"Bash," I whispered, my voice scratchy. "Where are we?"

"At The Mansion."

I scanned the room half the size of the one we slept in last night. "Whose room is this?"

"Sonny's."

My chest still felt heavy from all the fumes I'd inhaled. "Why do people keep trying to rape and kidnap me?"

"Because you're ours." He slid a curl behind my ear and smiled. "We have a lot of enemies who want to hurt us."

I draped my arm over his stomach and breathed in the delicious scent of his cologne. "Where's Damian?"

"Right here, Pet." He clutched my thigh from behind and pulled my back into his chest. His lips grazed my neck. "Fuck, you smell so good."

I whimpered when his teeth trailed across my skin. "Where's Luca and Marcello?"

"Taking care of business." As I tilted my head to the side, Damian kissed my neck and bit me.

"Damian." I reached behind me to grab his hand and moved it between my thighs. "Mmm... You feel so good."

I was barely awake, but their warm bodies pressed into mine were distracting, especially when Damian touched me like he wanted to devour me.

"Well, aren't you three fucking cozy," Luca said in a nasty tone, standing in the entryway to the room with his hand on the frame like he was holding up the wall. "It's time to get up. You've slept for long enough."

I rolled my eyes at him. "Don't be a dick. We just woke up."

He entered the room, hands stuffed into his pockets, dressed in his usual three-piece suit. "No, you just woke up. These two have been in here feeling you up like fucking perverts."

"They can touch me all they want."

"Damian's into a lot of sick shit," Luca commented with an evil glint in his eyes. "But necrophilia, that's a new one."

"I was sleeping, not dead." My men moved with me as I sat up. "And who are you to judge anyone, Luca?"

"I hate it when Mom and Dad fight," Bastian quipped with a cocky smirk, glancing over my shoulder at Damian. He kissed the top of my head and laughed. "You bring out that fire in him, Cherry."

"Don't you dare patronize me, Bash." Luca put his knee

on the bed and then raised his hand to beckon me. "Get over here, Drea."

"Luca," I groaned. "What is up your ass today? We're not even awake yet. Give us a minute before you bark orders."

He got on his knees and grabbed my legs, pulling me across the mattress to him. His lips brushed mine. "Don't tell me what to do, woman. I'm in charge. When I tell you it's time to get out of this bed, you say yes, sir."

I shoved my hands at his chest, but he didn't move. "Why did I think you would be different after last night?"

Luca shook his head, and a strand of his dark hair dropped onto his forehead. "You have to do more than suck my cock and spread your legs to change me."

"If you don't get off me and out of this room, I will kill you." Again, I slammed my palms into his hard chest. This time, he loosened his grip on my legs. "I'm serious, Luca." I pointed at the door. "Get out!"

"Seriously, bro," Bastian grunted. "Give her some space. We'll be out in a few minutes."

"Go direct all that big dick energy somewhere else," I added. "I'm sick of your attitude."

Luca flexed his jaw, his hands balled into fists at his sides, aiming those pretty but scary blue eyes at me. And then he slid off the bed, slamming the bedroom door behind him.

I sat back on the mattress with a sigh. "He's so infuriating. How have you put up with him all these years?"

Bastian rolled onto his side, running his fingers down my arm. "Luca's not bad. Just difficult and demanding."

"Our brother is used to getting his way." Damian moved behind me, resuming his previous position. "Even our dad doesn't tell him no."

"But our little vixen always puts him in his place." Bastian laughed as he pressed his lips to mine. "Don't you, baby?"

"I don't take any of your shit."

Damian slid his fingers beneath my chin and tilted my

head back. A creepy but sexy grin stretched the corners of his mouth. His lips looked red against his pale skin like he'd just drank blood. "You're a good girl, Pet."

Bastian sat up, stretching his arms above his head, and yawned. "Time to get up, pretty girl. We need showers."

"I'm starving." I rubbed my grumbling stomach. "Whatever drugs those assholes gave us are wreaking havoc on my insides."

Damian lifted me from the bed and walked me into the ensuite bathroom. My head wouldn't stop pounding, and after that encounter with Luca, it was only getting worse.

Why did he have to act like such a jerk? He only had two modes: raging asshole or sexy savage. I liked when he turned into the sex god I saw last night. But his attitude outside of the bedroom was grating on my last fucking nerve.

After I showered with Bastian and Damian, we dressed in Sonny's clothes and headed into the living room. Marcello sat on the leather sectional couch with his phone in hand, his fingers flying across the keys.

Luca was on the phone and screaming at someone in Italian, pacing across the tiled floor in the dining room. His nostrils flared as he spoke, and as his voice reached a higher octave, Marcello snapped his head at him. Whatever he was saying to the person on the phone must have shocked Marcello because his eyes widened.

"Someone is PMSing," I said under my breath to Bastian. "He needs to calm down."

I sat on the couch between my two handsome protectors, claiming one of my thighs with their big hands.

I was theirs.

They were mine.

"He's worried about you, Cherry." Bastian snaked his arm around me and lowered his voice. "You don't know what Luca has given up for you. All the things he's done to make you happy."

I let his words hang between us before I looked up at him. "Happy? When has he ever made me happy?"

"You're talented, baby." He grabbed my breast over top of Sonny's T-shirt and winked. "But you need Luca's connections to get ahead in your career. His mother's name opens many doors in the art world."

I knew he was right. The Blackwell Gallery was one of the top art galleries in New York. A sold-out show at Blackwell would change my career and propel me to the next level. You needed an introduction from someone important to get the owner to consider looking at your work.

My grandfather probably could have made my dream a reality. He had even more money and connections than the Salvatores. God forbid he did anything that would allow me some freedom from this arrangement. But after last night, I didn't want to leave anymore. I was in the arms of my savage Knights and right where I belonged.

I leaned into Bash and whispered, "Then why does he act this way?"

Bastian rolled his broad shoulders. "He hasn't been as bad since you moved into the house with us."

I chuckled. "He was worse before? I doubt that."

"You mellow him out. Just knowing you're under our protection brings him some relief."

"Because he's afraid of losing his pawn, not because he gives a shit about me."

"Not true," Marcello said in a deep tone that forced me to look at him. "We all care about you, princess. Even Luca. He has a different way of showing it."

Damian nodded to confirm. "The Knights will do

anything for you, Pet. Kill for you. Die for you. Whatever you need. We take our oath seriously."

This wasn't the first time I'd heard the same thing from the other guys. They must have all rehearsed this oath, a vow to protect their queen at all costs.

Luca hung up the phone a minute later and spun around to face us. I could see the madness dance across his handsome face, twisting his gorgeous lips into a snarl.

I pushed myself up from the couch and walked toward him. Luca just stood there, hands on his narrow hips, pushing his suit jacket to the side. He had two guns holstered on his chest. My devil looked so damn sinister and tempting.

I stopped in front of him and inched my fingers up his muscular arm. "Thank you, Luca. I know you saved me from those men. That I wouldn't be here if it weren't for you."

His snarl quickly transformed into a semblance of a smirk. Would it have killed him to smile?

"I know you mean well, even if your approach is terrible."

He snickered. "My approach is effective."

"Not quite," I remarked.

He stared into my eyes for the longest few seconds of my life. When Luca looked at me, it was as if he stared through me. Like he was searching my soul.

Of all the Salvatore boys, he was my biggest weakness. The one I wanted the most because I couldn't have him. He never let me get too close. He never wanted me to see the darkness inside him, even though he couldn't hide from me.

That was my skill.

I could draw the truth out of anyone. With the swipe of my brush, I told the world stories about all of them. My handsome princes. The men I couldn't imagine living my life without now that we had formed those bonds.

Since he didn't recoil from my touch, I took that as a sign I could let my hands wander. Luca often looked disgusted by any form of affection. He hated intimacy and made that abundantly clear over the years. So it surprised me when he didn't push my hands off his chest. I moved them higher and wrapped my arms around his neck.

Luca lifted my feet off the ground, his lips inches from mine. We looked into each other's eyes and breathed against each other's lips. I thought he would kiss me, but he pulled his head back and set my feet on the floor.

"I have to ask you something."

He peeled his hands from my waist and got on one knee as he reached into his pocket. A dark blue box sat in his palm. I gasped as he opened the top, revealing a massive round diamond. It twinkled when the light hit it just right. The ring must have cost him a small fortune.

"Drea," he said as he held out the box for me to get a better look at the ring. "Will you marry me?"

Chapter Four

ALEX

I stared at Luca down on one knee, holding a gorgeous diamond ring. I blinked a few times to clear my vision because this had to be a dream.

But it was so real.

No one spoke a word as they awaited my response. This wasn't how I thought I would get engaged. Luca wasn't the man I thought I would marry.

When I was a girl, I dreamed of marrying a handsome prince who would sweep me off my feet. That was how I escaped all the trauma. I had to believe in fairy tales and things that didn't exist. Then, I grew up and realized the world was full of monsters and that people are never what they seem.

As I considered Luca's proposal, I thought about my last year at Astor Prep. Luca treated me like shit and did horrible things to me. Of all the Salvatores, I wanted him most. But I also hated him the most.

I wouldn't have thought twice if Marcello or Bastian were on their knees. Even Damian would have been a better choice.

I bit the inside of my cheek as I looked down at him,

knowing he would flip the fuck out when I shook my head. "No."

Luca shot up from the floor so fast that I had to step back to create some space between us. His nostrils flared as he glared at me. "Why the fuck not?"

"Regardless of what happened last night, I still hate you."

His jaw clenched so tightly it looked like it would snap in half. "What the fuck is your problem now?"

"You." I took another step backward toward the living room. "Why is it so hard for you to understand? Have you forgotten how you've treated me?"

"Bash and Damian did worse things to you." He sneered, hands balled into fists at his sides. "I never even touched you."

"No, you just fucked every girl at school and made me watch. Made your brothers hold me down as you bent those skanky cheerleaders over the sink in the bathroom. Forced me to see who knows how many blow jobs. I will never forget the shit you did to me."

"Get over it." He stuffed the ring into his pocket and rolled his eyes. "That was years ago."

"I hate you, Luca." My arms flew up in the air, my skin burning with flames. "I don't know if I will ever forgive you."

"He's not the same asshole from high school," Bastian said in his defense.

I angled my body to look at Bastian and pointed my finger at him. "No, don't stick up for Luca. Nothing you say will redeem him in my eyes."

"Why not, Cherry?" He leaned forward on the couch, giving me one of his sexy smirks. "Luca's done a lot of good shit for you."

"Was he doing good things for me when he woke me up in the middle of the night at Wellington Manor? When he made The Serpents chase me through Beacon Bay."

"We were all there." Damian ran a hand through his black hair, his face expressionless. "It wasn't just Luca."

"But you all listen to Luca." My eyes shifted between the three of them. "Tell me I'm wrong about that."

Damian looked away and groaned. Marcello scrubbed a hand across his jaw. He knew I was right. They all did.

I glared at Luca and aimed my finger at his smug fucking face. "Mirror, mirror on the wall, who's the cruelest prince of all."

Bastian got up from the couch. The scent of his cologne filled the air as his strong muscles wrapped around me. "C'mon, baby." He brushed my hair behind my ear and kissed my cheek. "You forgave me, right?"

I leaned into his warm embrace. "Yeah. So?"

He sucked my earlobe into his mouth, tightening his grip on me. In his arms, I felt safe, wanted. I didn't think about the stupid shit he did to me in high school. I liked Bastian and Damian's sexual advances. I couldn't get enough of them.

"Bash," I whispered, clutching his wrist as he licked my skin. "Mmm, stop that."

"Yeah, stop that," Luca hissed. "We're having a conversation, motherfucker." He pointed at the couch. "Sit your ass down and let me deal with my girl."

"You need to chill the fuck out," Bastian grunted as he released his hold on me. "I can kiss *our* girl all I want."

Luca's mouth twisted in disgust. "Are you going to tell her you love her back?"

Bastian's hands fell from my body.

"That's what I thought," Luca shouted at his brother. "Stay the fuck out of this. It doesn't concern you, Bash."

Bastian plopped down on the couch, shooting daggers at Luca. "It's easy to see why she can't forgive you, bro."

Luca raised his hand. "Enough."

I stood on my tippy toes and got in Luca's face. "You're a bully. Always have been, and you always will be."

His eyes flashed with anger. "No, I'm not."

"How many times did my grandfather have me hospitalized because of your cruelty? I'm still not allowed to make my own medical decisions because of the hell you put me through."

"My brothers played their part," he said through gritted teeth. "They're not innocent."

"Damian and Bash never fucked another woman in front of me. They never made me watch some whore suck them off! They may have helped you, but they weren't the masterminds. We all know you run the show. All the vile shit any of you did to me came from your sick mind."

"It's in the past, Drea." His eyes narrowed into slits. "Why does it bother you so much?"

"Because I wanted to be the one you were fucking!"

Luca dug his fingers into my hips and lifted me onto the dining room table. "I've always known how much you want me, baby girl." He licked his bottom lip as he looked at my mouth. "You make it so obvious."

"Luca, stop torturing me."

"When you first moved to Devil's Creek, I watched you watching me." He stroked my cheek with his long fingers, but it wasn't sweet. "You thought I would touch you like those girls. Just once. Isn't that right, baby?"

"Stop it."

He inched his hand up my inner thigh, and my breathing quickened to an abnormal rate. "I bet you went back to Wellington Manor and fingered your tight pussy, hoping one day I would bend you over that sink and make you scream like a dirty little whore." His fingers dipped beneath the boxers I'd borrowed from Sonny. "You still think about me doing that, don't you?"

I pressed my lips together and nodded. "Fuck me, Luca."

He shook his head. "Not today, baby. Only good girls get the pleasure of coming on my cock."

"You just asked me to marry you. But you won't fuck me?"

I pushed his hand off my thigh. "Get away from me. I'm sick of your mind games."

Ignoring my request, he moved his hand back to my leg and tapped his fingers. "I've done a lot to protect you. To keep you alive. Things I wouldn't do for another woman."

"I know you wanted to fuck me back then. You still do. So what's the problem?"

"Sex is just sex." He slid the pad of his thumb across my bottom lip. "Nothing more. It's a physical response to a necessary bodily function."

"That's a strange way of putting it."

He shrugged. "It's the truth."

"You're so mean, Luca. I can't keep doing this with you. The back and forth, tit for tat, is very draining."

"If it weren't for me, you wouldn't be here right now. I signaled the Knights to locate you. Be glad I'm in control of this family, baby girl. Because as long as I am, you will never have to worry about a fucking thing."

"Luca." I sighed. "I can't stop hating you overnight. You need to show me another side. There has to be some good in you."

"And do you think Bash is good? How about Marcello or Damian?" His wicked laughter filled the air. "They are no better than me. None of my brothers are saints. Wait until you see what you've signed up for, Drea. You won't like any of us."

"Maybe not. But I've seen other sides to your brothers. They let me in when you do nothing but shut me out."

He folded his arms across his chest, rage shaking through him. "So you would marry one of my brothers over me?"

I shrugged. "I don't know. After last night, I can't choose. I'm with all four of you."

His dark eyebrows raised. "You want me to make you come, but you don't want to marry me?"

"I'm attracted to you, Luca. Most women are." He grinned at that. "It means nothing other than my body likes you. My heart? Not so much. My head? Not at all. I'm not ready to let go of the past. You haven't let go either. Tell me why you hate me because I've done nothing to you."

He clenched his jaw. "Your existence is troubling."

I pushed out my chest. "Tell me why my existence bothers you so much."

His brothers shifted awkwardly in their seats. Marcello turned his head to look out the window. Bastian leaned forward on the couch and stared at his shoes. Damian glanced at Luca like a little boy waiting for his dad to tell him the universe's secrets.

He idolized Luca.

They all did.

Luca was their god.

Their bully king.

"Your grandfather needs to be there when I do it." Luca couldn't meet my gaze. "You need to hear it from him."

My lips parted in shock. "Why?"

"Because I promised to wait until he was there to tell you. As much as I hate Carl, I respect him. I owe him that much."

"You hate me because of my grandfather?"

He shook his head. "Just drop it, Drea. I'll schedule a meeting with Carl and my father. You need to hear it from them."

"Are you going to make more of an effort?" I looked up at my handsome prince. His jaw ticked as he thought over my question. "I need you to be better, Luca." I slid my hand up his arm and squeezed his bicep. "Even Damian has been trying."

He snorted. "Damian choked you and almost killed you."

"Damian apologized."

He stuffed his hands into his pockets and glared at me. "You believe him?"

"I think he did it for Bash, but it doesn't matter. At least he tried." I inched my hand higher up his arm, and he stiffened from my touch as I invaded his personal space. "That's all I want from you. Just stop being such an asshole all the time. Stop pushing me away."

He studied my face, regarding me with curiosity. Like he didn't know what to make of my declaration.

"I know it's hard for all of you to let go of your hatred. But it's the only way this arrangement will ever work."

He removed his hands from his pockets and placed one of them on my lower back. "Are you reconsidering my proposal?"

"No." I pressed my chest against his and put my palm over his heart. "But I will think about it. You need to give me some time. And I swear to God, you better not try to break my finger to put that ring on it."

His nose wrinkled, and then his lips stretched into a thin line. "It won't come to that. You'll change your mind."

"Okay," Bash said, his voice a few octaves louder than usual. "Now that we've all kissed and made up, can we order some food? I'm fucking starving."

Marcello reached for a room service menu on the table and threw it at Bastian. "Order one of everything."

Damian rubbed his toned stomach. "I can eat."

But when he said it, he licked his lips, staring right at my pussy. A flush of heat rolled down my arms, spreading to my legs as I thought about last night. He ate my pussy as if he would never eat another thing in his life. And for a moment, I held his gaze, communicating I wanted him to do that again.

Marcello noticed the exchange and laughed. Damian raised his hand and beckoned me with his finger. I slipped out of Luca's embrace and climbed onto his lap. He flatted my back on the couch and ripped off Sonny's black boxers.

"You guys can eat whatever you want. I'm not hungry for anything else," he said before his tongue parted my slick folds.

His fingers etched into my thighs as he lifted my legs over his shoulders and devoured me.

"You'll let this psycho do whatever he wants to you." Luca shook his head as he approached the couch. "But not me?"

I raised my hand and gestured for him to come closer. "Get over here."

Luca closed the distance between us. Bastian hopped off the couch and was at my side within seconds. He beat Luca to the space in front of my head and started stripping off his clothes.

"Get the fuck out of my way, Bash." Luca gripped the back of his neck and pulled hard. "You took her virginity. It's our turn now."

I gasped at his comment, and then my eyes drifted up to Bastian. "So it was you?"

He nodded.

"The whole time?"

"Yeah, Cherry. You rode my cock like a good girl." His lips brushed mine, his tongue sweeping into my mouth as Damian drove his tongue into me. "Your cherry was always mine. Isn't that right, baby?" He stroked his fingers across my cheek. "Mine."

"I couldn't tell you apart, and it was so dark. None of you talked."

"But you knew," he said against my lips.

"I'm glad it was you, Bash."

He kissed me one more time and then moved over a few cushions to make room for Luca, who sat at my head. Luca didn't waste any time stripping off his clothes. His chest was bare and marred with dozens of scars from his abusive childhood.

"D, time to flip her over," Luca ordered.

Damian stopped licking me and turned me over and onto my stomach. He pulled me toward him and then bent me forward so I could palm the cushion.

Luca kneeled in front of me. His cock was so long and thick that I wondered how I fit him in my mouth last night. I was a little drunk when we went upstairs to the room. But now that I was sober and seeing him in the light, holy fuck.

Luca was huge.

He took my right hand and folded my fingers around his shaft. "Wrap your pretty lips around me, baby girl." Luca leaned forward to rub the tip across my lips. "Be a good girl and show me how much you like sucking my cock."

"Our girl is a natural," Bastian said.

Luca's palm dropped to my head, forcing me to take more of him. I choked on him right as Damian spread my thighs apart and licked my pussy from behind. I made a humming sound from the moans Damian stole from me. That only made Luca more aggressive.

He must have liked what I was doing because he fisted my curls so hard I thought he would rip the hair from my scalp. I slapped his hand, afraid I would choke on his big dick if he didn't ease up on his death grip. He finally stopped being a jerk and loosened his hold on me, so I could maintain a more steady rhythm that ripped several grunts from his mouth.

Marcello moved to the floor beside me. He rubbed my clit as Damian spread me open with his tongue. Then Marcello twisted my nipple between his fingers, the sensation sending a shock wave of pleasure throughout my body.

Luca helped me stroke his cock, jerking himself so hard that I couldn't match his movements with my mouth. I assumed he was close with how violent he was getting.

I came on Damian's tongue right as Luca came on mine, his salty cum filling my mouth. Damian's fingers dug into my ass cheeks as my entire body trembled. He held me tight, marking me as his property.

Claiming his Pet.

"Fuck, Drea." Luca groaned. "Goddamn, baby. Are you sure you weren't sneaking out on us all these years? Fucking men behind our backs. What happened to our sweet little virgin?"

I slapped his leg and laughed. "Stop being an asshole."

"I'm serious." He dropped to the couch and ran a hand through his spiky black hair, a look of pure ecstasy on his handsome face. Luca tugged on his semi-hard cock that glistened with my saliva and his cum. "Fucking hell, woman. I've never come like that before."

I sat between Luca and Damian, my legs spread for Marcello, who kneeled between them. He wanted his turn to make his queen come, lifting my right leg in the air. I leaned back against the cushion and pulled on his dark, messy hair. His eyes met mine as his tongue rolled across my clit. He sucked on the tiny nub a few times, and I hissed each time he did it.

I gripped his hair in my hands and moved his head closer, needing more of his tongue. "Make your queen come, Marcello."

"I love seeing this side of you," Damian whispered in my ear, sucking the lobe into his mouth. "You're not a shy little virgin anymore."

He rubbed my clit with the pad of his thumb. Marcello licked me straight down the middle while his brothers watched, my chest heaving, my lungs ready to explode.

"She was never shy." Bastian snickered. "Remember the first time we touched her? She pretended to hate it when she was so wet for us." He scratched the corner of his jaw and groaned. "Fuck, I almost blew my load right there in the hallway at school."

Damian dipped his head down and spoke against the shell of my ear. "We had to jerk off in the bathroom after that. You don't know what you did to Bash and me. Your pussy was so tight I couldn't stop thinking about you." He breathed me in like he was trying to memorize my scent. "You smelled so good. I didn't want to wash your cum off my fingers."

I smiled between moans, trying to give equal attention to all of them, even though Marcello was working his magic between my thighs. "Is that why you forced yourself on me every day?"

He nodded. "I'm addicted to your smell."

"You got off to a girl you hated," I choked out, my eyes closed as Marcello swirled his tongue around my clit, driving me fucking wild.

"I never hated you," Damian admitted. "I hated I couldn't fuck you."

Marcello stopped licking me for a second and looked up at Damian. "This isn't storytime, D. Go order the fucking food while I take care of Alex."

"Already did it," Bastian said from the other side of the sectional couch. "Hurry and make her come, Marcello. They'll be here any minute." Then he shot up from the couch, hovering over Marcello as he watched him lick my pussy. "Remember that day in my car on our way to The Founders Club?"

I bobbed my head and forced Marcello's tongue deeper inside me. "Uh-huh."

"Same deal, Cherry. If you don't come before room service knocks, you don't get to come."

"Fucker," I muttered, eyes closed so that I could focus on Marcello and his tongue.

"C'mon, Cherry." Bash's knee dropped to the couch between Damian and me. "It's time to come for us."

My entire body trembled from the intense orgasm ripping through me as if on command. A wave of heat, then cold, shot down my arms and legs, all the way to my toes. I felt numb all over by the time my moans ceased.

Luca glanced over at Bastian. "Didn't I tell you we could train her?"

Bastian's gray eyes met Luca's blue ones, a smirk tipping up the corner of his mouth. "That was all me, brother."

Marcello was still between my legs, staring up at me with his lips soaked with my juices, his black hair a mess.

Damian slid his arm across the back of my neck. "Why do you think I call her Pet?" He rubbed the top of my head. "She's such a good girl."

A loud bang interrupted our moment of bliss. Until that morning, I'd never heard a gunshot before, but now the sound was unmistakable.

We were under attack.

Chapter Five

ALEX

Luca headed toward the door, butt ass naked and with a gun in each hand. What a sight. His body was like a work of art, tanned and toned, sculpted to perfection.

Bastian walked over to a screen on the living room wall and hit a round button below it. A keyboard popped out from the wall like something out of a spy movie. He started typing, and then several camera angles appeared on the screen. "We're surrounded," he told Luca.

"Anyone on this floor yet?"

"No, but they're on their way. It looks like they went straight to our apartment."

"That buys us some time," Luca said in a calm, even tone, not the least bit affected by the situation.

Damian gripped the gun as Luca cracked open the door to look into the hallway. Not giving a shit about his nakedness, Luca leaned his back against the doorframe. My God, he was so big I couldn't take my eyes off him. All of them were well above average, but Luca was something else.

Marcello lifted me in his arms. "Time to go, princess."

"Where are we going?" I clutched his thick bicep. "We're in the middle of nowhere."

He flashed a cute grin and carried me toward the bedroom. "You should know by now we have our ways."

"But the exit is the other way, Marcello."

He laughed. "Patience, woman. I'll get you out of here in one piece."

Luca turned around, his massive dick smacking his thigh. *Lord, save me when he tries to fit that inside me.* Putting him in my mouth was hard enough.

"We'll follow you," he told Marcello. "Go!"

"Are you seriously going into a gunfight naked?" I laughed at the idea. "Put some clothes on, Luca."

He waved his hand to dismiss me. "Just worry about getting out of here alive, baby girl."

Marcello glanced down at the unusual watch on his wrist. It differed from the Chopard watch he usually wore with his suits. "Alpha Command will be here in fifteen minutes. They're blocking off the main road now."

"Good," Luca bit out. "Make sure they send a team here to create a diversion. Who knows how many Russians are out there, waiting to ambush us."

"At least a hundred men," Bash commented."

"You can't fight a hundred men," I shouted as Marcello entered the bedroom.

"They won't have to shoot their way out of here," Marcello confirmed with a wink. "We have an escape plan."

Once inside the bedroom, Marcello entered the walk-in closet and set my feet on the floor. He pushed a key into a lock on the side of the tall shelf in the right corner. Then, he unlocked it and moved the shelving unit out from the wall.

"You guys have so many secrets." I shook my head in disbelief. "I don't know if I'll ever get used to all this spy shit."

He tapped my ass and shoved me toward the dark hole in the wall. "Get in there, princess. This is our only way out."

I glanced up at him, a frown in place, my arms crossed

under my breasts. "Are you fucking kidding me? Another dark, creepy space. You know how much I hate the dark."

"You adjusted just fine last night." A sly grin pulled at his lips. "Didn't mind when we were giving you multiple orgasms."

My core ached at the thought of their hands, mouths, and tongues on my body. He bent down to suck on my earlobe and then grabbed my ass. "Imagine four big dicks at the end of that tunnel."

"Well, when you put it that way." I giggled when he tapped my ass again. "Maybe the dark isn't so bad after all."

As we stepped into the dark space, lights built into the walls flicked on, making it less scary. Maybe one day, I would overcome my fear. Not today, though. I still had a lot of shit to work out before getting used to the darkness.

"Better, princess?" Marcello asked as he followed me into the tunnel, his hand on my lower back.

"Yeah. Not as bad as your spy shed tunnel."

He laughed. "It's not a spy shed."

"I still find it slightly unnerving that you watched me from that room."

"Consider yourself lucky I did. If I hadn't spotted the threats in Brooklyn, someone would have taken you a long time ago."

A shiver rushed down my arms, dotting my skin with tiny bumps. I rubbed my hands down my arms to get the gross feeling to go away. "How many times?"

"This year... or ever?"

I halted in place, my heart pounding in my chest, and looked over at him. "How many total?"

"Since before you moved to Devil's Creek?" Marcello ran the pad of his thumb over his bottom lip, deep in thought. "Over a hundred. Maybe more."

I gasped at his confession. "And this year?"

"We're only halfway through the year and at thirty-seven rescues."

"Wow," I choked out, nerves shaking through me. "Why do these men want me so badly? Don't say it's because I'm with you and your brothers because Bash gives me the same response every time."

"He's not lying to you, Alex. It's the truth." He hooked his arm around me, resting his hand on my shoulder. "The Devil's Knights don't just loan money to the criminal underworld. We make investments for our clients, handle secure transactions for illegal items, import and export guns, drugs, and anything you can't get through customs."

My jaw unhinged at his confession. They were even worse than I had thought.

"How do you ship drugs and guns?"

"Through Sonny's company. Mac Corp. We use their shipping containers and connections to circumvent the usual channels."

"So the Russian men who keep trying to steal me... Are they customers?"

"No. We deal with a lot of shady people, but not the Bratva. It's a conflict of interest for our other clients."

"Who do you work with?"

He steered me down the lit pathway as we walked farther into the never-ending cave of wonders. "Drug cartels, the Sicilian Mafia, the Italian-American Mafia, motorcycle clubs, street gangs. You name it, and we've probably worked with them."

"The Knights come from wealthy families. So why do you need to work with those kinds of people?"

"We don't." Marcello rolled his broad shoulders. "My grandfather got us into this business. He already had a relationship with the Mafia in the States and wanted a connection with the Sicilians. My mother was the granddaughter of a

Mafia boss. So my grandfather sent my dad to get information. But he ended up falling in love with her."

My lips parted in shock. "Really? In interviews, people always asked her about her humble upbringing."

"My grandparents left Italy to get away from the violence. Vincenzo Basile is my uncle. He runs the family now from Calabria."

"I thought the Salvatores weren't in the Mafia."

"My great grandfather was a Made man," he said as we neared the end of the tunnel. "After the Salvatores fled from Italy, they became bootleggers and worked for the Five Families in New York. My dad wanted to make us legit. He's the reason we have Salvatore Global."

"Now I understand why it's so important for one of you to marry me. It's not about the money. In the eyes of the Founders, you are all thugs."

He stopped in front of a steel door and produced another key to open the lock. "Exactly. They will never see us in the same light as you, Bash, and Damian. You need to marry Luca. It will make all of our lives easier if you do."

"I can't marry him, not until he changes his attitude."

Marcello clutched my shoulders, those sad blue eyes searing into my soul. "If I had asked, would you have said yes?"

"Yes," I said without hesitation.

"Then pretend he's me."

My heart cracked in half at his words.

"Marcello, I can't." I slid my fingers up his muscular bicep and pulled him closer. "You're not like him."

"Your choice affects me, too. So if you care about any of us, you'll accept Luca's proposal."

I shook my head. "Not yet. I'm not ready."

"My brother won't change, Alex. Accept him, faults and all. He's been like this his entire life. Luca is used to getting what he wants and doesn't care who he fucks over to get it."

"How much longer do you have before choosing who I want to marry?"

He scrubbed a hand across the dark stubble on his jaw. "The end of the summer."

"Luca said he wants a queen. So then he needs to treat me like one." I smiled. "Maybe you can teach him a thing or two."

Marcello winked. "Yeah, I can do that for you. But I don't know if he'll listen."

I followed him through the doorway that dumped us into a tiny, dark room. Marcello got on his knees and gripped a steel panel on the floor, using his strength to lift it.

"Great," I deadpanned. "Another spy tunnel. What is with your family and secret passages?"

"In our line of work, this is necessary. We would have died in a hail of gunfire if my father didn't think to have these tunnels built before he opened the club."

Marcello climbed down the first few rungs. "Let's go, princess. Get your sexy ass down here."

I laughed at his comment. If only Luca were more like Marcello, I would have married him in a heartbeat.

I peeked into the dark space and cringed when I couldn't see the bottom of the scary pit. "How far down do we have to go?"

"This tunnel is deeper than the one at my house."

My arms and legs trembled as I looked down. "How much deeper?"

"I can go as deep as you want, princess." He snickered, a sexy grin in place. Then he wiggled his fingers. "C'mon, get down here. This is life or death. My brothers will run through here any minute. You don't want to be the holdup, or Luca will throw you down here."

I shivered at the thought. "Your brother is so vile."

"He gets the job done."

My sweaty hands slipped on the metal rungs, so I had to

take turns wiping them down my sides. Accepting my place with the Salvatores came with its challenges. Like being forced daily to conquer my fears. They were testing the limits of my mental illness. I intentionally avoided situations that could trigger an attack. And if this shit with the Russians continued, it wouldn't be long before they had to hospitalize me.

I hated feeling like the crazy girl. None of my men feared anyone or anything. They dove headfirst into situations that could get them killed without a second thought.

As I moved down the ladder, I reminded myself I was a Salvatore girl. One day, I would marry one of them. So I had to act like them and be brave.

Once I could see the bottom, Marcello grabbed me from behind and lifted me off the ladder. He held me in his strong arms and softly brushed his lips against mine. "You did good, princess."

I smiled. "How much farther do we need to go?"

He pointed down another dark corridor. "Five more minutes in that direction."

"And then what?"

"Our ride is waiting for us."

I heard loud noises above us, followed by shoes slapping the ground. My heart thumped in my chest, and I hooked my arms around his neck.

"It's just my brothers." He cradled the back of my head. "Don't worry, princess. We won't let anyone touch you."

"Marcello," Luca yelled.

He cupped his hands around his mouth and shouted, "Down here."

Luca climbed down the ladder with Bastian and Damian in tow a moment later. They hopped down from the ladder, and Luca shot Marcello a strange look.

"What the fuck are you still doing here?" Luca slammed his palm into Marcello's back. "Get fucking moving, asshole. We don't have time to dick around."

Marcello shook his head and groaned, but he didn't argue with his brother. All five of us headed into the darkness. I slipped my fingers between Marcello's, feeling less scared with him by my side.

Luca pushed open a metal door at the end of the hallway. Bright light filled the space, forcing me to shield my eyes with my forearm. I blinked to clear my vision. We were in the middle of a field with tall grass.

From a distance, I heard gunshots. I turned my head to my right and spotted The Mansion. It sat at the edge of a cliff overlooking the Atlantic Ocean. Such a beautiful place for horrible people.

"Time to move." Marcello yanked on my arm and steered me through the grass behind Luca, who led the pack. "Our ride is on the other side of this field."

More gunshots penetrated the quiet air, and a whimper escaped my lips. A sharp pain pierced the side of my head, and for a moment, I struggled to hold myself up. I staggered to the side, squeezing my eyes together to regain my bearings. "Oh, no. Not now."

Marcello dug his fingers into my bicep. "What's wrong?"

I rubbed my temples. "Migraine from the gunshots and the darkness. It's too much."

He lifted me in his arms and ran through the grass. "Just hold on."

His brothers surrounded us, never breaking stride as we bolted through the field. A few minutes later, we hit the end of the area, where a black Escalade waited for us. The back door opened as we approached, and a blond-haired man with tattoos from his fingers to his neck stepped down from the back seat. He had tanned skin, a dimple on his right cheek, and pale blue eyes.

Marcello set my feet on the ground and cupped the man's shoulder with a grin. "You remember Morpheus, right?"

The Serpent Society's second in command.

I gritted my teeth at the memory of the last time I met The Serpents. "Oh, I finally get to meet the elusive Serpents without them chasing me through Beacon Bay first?"

Bastian moved behind me, his hands on my waist, and kissed the top of my head. "It's time you meet your loyal subjects."

"Subjects?"

"The Serpents are under The Devil's Knights' command," Luca informed me. "Which means you will be their queen one day, too."

I stared at the tall, blond, tattooed god and drew a breath from between my teeth. "Then you better get us out of here alive."

Chapter Six

ALEX

We piled into the SUV with The Serpents. They had half of their faces painted with scales the last time I saw them, each representing a different snake. After they chased me through Beacon Bay, I was so traumatized that my grandfather had to hospitalize me for a week.

I hadn't forgotten that night and still dreamed of those vicious psychos who tormented me until I lost my mind.

Hades sat in the passenger seat, his hands steepled on his lap. Like his friends, ink spread from his neck down to his fingers. He was the group's leader, named after the God of Death. His spiky black hair reminded me of Luca's, only his hair was longer on the top and shaved on the sides.

He could have been a Salvatore.

Years ago, he had painted his face to look like a black mamba. The scales were dark brown, and when he opened his mouth, I screamed at the sight of his black tongue. That was the last thing I remembered before waking up in the psychiatric ward at Beacon Bay Memorial Hospital. One of the many times my grandfather had to commit me because of my bullies.

I sat in between Bastian and Luca, both of which kept their hands on my thighs as if they were afraid I would vanish.

"Hello, Alexandrea," Hades said in a calm, deep tone that sent a chill down my arm. "It's nice to see you again."

Yeah. Fucking. Right.

I cleared my throat, narrowing my eyes at him. "Wish I could say the same."

Bastian grabbed my inner thigh with possession. "That's my girl."

Hades laughed. "Still got that fire." A grin tipped up the corners of his mouth. "You will need it when you become our queen."

The bastard acted as if he hadn't chased me. Like he didn't almost give me a fucking heart attack. I woke up screaming for years, convinced snakes were trying to kill me in my sleep. Aiden was my only saving grace. He held me in his arms and coaxed me back to sleep.

I rolled my eyes at Hades and turned away to glance out the window. Luca etched his fingers into my thigh, piercing my skin. He was so rough. But it's not like I would want him to be sweet. I liked it when it hurt, when he was mean and made me beg for more.

"Be nice to my cousin," Luca whispered. "He'll be your family someday."

Morpheus drove the SUV out of the field and onto the dirt road. We were in the middle of nowhere. He floored the gas, and my heart fluttered like it was about to break through my chest. I held my hand over my heart to still the rapid beating.

"Who said I want to be your family?" I smiled, and he gave me a nasty scowl. "Chill, Luca. I'm going to marry one of you. Eventually."

"No, baby girl." He tightened his grip on my thigh and pulled my leg on top of his. "You're marrying me."

I pressed my lips together, smiling at him with my eyes. "Then you better step up your game."

Luca's blue eyes filled with the usual rage, which brewed at the surface. "Challenge accepted." His hand slowly inched toward my aching core. "Your pussy is mine." He cupped me over top of the boxer briefs I borrowed from Sonny. I had to bite my bottom lip to stifle the moan ready to escape past my lips. "This king needs his Queen D."

I loved when he called me that. So over the past few weeks, I signed my paintings with that name.

"Luca," I whispered as his fingers slipped beneath the briefs. "No, not like this. Wait until we get home."

Bastian groaned as he stared down at Luca's hand between my legs, his left hand on my other thigh. He licked his lips. "Goddamn, Cherry. You make my cock so fucking hard."

Marcello and Damian grunted their agreement from the back seat. My men were dangerous in and out of the bedroom. If we weren't with The Serpents and on the run from Russian Bratva, I would have made them pull over the car and have their way with me.

Brushing his lips on my earlobe, Bastian whispered, "I'm so fucking lucky. They don't know how good your pussy feels. It's our little secret for now, baby."

Morpheus checked the rearview mirror, a concerned expression crossing his face. He ran his fingers through his blond hair, then placed his hand back on the steering wheel. Then he glanced in the mirror again.

Named after the Greek God of Sleep, Morpheus killed his victims using hypnotics. When I first heard his nickname, I thought of The Matrix. I could see him giving his victims the option of taking the blue or red pill: a painful death or a quick death.

In some ways, he reminded me of Aiden. Dark tattoos and the same wavy blond hair gelled into place.

The Serpents were also artists.

Like my brother, they specialized in street art. They turned their crimes into murals of the Greek underworld. It was all about the big splash with The Serpents. To make a statement. My brother once told me if my grandfather forced him to join a secret society, he would want to work with them.

I angled my body to follow Morpheus's line of sight out the back window. Marcello and Damian sat in the row behind me, next to Charon and Lethe. Of course, no one knew their real names. That was the best-kept secret in Devil's Creek.

Charon was stocky and built like a professional boxer. His arms were thicker than Marcello's, corded with muscle and dark tattoos. He had dark reddish-brown hair styled into a faux hawk. Named after the ferryman of the Greek under-world, he was the undertaker of the group.

The fixer.

Body disposer.

Kind of like Damian.

Lethe was tall, at least six foot five, and muscular but lean. He had dark brown hair, short on the sides and long on the top, with errant strands flopping onto his tanned forehead. Like his friends, all of his tattoos had a theme, specific events from the Greek underworld. I recognized a few of them from my brother's art. Aiden loved Greek mythology and often spray-painted murals inspired by his favorite stories.

Luca removed his hand from my briefs so he could turn to look out the back window. All the guys had their eyes on the SUV, barreling toward us. Three men hung out the windows with machine guns in their hands. My nails pinched Luca's bicep.

He hooked his arm around me and reached for his gun. "It's okay, baby girl. I'll burn down the world before I let them touch you."

A bullet sank into the bumper, and I screamed. The windows rolled down, each of my men hanging out the window to shoot at the assholes following us. Marcello joined Luca on my left, Damian helping Bastian on my right.

"Put your head between your legs, princess." Marcello's deep voice comforted me, even in times of distress. "Do it. Now!"

Shaking uncontrollably, I obeyed his command and tucked my head between my legs, gripping my knees to steady my nerves. Tears leaked from my eyes and streamed down my cheeks. I thought we were safe. That all the bullshit we went through to leave The Mansion meant we could drive back to Devil's Creek without a fight.

"Alpha Command is five minutes out," Marcello shouted over the gunfire.

Another shot hit the back window, but the car must have been bulletproof because it didn't shatter the glass. None of their bullets seemed to do much to our vehicle. Knowing my guys, this was the equivalent of an armored truck.

Morpheus swerved when another shot hit a tire.

"You better be waiting at the rendezvous point," Marcello yelled into the watch on his wrist. "We can't hold out much longer."

He was talking to one of his Alpha Command team members.

I covered my ears, keeping my head low as shots hit the car. My men fired back, keeping pace with the assholes behind us. The vehicle veered to the right, and we hit a bump into the road, throwing me into Luca's side.

He snaked his arm around me and pushed my head back down. "It will all be over soon, Drea." His fingers ran up and down my back in a soothing motion that seemed unnatural for him. "Breathe, baby girl. We'll get you home soon."

I closed my eyes and listened to the sound of his deep voice. Bastian ducked to allow Damian to cover his side. And then he was on top of me, pressing his hard chest to my back.

"I got you, Cherry." He tucked my curls behind my ear

and then rocked me. "It's okay."

I must have been acting worse than I realized. Sometimes, I went to a dark place inside my mind where no one could reach me.

Had I done that?

That was the problem with my medical condition. I had highs and lows, extreme ups and downs. Sounds, smells, and high-stress situations brought back all the awful memories. All the unwanted feelings I'd spent years trying to bury.

"Bash," I whispered, hoping he could hear me over the gunfire.

He leaned down. "Yeah, Cherry?"

I peeked up at him. "In case I die today, I need you to know I meant what I said last night."

His gray eyes illuminated from a genuine smile that graced his full lips. "I know, baby."

"It's okay if you don't feel the same way about me."

Bastian kissed the top of my head, cradling the side of my face with his big hand. He lowered his voice so only I could hear him. "What I feel for you goes beyond love. It's unnatural."

I laid my head back on his muscular chest and smiled. The moment was perfect until we swerved off the road.

Morpheus attempted to maintain control of the vehicle. "Fuck," he groaned. "Put on your fucking seatbelts and hold on."

I clung to Bastian's side, fear rocking through me as I gripped his arm. We drove toward a storm drain at full speed, the tires flattening with each step closer to our deaths.

Bastian held my head against his chest and whispered, "Don't look, Cherry."

Luca slid closer, then threw his body over mine to shield me from the crash's impact. I felt Marcello and Damian's hands on my shoulders. At least if we were going to die, we would go out together.

Chapter Seven

MARCELLO

The tires flattened as we reached the entrance to the storm drain. Alex would not like our next move, but we didn't have a choice. Our enemies had outsmarted us again, and they wanted to get our girl to that auction.

There was a two million dollar bounty on Alex's head. It wasn't just the Russians looking for her, but I kept that minor detail out earlier. The less she knew, the better. I could see her slowly falling apart, her PTSD rearing its ugly head. If we weren't careful with Alex, she could crack under all the stress.

I removed my cell phone from my pocket and checked the Salvatore Global security app for the movements of Alpha Command. My men would be here soon. But we had to get over one hurdle, like convincing Alex to crawl through a dark storm drain, before we could meet my team on the other side.

Hades, Charon, Lethe, and Morpheus stood beside Luca and Bastian, their backs to us as they discussed the new plan. None of us would bat an eyelash at crawling through sewer filth to safety. I glanced down at Alex, who curled her body into mine, her nails digging into my back like she was afraid to let go.

By the terrified look in her eyes, I could tell that she understood we had one move to make. It was hard enough getting her into the secret passage at The Mansion.

I brushed my lips onto her earlobe. "Alex, I need you to listen to me. You won't like this, but I will be there with you every step."

"I can't," she whimpered, clinging to me like a koala hanging on its mother. "Don't make me get in there, Marcello."

I hugged her, resting my chin on top of her head. "It's this or death. We don't have time to deliberate. There's no other way out of here."

A bullet grazed past my ear, missing me by a few inches. It hit the pipe with a loud bang, and Alex screamed at the top of her lungs. She ran toward Bastian, who lifted her in his arms.

"Time to move, Cherry." He raised her high enough for her to climb into the pipe. "Get your pretty ass in there before you have a bullet in it."

"No," she screamed, her chest rising and falling with each shallow breath she took. "No, I can't."

"Yes, you can." Bastian set her at the edge of the pipe, and then he climbed in after her. He tapped her ass. "Get a move on, woman, before you get us killed."

"Marcello," she whimpered, her pretty blue eyes aimed at me.

My brothers didn't know how to deal with her fears or mental illness. They had issues and couldn't handle hers.

I pushed Luca and Hades out of the way and gripped the edge of the pipe. "Bash, get in front of Alex. I'll take the rear." Then I glanced over my shoulder at Luca. "Cover us."

My brother nodded. "Get her out of here."

"We'll meet you on the other side." I got inside the pipe that barely fit me without banging my elbows. Then I traced soothing circles on Alex's back. "C'mon, princess. Bash is in front of you. I'm right here. Just listen to our voices, okay?"

48

She turned her head to the side to look at Bastian. "Okay, but…" Her top lip quivered.

"No buts," Bastian told her. He bent down and kissed her cheek. "We have to go, baby. Follow me. There's a reward for you on the other side. All you have to do is follow me down the rabbit hole."

With her back to me, I grabbed her ass cheeks and pretended like I was burying my face between her legs to distract her. "You can have all the rewards you want, princess. They're waiting for you at the other end of this tunnel."

She listened to my command and moved along with Bastian. He used his cell phone for some light, which seemed to calm Alex down. Though, I wasn't so sure she would make it to the other side without screaming about a rat or a bug. There was a ton of nasty shit in the pipe, which stunk like rotten ass.

I heard more bullets from a distance and assumed Luca and Damian were with The Serpents, firing back at the Russians. We needed them to buy us enough time to get Alex headed toward safety before they could meet up with us.

I was going to stay behind since it was my job as the head of security and the leader of Alpha Command.

But Bastian handled the situation poorly. Damian would have terrified her more. And Luca would have just dragged her through the pipe without a second thought.

So it had to be me, and I felt guilty about it.

There was a chance one of my brothers wouldn't make it to the other side. We had all accepted our fates years ago.

Protect our queen at all costs.

That was our mission.

Our duty.

Chapter Eight

ALEX

Bastian helped me down from the storm drain, hugging me hard against his chest. "You did good, Cherry. Nothing to it."

I forced a laugh, my body shaking uncontrollably. "Yeah, easy for you to say. Nothing scares you."

"Everyone is afraid of something." He wiped the dirt off his face. "You'll learn to overcome your fear."

I looked into his gray eyes. "What are you afraid of?"

He stared into the expanse of the field before he looked at me. "Losing you."

Marcello tumbled out of the metal pipe with the grace of a tiger. He was naturally athletic, while I must have fallen flat on my face a dozen times.

"You won't lose me," I told Bastian. "I'm here to stay."

Bastian put his hand on my shoulder, a smile still in place. Marcello came up behind me and clutched my hip, digging his long fingers into my skin. I spun around to face him, and he surprised me by planting a soul-stealing kiss on my lips.

Hooking my arms around his neck, I lost myself at the moment. It felt like an eternity before our lips separated. And when they did, I couldn't breathe as I looked up and into his dark blue eyes. He was so beautiful, even covered in mud and sewer filth.

"Where are Luca and Damian?" I glanced over Marcello's shoulder to see if his brothers were close behind us.

Not a sight.

Not a sound.

"They should be here any minute," Marcello assured me. "Don't worry about Luca. He's indestructible."

"And Damian?"

He shook his head. "Our enemies should be more afraid of what he will do to them."

"He's a man, not a god. They can kill all of you, and yet you act like it is nothing. Like we didn't just run from Russian gangsters, get shot at, or climb through a fucking storm drain."

He rolled his broad shoulders. "It was nothing. Just another day for us."

Bastian moved to my side and pulled me from Marcello's arms. "Damian is fine, baby." He kissed the top of my head, wrapping me in his warm embrace. "So is Luca. You don't have to worry about them."

Ten minutes later, I heard a loud groan and rushed to the metal pipe. I breathed a sigh of relief when Luca's black hair and pretty blue eyes came into focus.

"Why do you look like you've just seen a ghost?" Luca asked me.

I put my hands on my hips to calm the nerves shaking through me. "Because I was worried about you."

He smirked. "You can't kill the Devil, baby girl."

Annoyed by his arrogance, I blew out a deep breath. However, I found it kind of sexy. Luca was confident and in control of every situation. I could put my life in his hands, and everything would be okay.

We all trusted him.

After Luca hopped down, he extended his hand to

Damian, who jumped out of the pipe. They made it look so effortless. Like they hadn't crawled through shit and sludge to get to safety.

Marcello hit a button on his watch and raised his wrist to his mouth. It had several buttons that allowed him to communicate with members of Alpha Command. My broody protector was like a more muscular, scarier version of GI Joe.

A few minutes after we climbed out of the drain, Hades, Charon, Morpheus, and Lethe joined us. Three black SUVs arrived in the middle of nowhere, a field that seemed endless.

Marcello spoke to a blond man with a severe jawline dressed in black fatigues. He had a buzz cut and thick biceps and looked like he'd spent years in the military.

The Serpents walked over to the first SUV and climbed into the back. Marcello finished up with his team member, who took his place in the driver's seat of the second SUV. Then Marcello tapped my back and ushered me over to the last SUV. Luca offered to drive. Bastian got into the passenger seat beside him, and Damian hopped into the last row by himself.

My heart wouldn't stop racing as I got into the back with Marcello beside me, his arm draped across my neck, holding me close. With him, I truly felt safe. The others said they would kill for me, and I believed them. But when Marcello said he would die for me, I knew it was true.

I loved him.

I never thought it was possible to love more than one man. And yet, I loved both Marcello and Bastian.

Maybe not equally.

My love for each of them differed from the other because I loved them in different ways. I loved each of them for their faults, for their strengths. And I loved the way they loved me, even if they couldn't say the words aloud.

Luca drove like a maniac while Bastian sat in the passenger seat beside him and navigated the way home using the GPS on his cell phone. They worked well as a team. The two of them were the alphas of the group and always had to be in charge. It surprised me Luca let Bastian take my virginity.

I leaned forward on the bench. "How come you let Bash take my virginity?" I asked Luca.

Luca breathed through his nose, eyes on the road with his fingers clutching the leather steering wheel. "Does it matter?"

"I'm just curious why you would give up the honor."

"Because the better man won," Bastian said with laughter in his voice, shoving a hand through his messy, dark brown hair.

Luca snickered. "Not quite, dickhead."

"So, tell me," I demanded. "I want to know why it was Bash and not you."

I'd always known it would be one of them. Luca would have killed Marcello and Damian if they had even attempted it. But the relationship Luca had with Bastian was different. He respected him as a true equal. When Bastian offered suggestions, Luca at least considered them. Whereas with the others, he usually dismissed their ideas because he thought his way was right.

"Fine," Luca hissed. "You want to know why it wasn't me?" I watched him grind his teeth as he focused on the road ahead of us. "Because I didn't want to be your first."

My mouth dropped in shock. "But you said... You used to fight with Bash over me."

"Don't sound so disappointed, Drea. We both know you wanted it to be Bash." His eyes met mine in the rearview mirror. "Are you upset with the outcome?"

I shook my head.

He forced a grin. "Then why do you care so much it wasn't me?"

"I don't," I bit out. "I'm just... curious, is all."

"Uh-huh." Luca clicked his tongue. "Don't worry, baby

girl. I'll fuck you. And when I do, you won't even remember Bash's name."

Bastian punched his arm. "You're just mad I fucked her first."

Luca turned off the dirt road and drove onto a two-lane paved highway. I was annoyed with Luca's attitude, so I sat back against the leather bench and leaned into Marcello's warm embrace. Why couldn't Luca be more like his brother?

I slipped my hand beneath Marcello's shirt, feeling the rough edges of his well-defined stomach. He had at least a six-pack, maybe even more. He groaned as my hand slipped lower, my fingers wedged beneath his boxer briefs. His long, hard length poked my arm through his slacks.

After everything we'd gone through, I wanted to feel closer to him. We could have died at any minute. That much was true after the last few hours of running from danger.

I unbuttoned his pants and slid down his zipper so I could fit my hand in his boxer briefs.

"What are you doing, princess?" Marcello whispered in my ear before he sucked on the lobe. "We're not out of the woods yet."

"I don't care," I breathed. "If I were to die ten minutes from now, at least I would die doing the one thing I've wanted to do for a very long time."

I climbed on top of him and kissed his lips, hooking my arms around his neck. He grabbed my ass and pressed my soaking wet pussy into his hard cock. Luca was a little longer than him, but Marcello was so damn thick it wasn't easy to wrap my hand around him.

"What the fuck are you two doing?" Luca growled. "This isn't the time to fuck around. We barely escaped with our lives."

I peeled my lips from Marcello's, breathing hard. "All the more reason to fuck around."

"He's right," Marcello pointed out. "We need to stay sharp. Focused."

I kissed him again. "I think your brothers can take over for a little while, don't you?"

"Drea," Luca warned.

"Just drive," Bastian cut in, tapping Luca on the shoulder. "She's right. We almost died back there."

"Don't tell me what to do!" Luca shouted.

"Marcello," Luca snapped. "You're fired as head of security if you don't get your fucking shit together."

Marcello laughed. "We both know Dad would never let you do that."

"Stop testing me, little brother."

Ignoring the cruelest prince of all, I slid off Marcello's lap for a second to strip off my shorts. Then I resumed straddling his muscular thighs. With my hand wrapped around Marcello's length, I leaned forward and lifted my hips, pushing him inside me.

He was so big.

Just a few inches of him stretched me out. I bit my lip, and he moved his hand to my back to encourage me to keep going. As I took all of Marcello in one quick thrust, my eyes met Damian's. His blood-red lips parted with desire as he gripped the back of the bench and watched me.

Marcello's fingers burrowed into my ass cheeks as he stretched me out, thrusting his cock deeper and deeper. I moaned against his neck and rocked my hips. Then, letting him take charge, I moved with him, focused on Damian the entire time.

"Goddamn, Cherry," Bastian groaned from the front seat. "Look at you taking my brother's cock like a pro. Fuck, girl. Turn around so I can watch you."

"But then Damian can't watch," I moaned.

Bastian snapped his fingers. "D, get up here with them."

Marcello drew a breath from between his teeth. "Why the fuck do all of you have to keep getting in the way?"

"Because she's ours, brother," Bastian shot back. "Now turn her around, so we can watch."

"I'm driving," Luca said in a nasty tone. "Unlike you assholes, I take getting home alive seriously."

"Loosen your tie, would ya?" Bastian laughed. "You're so fucking uptight."

Marcello lifted me off him, and in one skilled movement, he turned me around. I palmed the seat beneath me and rocked my hips, feeling every inch of his thick cock push inside me.

Damian dropped onto the bench beside me and twisted my nipple between his fingers. He pinched so hard the second time I screamed. Bastian raised his phone in front of his face, biting his lip.

"Bash, what are you doing?" I asked as I rode Marcello in reverse cowgirl, leaning my back against his hard chest.

"Filming this for later." He waggled his eyebrows, giving me one of his delicious smirks. "It gets boring sitting in meetings all day. This will give Damian and me something to watch when you're not around."

Damian grunted his approval right before he pushed up my shirt and took my nipple between his teeth.

"Luca," I moaned. "Watch me."

"Nope." He kept his gaze on the road, his fingers curled around the steering wheel so hard his knuckles turned white. "Like a bad girl, you didn't listen to me. So don't expect any praise or admiration. The only thing you've got coming from me is a punishment I'll reserve for later."

"You're impossible."

"I'm the one who will keep you safe," he said through clenched teeth. "Consider yourself lucky I put your safety before sex. Because if it were up to my brothers, we would have stopped in the middle of the road taking turns with you. Sitting ducks for our enemies."

"That's not true," Bash added. "We all take her safety seriously."

"Is that so?" He snickered. "Act like it then."

Bastian continued filming Marcello slamming his big cock into me, ripping a series of moans from my throat.

"Luca," I whimpered, "stop being such a buzzkill. You're not mad that I'm fucking your brother. You're mad that you're not the one fucking me."

His lips pressed into a thin line, and that was the end of the conversation. He didn't yell at Bastian again. In fact, he didn't even look at or speak to anyone. Not even when Bastian told him where to turn or that he needed to detour around an upcoming traffic jam in the city. Marcello fucked me for a solid thirty minutes, all the way to the main road. He squeezed both arms around me after I came for the fifth time, holding me in a vise as he spilled his cum inside me.

I slid off his lap, our juices dripping onto the seat. Damian noticed and lapped up our cum with his finger. And then, he surprised me by sucking on his finger. My eyes widened as I watched him.

He was so strange.

I didn't quite understand his dynamic with his brothers or how it would work between us. After Bastian took my virginity, Damian got on his knees and feasted on my pussy, licking every bit of blood and cum from me. I hadn't made the connection until Bash reminded me of his obsession. He liked blood, which he'd made clear when he almost killed me.

Still bottomless, I hopped onto Damian's lap and licked his lips. He palmed the back of my head but made no move to kiss me. Of all the Salvatore boys, he was the only one never to kiss me. I wanted to feel intimacy with Damian.

"Put your fucking clothes on!" Luca shouted. "Playtime is over, baby girl."

Damian's big hand skated down my back, ass, and then between my thighs. He spread me open, and I felt our cum drip out of me and onto Damian's lap. He lifted me just enough to see the stain on his pants, and then he grinned like a maniac.

"Does that turn you on?" I asked him.

He nodded.

"You enjoy watching me with your brothers?"

Another nod.

"Are you ever going to touch me?"

"I'm touching you right now."

I frowned at his comment. "You know what I mean, Damian."

"My cock is a reward reserved for good girls." He slid his tongue across his bottom lip. "And you've been a very bad girl, Pet."

I took his hand and shoved his fingers inside me, so he could feel how much I wanted him. "You wouldn't know what to do with a good girl."

"Clothes," Luca growled. "Now! You're showing your ass and pussy to every fucking person sitting in traffic with us. Must I remind you of the consequences for sharing what's ours with other men?"

I hopped off Damian and grabbed my borrowed clothes from the floor with a groan. "No, sir." I leaned forward, elbows rested on my thighs, and his gaze finally met mine in the rearview mirror. "But I'm looking forward to that punishment later."

Chapter Nine

LUCA

We hadn't been home for ten minutes before I got back to work. Protecting our queen was my number one priority. That girl drove me fucking crazy and gave me a rush unlike any high I'd ever experienced. She was the reason I did many things that forced me out of my comfort zone.

I leaned back in my chair, resting my dress shoe on my knee as the vein in my neck pulsed. The men on the other line were grinding my ass into the pavement for one fucking favor. Now that everyone in the criminal underworld knew I had a weakness, those motherfuckers were out for blood.

Marcello listened to the heads of each crime family offer suggestions about our issue with the Russians. We were on a secure line, one the FBI could not touch. I didn't make a habit of speaking over the phone, but these were desperate times.

"I will pay ten million dollars to whoever brings me the heads of the fucking Volkov Bratva," I shouted into the speakerphone on my desk.

"Ten plus a free shipment, no questions asked," Adriano Alteri said sternly.

No questions. Exactly what I tried to avoid to limit my liability.

Adriano was the boss of the Alteri crime family in New York. The Mafia Don had given me the best deal of the bunch. While everyone else was content on raking my ass over hot coals, I respected him for throwing me a bone.

"Done." I loosened my tie, already feeling ten million dollars lighter. "As for the bounty on my fiancée's head, I will pay triple to make it go away."

Alex hadn't accepted my proposal yet, but word had already spread that we were getting married. She would say yes eventually. I had a way of wearing people down until they gave me what I wanted. Money ruled my world, and my family had tons of it. A few million here and there meant nothing if it kept my girl safe.

"You know the rules, Luca," Vincenzo Marchese said.

He was an old friend of my father, who ran a small operation from his mansion on the Long Island Sound.

"The man who set the bounty has to lift it," I growled. "Yes, I know. And if I could locate the motherfucker, I would force him to cancel the contract."

"Let us handle the Russians," Adriano said.

"I need assurances," I countered.

"I will tell my men to ignore the bounty for Alexandrea," Vincenzo promised. "You have my word."

I tapped my platinum and onyx serpent ring on the desk to steady my nerves. "Adriano?"

"Agreed."

The other men on the phone muttered similar responses.

"I'll have an update on the Russians within the next twenty-four hours," Vincenzo said before dropping off the line.

After everyone hung up, I felt like I was sitting there with my dick in my hand. My mistakes were costing me a fortune. And if I didn't find the men who wanted Alex in time, they would take something more valuable.

"That went well," Marcello deadpanned.

"I feel like I've just had a root canal and a colonoscopy." I raked a hand through my hair. "Fuck, that was brutal. I'm going to owe favors to the Five Families for the next decade."

"We don't have a choice," he confirmed. "Even Dad thinks this is the best move. But, until we replace the Knights we've lost over the past few months, we need help from our allies."

Some of our family's power came from the help of our associates. I hated we needed them to find the Russians and whoever else was vying for the bounty on Alex's head. But none of our attempts to locate the bastards had proven successful.

Marcello leaned forward in his chair, his shoulders slumped. We were all tired but not yet defeated. "You should call Dante. Let our cousins get involved with the bounty."

I shook my head. "Not yet. Let's see how this pans out with the other families. Besides, Dante and his brothers have their war to fight."

"They're family, Luca."

Dante Luciano was the new head of the Atlantic City crime family. He was my cousin on my mother's side. They had gotten into the casino business when my father started building Salvatore Global.

"We have all the family we need right now," I assured him as I shot up from my desk and walked over to the screen on the left wall. "Once Alex accepts my proposal and becomes our queen, we will have more bargaining chips at our disposal."

He moved beside me and placed his hand on my shoulder. "We need Wellington's black book."

"I know," I said with my eyes on the security feeds. "So you better do your best to convince Alex that marrying me is her only option."

"You could try being nicer to her," he shot back. "Ever think of that, dickhead?"

I snapped my head at him, nostrils flared. "Nice? What the

fuck is wrong with you, Marcello? That girl doesn't want nice from me. She has you for that." I got in his face, our noses so close they could touch. "Our queen wants to dance with the Devil, and I plan to drag her back to Hell with me."

He crossed his arms over his chest, returning his gaze to the security monitors. "I know what she wants, Luca. You gotta trust me."

"I do trust you. But you need to trust that I know how to handle our girl. What she thinks she wants is not what she *needs*."

"Alex doesn't need any more of your cruelty. She's teetering on edge after what she's been through in the last twenty-four hours. One more push and her sanity will snap like a twig. Don't try to break her or bend her to your will. She's too close to having an episode. I barely got her into that storm drain without her losing it."

"You didn't think she was ready to break when you fucked her on our way home." I turned up my eyebrows at him. "I don't recall you giving a fuck about her sanity each time you slammed your cock into her pussy."

He tipped his head back and laughed. "You're just jealous. Fuck her already, you miserable bastard. Once you do, you won't be so fucking uptight."

"I'm not touching her. Not until it's time."

"Stop planning every second of your life. It's fucking stupid. Bash is right. You need to live a little."

I shot daggers at him, my anger seething through me. "Who are you to judge my decisions? You spend most of your time watching Alex on the security feeds and jerking off to her."

He clenched his teeth. "No. I. Fucking. Don't."

"You forget I see everything that goes on inside and outside this house. There's nothing any of you can hide from me. Damian and Bash and their sick and twisted shit. You and your obsession with Alex. I see it all."

"I watch to keep her safe," he insisted with venom in his tone. "You should try being more like me. Maybe she would have said yes to your sad fucking proposal."

Blinded by rage, I gripped his collar and pressed my nose to his, breathing through my mouth. "Just because you have a crush doesn't mean I should act like you and swoon every time she walks into a room. I'm the man of this family, little brother. If you want to play house with our queen, go right the fuck ahead. No one is stopping you. But you need to stay the fuck out of my business with her."

"Your business with her is our business." He peeled my hand from his collar, his blue eyes wide and full of rage. "This is a partnership. We're all in this together. So start fucking acting like it."

Marcello took a few steps back and fixed his tie, pulling on the fabric as his focus shifted to Alex, in her bedroom one floor below us.

She stood between the open French doors in a pair of silky pajama shorts and a matching top. She wore a similar pair every night.

"Do yourself a favor and fuck her." He tugged at the ends of his black hair, which was always messy from him pulling on it. He licked his lips as our eyes met. "She was worth the wait. Trust me, you'll never think about anything else again."

Ignoring him, I stared at Alex on the screen. Her long blonde curls trailed midway down her back, moving as she swayed her hips. She was fucking perfect.

Maybe Marcello was right.

I'd been dreaming about splitting her open with my cock for years. I envisioned every moan I would steal from her pouty lips as she took all of me. But, like a piece of art, I wanted to preserve her so no one could touch her.

I waited too long to have her.

My brothers had already defiled her, ruined the pretty

image of her in my mind. But I had more important things to think about other than sex—like saving her life.

At least she was safe.

For now.

Chapter Ten

BASTIAN

W e were home. *Safe.* That was a close call with Alex, too fucking close for comfort.

I dropped my bag on the floor beside my closet and sat on the mattress, slumping forward on my elbows. Damian walked into the room a few seconds later. He hadn't spoken a word about Alex or the attack at The Mansion. It was business as usual for us, but this time it was different.

We could have lost her.

I knew without communicating that he was just as fucked up over it. He dropped to the bed beside me, his hand on my knee. I covered his hand with mine. We didn't look at each other, didn't say a word. He stared at the black and white wall as I hummed the tune to Alex's song.

Damian liked when I played the piano for him. It calmed him down when he was out of control.

He was okay for now.

But I could tell he was close to snapping again. It was only a matter of time. His condition was incurable, a sickness he would live with for the rest of his life. Stress seemed to exacerbate the problem. If we had lost Alex, he would have gone full-blown psychopath.

"Bash," he said after twenty minutes of listening to me hum Alex's piano sonata on repeat.

I tapped my fingers, my gaze on the dark walls. "Yeah, D?"

"You were right about her." He shifted his weight on the mattress to look at me. "She's good for us."

I turned my head to look into his green eyes that were so damn dark they looked like emeralds. "I told you she's a keeper."

"Yeah, but…" He shoved his hand through his black hair. "She'll never accept me. Not the way you do. As soon as she sees what I'm like, I will chase her away."

I grabbed his shoulders, forcing him to look at me. "Listen to me, D. You're not a bad person. You just do bad things that are out of your control. If you were bad, would I still be here?" He shrugged, and I continued, "Do you think Dad would have put up with your sickness? Or our brothers? They didn't have to take us in when we were kids."

"Dad had his reasons for adopting us." He curled his hand into a fist on the mattress, teeth gritted. "It wasn't completely out of the kindness of his heart."

I lowered my hands to his biceps and held him close. My touch always seemed to quell his dark emotions. We had a special bond no one would ever understand.

I did things for him—and with him—that neither of our brothers would do. The few times they had caught us in the act, they looked down-right disgusted but never said anything. We all had our demons to feed.

"What if she sees what Eva saw in me?" He pressed his lips into a thin line, staring out the patio doors. "She hated me. If she had lived, Dad wouldn't have kept us."

"She didn't like the circumstances of our parents' deaths. I don't think it had anything to do with us."

That was a fucking lie.

The great Evangeline Franco was the queen of this household. Loved and adored by her husband and sons, she didn't want us disrupting her life. After the second time Damian brought home a dead bird he killed, she begged Arlo to give us back.

Except we had nowhere to go.

We had family who would have taken us for the money. But Arlo had adopted us as a favor to the Grand Master of The Founders Society.

My grandfather was the wealthiest man in the world—number one on the Forbes Billionaires list. He was also the leader of the secret societies in the United States. Fitzgerald Archibald Adams IV was a cruel, brutal man.

He made Arlo and his beatings seem like fun. I was glad we avoided having to live with old Fitzy. But the first six months of living with the Salvatores were pretty rough.

Evangeline would whisper *diavolo* whenever she looked at Damian. *The devil.* She often spoke in Italian. Her parents were Italian immigrants. On her mother's side of the family, they were the Sicilian Mafia. Made men who controlled Calabria.

The Basile family.

We worked with them monthly on illegal shipments from Europe to the United States. They blamed Arlo for Eva's death and held it over his head. To avoid a war, The Devil's Knights handled many shady transactions for the Sicilians.

Luca was contemplating asking them for help with the Russians. The Italians hated them and had every reason to want to wipe them off the map. But they had too many requests. Too many favors we would need to repay for the rest of our lives.

"Alex wouldn't have let you touch her again if she wasn't okay with your sickness."

"Stop calling it that," he snapped.

Laughter shook through me. "What would you call it? Getting aroused over murder is a sickness."

"You like it, too." He waggled his dark brows at me. "Just admit it."

I shook my head. "Nah, D. Murder is a necessity for me. It's kill or be killed."

"Now it's hunt or be hunted," he fired back with venom in his tone.

"It will never be over. We will always have another enemy, another person who wants what we have."

Someone knocked on my door. A light tap that could only come from one person.

"It's open, Cherry."

Alex pushed on the door, standing in the entryway with long blonde curls spilling past her shoulders, stopping right below her big tits. She wore a pair of black silky shorts that showed off the definition in her thick thighs. The short top had thin straps and rode up her stomach.

She didn't look like the same girl from high school. Even back then, I couldn't keep my hands off her. But now that she'd filled out her body with curves, I wanted her even more. I licked my lips, already thinking about pulling those thighs apart and shoving my head between them.

As his eyes flicked up and down her body, Damian leaned forward, palms on his knees. His thumb rolled across his bottom lip as if he was hungry and dying for a taste.

I patted my thigh. "Come here, Cherry. It's time for bed."

Her eyes moved between us as she approached the bed. "Are you both sleeping in here?"

"Damian likes to sleep alone," I told her.

"He didn't last night." She stood between us, her pretty blue eyes aimed at me. "All five of us slept in that bed."

"Do you want him to stay?" I asked.

She glanced at Damian and nodded.

He looked as if he were holding his breath, still unable to relax, even after Alex's confession. I didn't know why he was so afraid of Alex not accepting him. He worried she would rip us apart. That she would get rid of him like Evangeline had tried to do all of those years ago.

Alex sat on Damian's lap, and he hooked his arm around her, digging his fingers into her hip. She shoved the hair off his forehead and smiled. "Can I paint you?"

He stared at her, not even blinking.

She rubbed her thumb across his cheek, smile still intact and growing larger as she touched him. "You're beautiful, Damian. Perfect." Alex tilted her head to the side to study his face. "My fingers are itching for the chance to paint you."

Alex had accepted us years ago, faults and all. She was just as fucked up as the four of us and wasn't going anywhere. We had her right where she wanted to be.

"I'm not beautiful," Damian said in a pained tone, looking at her lips. "Or perfect. If you peel back the layers, you won't like what you see."

"I see darkness in all of you," she confessed with a beautiful smile. "I see your anger, all the violence, and the hatred. But I know there's good in each of you. The light to your dark is there, and I want to draw it out. Show the world there's beauty in my beast."

He lifted her hand to his mouth and kissed her soft skin—a rare display of affection I'd never seen before.

Damian hugged me—and only me. But with Alex, he was showing signs of compassion. I wasn't so sure he could ever love her, but he was making progress.

Alex blushed as Damian lowered her hand to his thigh. "Is that a yes?"

Damian nodded. "Yeah, you can paint me."

Between Luca and his rage and need for revenge, and Damian's illness, I was afraid Alex would bolt before we could make her ours. But they were both changing. Maybe not all at once, but the signs were there.

Alex hooked her arm around Damian's neck and kissed his cheek. He didn't recoil from her touch. They'd never kissed.

"I'm tired." Alex raised her hand to her mouth and yawned. "Bash, can you turn on my music?" Then she slid off Damian's lap and rolled onto the bed, moving to the dead center. "Damian, you can light the candles."

"Oh, can I?" He laughed. "We still give the orders around here, Pet."

We turned to face her, and she got on her knees, palms flattened on the mattress. "The last time I checked, I'm the only one with a wet pussy in this room. So I make the rules."

I lifted my phone from the table to check the time. It was too close to midnight to fuck around with our girl. That was one rule I never broke. The structure was essential to Damian and me.

We both needed it.

But we could make her come in the next fifteen minutes. We crawled across the king-sized bed and pushed her back to the mattress. We pulled her thighs apart like savages on the hunt. Damian kissed her leg while I planted carefully placed bites up her inner thigh. She squealed each time my teeth nipped at her flesh.

Alex gripped the waistband of her shorts and panties, sliding them down a few inches. "Take these off me."

Damian pulled on one side, and I yanked on the other, tearing her clothes off her sexy body. I reached between her thighs to feel how wet she was for us. My fingers slid right into her tight pussy.

"Bash," she moaned. Licking her lips, Alex arched her hips to meet my thrusts. She grabbed Damian's hand and shoved it between her legs. Her eyes closed, chest heaving with each deep breath. "I want both of you to make me come."

"I have an idea." I removed my fingers, earning a nasty look from my sexy ass woman. "D, lie down." I pointed at the space beside Alex and slid off the bed to grab a satin pouch from the bedside table. "Cherry, sit on Damian's face and let him lick your pretty pussy."

Our queen licked her lips and then climbed on top of Damian. He gripped her thick ass and pulled her pussy to his mouth, diving in like he was dying of hunger and wouldn't live without a taste.

I opened the drawer and grabbed a bottle of lube. Alex glanced over at me, her eyes wide as I removed the vibrator from the bag.

"What do you plan to do with that?"

I approached the bed and smirked. "Guess you'll have to see. Don't you trust me, Cherry?"

She leaned forward and fisted Damian's black hair in her hands, pulling hard enough to rip it from his scalp. "In theory, yes," she whimpered. "Fuck, Damian. Mmm…"

I got on the bed behind her. "Don't cum yet, baby." I ran my hand over her ass cheek and opened the bottle of lube. "This will feel good. Heighten your orgasm."

"What are you doing, Bash?"

She whimpered as Damian shoved his fingers into her pussy and sucked her clit into his mouth. He'd obsessed over Alex and her scent for years. Ever since the first time he touched her. Like some fucking creepy vampire drawn to her blood.

I hadn't seen him like that before. Wild and out of control over a woman. His interest quickly turned to obsession, and it was usually deadly when Damian set his sights on someone.

Apart from Alex, he'd never touched a woman who wasn't on our payroll. He was too much of a savage for us to let him loose on the world. The women he'd fucked knew the drill and were into our particular brand of dark and dirty.

Alex wasn't sweet and innocent. She was just like us. Corrupted by evil, tarnished by the sins of her family's past. Marked by four savage Knights.

I pressed my palm to Alex's back and lubed her entrance, sliding my finger into her ass. She gasped as I moved inside her.

JILLIAN FROST

"Bash," she bit out. "What are you? Oh, my…"

Gripping her hip, I replaced my finger with the vibrator—just the tip. Enough to make her squeal right as she sang Damian's praise, screaming his name like a good girl.

"Bastian Salvatore," she said in that deep but sexy fucking voice as she turned her head to the side. "What are you doing to me?"

"Preparing you for the destruction of your pretty ass." I slapped her cheek hard enough to leave a red handprint, still pumping the vibrator into her. "How else do you think you'll handle four big dicks?"

She moaned as if she liked the idea of taking all of us. We needed to devise a system so each of us had an equal amount of time with our queen. I spanked her again, this time harder than the last. The nice girls always liked to be bent over, face down, ass up. But don't let this nice girl fool you.

Our queen was vicious.

I turned up the speed on the vibrator, and Alex screamed so loud it pierced my eardrum. "Oh, my God, Bash."

She moved her hands to each side of Damian's head, smothering him with her pussy. He wouldn't care if she choked him to death as long as he got to die with her taste on his tongue.

"That's it, baby." I slapped her ass again, sliding the vibrator in and out, increasing the speed with each thrust. "Open up for us."

Alex rolled her head to the side and moaned. "Why does this feel so good?"

"Because we're hitting all of your pleasure points at once." I grabbed a handful of her curls and tilted her head back so I could kiss her pouty, pink lips. "My God, woman. You're killing us."

She giggled, then another series of moans passed her lips. "Damian," she cried out, taking his hair in her hands, holding him in a vise as her body trembled. "Oh… Keep doing that."

72

Then she reached behind her back to clutch my wrist, pushing the vibrator deeper. "Bash. Holy shit! I'm going to…"

I pulled her hair again, forcing her to kiss me. "Cum for us, Cherry."

She was such a good girl and listened to my command. Her orgasms spilled out of her, one after another. After she stopped shaking, I slid the vibrator out of her ass and turned it off. She rolled off Damian, who could hardly breathe, covering his heart with his hand.

I hooked my arm around her middle and pulled her onto the mattress, curling her body into mine. Naked and beautiful, she laid her head on my chest.

Damian sat up, his lips covered in her juices. I'd never seen him look so fucking happy. That bastard never smiled. But I saw the semblance of one as he licked her cum from his fingers and aimed his gaze at Alex. A true hunter, Damian had a habit of obsessing over something, or in this case, someone.

"Damian, come here." Alex patted the space between them on the bed. "Cuddle with us."

He didn't reject the idea, though he didn't look all that thrilled either. It had nothing to do with Alex. Damian couldn't do normal shit like curl up with a woman, hold her hand, or even kiss her.

He wasn't wired that way.

But when Alex asked him to do something, he softened. He'd even surprised me when he brought her black dahlias and apologized. She had commented about him acting submissive, and it was the first time I'd ever seen him like that. He was sorry for almost killing her. The woman he'd vowed to protect at all costs.

Our queen.

"It's time for bed." I ran my fingers through her blonde curls to untangle them. "You know the rules, Cherry."

"Yeah, I know." She blew out an exaggerated breath and rolled her eyes. "In bed by midnight. No exceptions. Ever."

"Nope." I rolled onto my side to turn off the lamp, and she pulled on my arm. "Rules are rules, baby."

"Not yet," she whined. "Give me a few minutes. I need to use the bathroom and brush my teeth."

She kept some of her clothes in my closet and an extra toothbrush in my bathroom. I divided the other half of her time with Marcello. Neither Luca nor Damian wanted her in their beds.

But that would probably change.

My brothers were growing up.

She was changing all of us.

Alex climbed into bed, dressed in a silky spaghetti strap pajama top and matching shorts. She had dozens of them in every color and style. Luca made sure she had everything she would ever need.

He wanted to be the one who chose her clothes, dictated her schedule, and handled every aspect of her life. And then disappeared on her.

But I didn't complain because that meant more alone time with her. She was all mine most of the time. While the other two assholes worked out their issues, she took turns sleeping in mine and Marcello's beds.

Damian sat up, and Alex got on her knees, pushing his chest until he was flat on his back. "You're not going anywhere." She moved between us and laid her head on the pillow. Then she turned her head to the side to look at my brother. "Spend the night with us."

Damian gripped her hip. "Are you sure that's what you want, Pet? I'm not a good sleeper. I have nightmares. Sometimes..." He groaned. "Sometimes, I can't control myself in my sleep."

"I've lost count of how many times Damian almost choked

me to death in my sleep," I told her. "He'll spend the night with us, but it's your funeral, Cherry."

She rubbed her thumb across his cheek. "You won't hurt me. I think we're past that."

"It's not something I can control," he confessed.

"I have nightmares, too," she lilted. "Maybe we can help keep each other's demons at bay."

A rare smile tipped up the corners of his mouth as he pulled her closer, breathing in her delicious scent. He kissed her cheek, just a peck, but still a rare moment for my brother.

I lit the candles beside my bed and turned on Alex's playlist. The orchestra music from Tchaikovsky's Swan Lake floated through the speakers. Before Alex, I slept by myself in the dark and without a sound. But her routine was growing on me. It wasn't so bad once I got used to it.

I rolled onto my side and clutched Alex's thigh as Damian pressed her back to his chest. Her eyelids fluttered as she took one last look at me. And then she passed out in the arms of the last man I would trust to hold me in my sleep.

Chapter Eleven

ALEX

I woke up screaming. A strong arm snaked around my middle, pinning me against a hard chest.

"Shh," Bastian whispered, his grip tightening around me. "You're safe now, Cherry." He rubbed his fingers down my arm in a soothing motion. "We're in Devil's Creek. In my bedroom. It's okay, baby."

I knew he was right when I opened my eyes to the sun shining on my face. The soft light poured through the curtains on the French doors. Some nights, Bastian let me keep the doors open, so I could fall asleep to the sound of the waves crashing against the rocks. It was peaceful, perfect, and I wished for that soothing sound as my heart raced out of my chest.

"I won't let anyone hurt you, baby." Bastian kissed my forehead, his hand traveling down the length of my thigh. He curled his body into mine and rested his chin on my head.

I glanced at the empty spot beside me and sighed. "What happened to Damian?"

"He left after you fell asleep."

I rolled onto my back to look at him, staring into his gorgeous gray eyes. "Why? I told him to stay."

Bastian stroked his fingers down my arm, instantly calming me. "Because he's afraid of hurting you."

"Are his nightmares that bad?"

He bobbed his head. "I wasn't joking when I said he's almost killed me in his sleep. It wasn't bad when we were kids. I was taller and stronger than him back then. But now that we're the same size and strength, it's harder to fight him off when I'm in and out of consciousness."

"Is this going to work?" I wasn't sure why I was bringing this up, but I needed to know how they felt about me. About our situation. "All five of us. I don't see how you'll get what you need from one woman."

It pissed me off Damian left in the middle of the night. Marcello went into damage control with Alpha Command when we got home. And as usual, Luca disappeared into his office to make another shady deal with criminals.

Bastian wove his fingers through my hair. "We agreed to this years ago. Luca wants to marry you. I wanted your virginity. Marcello wants the first child. And Damian just wants to be included."

"But how does this work? Say I marry Luca and have Marcello's child. Then what?" I sat up and propped my back up against a stack of pillows. "What's in this for you now that you've taken my virginity? What about Damian?"

"I'm not going anywhere, baby." He dipped his head down and kissed my lips. "You're everything I have ever wanted. A queen. A woman who uses her trauma and turns it into a strength." His fingers continued their slow exploration down the length of my right side. "I would be a fool to walk away from you. All of us would be."

"I understand what Luca and Marcello have to gain. But not you and Damian."

"We want to share you." His tongue swept into my mouth just long enough to make me crave more. "We want to

77

worship you like a queen." He sucked my bottom lip into his mouth. "So let us."

"Promise not to leave me."

I hated how pathetic my voice sounded, but I was sick of everyone in my life using me for something and then abandoning me.

He nodded, his forehead brushing mine. "I couldn't walk away if I tried. I've never wanted anything as much as I want you, Cherry." Bastian bit my lip. "You're mine. Have been from the first second I laid eyes on you."

"If I agree to marry Luca or Marcello, you're okay with that? It won't make you feel differently about us?"

"Doesn't matter which of us you marry. It's a piece of paper. You'll still be a Salvatore."

He ended the conversation by pinning me to the mattress and ripping off my panties. I stared into his eyes and saw his love and devotion for me written all over his face.

Even if he couldn't process the word, I knew he loved me. Yet, a part of me feared what that love could do to me. Because something as powerful as love also had the power to destroy.

***

After Bastian fucked me twice, he washed every inch of my body. Then, he left to handle an urgent issue for work. He didn't talk about Atlantic Airlines much, but I knew he was a busy man. Damian wasn't emotionally aware. So that left Bastian to deal with the personal relationships they needed to maintain to ensure the success of their business.

I walked into the ensuite bathroom that adjoined my room with Damian's. Brushing my wet hair in the mirror, I studied the bruises Bastian left on my arms. He was rougher than I had expected. But I liked it all the same.

I glanced to my left, surprised to see Damian's door wide open. It was the first time I'd gotten a good look into his bedroom. The walls were black, the floors a dark gray wood. Even his headboard and sheets were black.

I poked my head into the entryway and found Damian dressed in a suit, his dark head lowered. He held a picture in his hand as if trying to commit it to memory. So I observed my hunter in his natural habitat.

"You can come in," Damian said after a moment of silence. "I know you're watching me, Pet."

His head lifted just enough that my eyes met his green ones. His skin was so pale and smooth that it looked like alabaster. I wanted to paint him. He was the only Salvatore I hadn't put brush to canvas yet. But I had plans to capture his handsome face and those haunting eyes for the world to see.

I inched toward him, apprehensive because his behavior was out of the ordinary. He never let me into his closed-off world. Hell, he couldn't even spend the night with us.

"What are you looking at?"

He showed me the picture in his hand. A beautiful woman with the same dark hair, smooth, pale skin, and wide green eyes stared back at me.

"Is that your mom?"

He nodded. "Today would have been her fiftieth birthday."

"What was her name?"

His eyes shifted to me. "Sofia."

I sat on the bed beside him and placed my hand on his knee. "I can see where you get your looks. She was beautiful."

"And smart," he said with a rare smile. "My mother was an electrical engineer. One of the best in her field."

"Wow, that's a cool job."

"That's how she met my dad." He clutched the picture, his

sole focus on his mother as he told me the story. "His original plan wasn't to start an airline. It was to build an aircraft. He hired her to spot the flaws in his design." He laughed, then his gaze flicked to me for a moment. "Of course, she figured them out. She was..." Damian looked at me as he considered his next words. "She was so much better than him. Too good for him."

I smiled at his confession and squeezed his knee. "She sounds like an incredible woman."

"I miss her," he said under his breath. "Her laugh. Her smile. She was the only good thing in my life..." He blew out a deep breath as he refocused on me. "And then, I met you."

"Damian," I whispered, covering his hand with mine. "It's okay to be yourself with me. I hope you know that."

He shook his head, and a long, dark strand of hair fell in front of his eyes. "No, it's not."

I swiped the hair off his forehead and forced him to look at me. "I'm not afraid of you anymore. I know you didn't mean to hurt me."

"No, I didn't. It was an accident." He sighed, his eyes downcast as he looked at my hand on top of his. "Sometimes, I lose control. I can't help it."

"Did your mother know about your urges?"

Damian bobbed his head, unable to look at me. "She thought it was a phase. That I would grow out of it. Back then, I hurt small animals." His hand clenched into a fist on the mattress. "The first time, it was a means to an end. To stop the suffering of a bird with a broken wing. I thought I was doing it a favor. But I liked it. I liked the power over another living thing. The doctors agreed I would eventually get over it. But they were all wrong. That obsession turned into something much worse."

I forced a smile. "Thank you for telling me."

"I figured Bash told you everything after I almost killed you."

"He filled me in on the basics, but it's not the same as hearing it from you." We sat in silence for a while, the air thick with tension. I looked at him, desperate to keep him talking about himself. "How did your parents end up starting an airline?"

"My dad thought he could build a militarized aircraft to sell to the government. But all the major contractors had already beaten him to the punch. So they started Atlantic Airlines instead."

"How did Bash's parents get involved?"

"Our dads were best friends." I slipped my fingers between his, and he let me hold his hand. "Bash's mom was an Adams. The daughter of Fitzgerald Archibald Adams IV."

"The Grand Master of The Founders Society?"

He nodded. "My parents had money but nothing like Bash's mom. She offered to float some of the operating costs until they turned a profit. Bash's grandfather wasn't thrilled about it. Fitzy wouldn't let Bash's mom invest in Atlantic Airlines without his dad agreeing to make Bash the company chairman on his twenty-first birthday."

"That's so young. Why would he want that?"

"He hated Marcus. Bash's dad," he said for clarification. "No one was good enough for his daughter. It didn't matter that Marcus Kincaid was a legacy. He never liked his family."

"So why did he agree to let his daughter marry him?"

He rolled his shoulders. "I've always wondered if Fitzy had something to do with the accident. Our moms shouldn't have been on the plane that night."

"Bash said you two were at his piano recital."

"Yeah." A smile turned up the corners of his mouth. "I went to all of Bash's recitals. Carolina, Bash's mom, she's the one who taught him to play. She never missed a recital until that night."

"You think Bash's grandfather had something to do with your parents' deaths?"

He nodded. "That old bastard would do anything to get what he wants. Even sacrifice his daughter."

"But why would he involve your parents?"

"My dad opposed his vote at the last F Society meeting before his death."

"Bash said his grandfather is why Arlo adopted both of you."

"They made a deal to keep us together."

He bit his bottom lip, staring at my mouth with a darkness that had suddenly washed over his face like a storm cloud. In an instant, his mood shifted. The dead look in his green eyes reminded me of the night he hooked his belt around my neck. The night I thought he was going to kill me.

"Damian, what is it?" I tapped my fingers over the top of his. "Where did you go on me?"

"Bash is the only one who understands me," he confessed.

"Yeah, I can see that." I stroked my fingers down his arm, and his lips parted with desire. "But what kind of deal did Arlo make with Bash's grandfather?"

He licked his lips and focused on my mouth. "He promised to give Arlo more time to produce an heir from a Founding Family." Damian grabbed my thigh and pulled me onto his lap. "You're our saving grace, Pet."

I felt his excitement through his pants and rocked my hips to meet his growing erection. "You don't need me."

"Yes, I do," he breathed, his lips inches from mine. "We all want something different from you."

"What do you want?"

He sucked my lip into his mouth and tugged hard, avoiding my question. I thought he would kiss me.

"Tell me, Damian." I rubbed my wet pussy against his hard cock and hooked my arms around his neck. "I want to understand you. I know you feel you can only be yourself with Bash, but I want to be that person for you, too."

He grabbed my ass cheeks and created some friction

between us. "I don't want you to be afraid. I want to teach you, to show you what I like."

"Okay," I agreed. "Show me."

He flipped me onto my back and stripped off my skirt and panties within seconds. Damian removed my clothes so quickly I couldn't even process what was happening. As he moved between my thighs, I yanked off his tie and then worked on undoing each of the buttons of his shirt.

Dark ink marked most of his chest, starting at his collarbone and dipping beneath his boxer briefs. He had both arms covered in sleeves with hardly any place left untouched. But I stopped moving when I spotted the tattoo right over his heart.

I pressed my fingers over the exact spot where it said *Alexandrea* in black script with a crown beneath it.

My lips parted in surprise as I looked up at him. "Damian, you have my name over your heart."

He looked away. "I got that a long time ago."

I turned his gaze back to me and smiled. "Until recently, I thought you hated me."

He shook his head. "I never hated you. I hated my feelings for you."

Feelings?

I didn't think he had any, but maybe I was wrong about him.

As if we had never had this conversation, he shrugged off his shirt and discarded his pants and boxer briefs. He kneeled between my legs, his long, hard cock aimed at me.

Even as a teenage girl, I knew he wouldn't be sweet or gentle. So when he thrust into me, filling me to the hilt, I had expected it. Though my body still hadn't adjusted to his size or the quickness of his movements.

He lifted his silky red tie from the bed with a smirk. I noticed the shift in his demeanor when he pinned my arms above my head and tied my wrists together.

"Damian, what are you doing?"

"You said I can be myself with you." His tongue glided across his full, red lips. "Let me show you."

"I thought bondage was Bash's kink."

An evil grin pulled at his mouth. "It's mine, too."

He pumped into me harder, raising both of my thighs over his shoulders as he slammed into me like he was trying to leave an imprint of his cock in my pussy. "Fuck," he hissed. "Your pussy is so tight." Then, my dangerous psycho went to a completely different place as he drove into me like a maniac, fucking me so hard I felt a lot of pain before it turned to pleasure. "Open up for me, Pet."

After destroying my pussy, he pulled out of me and reached for a black rope tied to the bedpost. My eyes widened as he wrapped the rope around my ankle, then moved to the other side to repeat the same process with my right ankle.

"Damian, I haven't even let Bash do this. So I'm trusting you."

He nodded. "You can trust me."

I'd never felt so vulnerable, exposed with my legs spread wide. But knowing Damian wouldn't judge me, I didn't care all that much. He'd never treated me like the crazy girl because he was crazier than me.

Damian moved me up toward the headboard, so my legs were open as far as they would go. The ropes rubbed my skin, but I tried to ignore it. I'd asked him to show me what he liked, so he would feel like he could talk to me. Even if I was a little scared, I had to pretend for him. I had to know what he was really like in the bedroom.

He untied my wrists and threw the silk tie on the floor. I let out a sigh of relief, which didn't last long. He pulled my arms apart and bound each of my wrists to the posts of his headboard. Damian climbed on top of me with a knife in his hand and unsheathed the blade.

"You're pretty, Pet." A sadistic look crossed his handsome

face as our eyes met. "But I need to put my mark on you. So my brothers know exactly where I've touched you."

I bit my lip to stop it from trembling. "Are you going to cut me?"

He nodded. "I want to taste you."

My blood.

Oh my God.

"Okay," I whispered. "But promise not to get too carried away. Bash isn't here to stop you this time."

"Don't you trust me?" His jaw clenched as his grip tightened on the knife. "You said you did."

I arched my hips, and the tip of his cock brushed my wet folds. "Yes. I trust you."

He leaned forward with the blade inches from my inner thigh. A wave of nervous energy rushed over me, sending a tremor down my spine.

"Damian," I bit out. "Wait."

His eyes lifted to meet mine.

"Kiss me first."

He shook his head.

We still hadn't kissed, even after all these years. I wanted him so badly I couldn't stand not having this moment of intimacy.

"If you ever want us to have a similar connection to what you have with Bash, you need to kiss me."

That seemed to catch his attention. He set the knife on the mattress, crawled up my body, and slid his hand beneath my chin.

"Have you ever kissed a woman?"

Another shake of his head.

Like Luca, he wasn't a fan of kissing, intimacy, or anything that required human contact. They were so fucked up. Yet, even after years of trauma, I could still feel love and compassion and normal human emotions.

"Kiss me." My tone was firm, demanding. "Now."

He bent his head down, his lips so close to mine I could feel his breath on my skin. "Will this make you happy, Pet?"

"I think it will make you happy, too." I smiled up at him with my eyes, trying to forget about the sting of the ropes on my skin. "You need this kiss as much as I do."

A dark chuckle escaped past his lips. "And you think you know what I need?"

"Yes, I do." I wet my lips. "Kiss me, Damian. Your queen won't ask you again."

He smirked with a wicked glint in his eyes, and then his mouth descended upon mine, his tongue parting my lips. I kissed him with every bit of pent-up frustration and desire I'd harbored over the years. We fought for possession over the other, our tongues tangling with a delicious fury that made me crave him.

When I rocked my hips again, he held me down and slammed his big cock inside me. He got rougher with each thrust, his kisses hot and angry. I loved this side of him. It was carnal, raw, and this crazy motherfucker was all mine.

He shoved his fingers into my mouth right as our lips separated and slid them down my throat. I practically choked on them as he fucked me like a possessed demon.

I didn't expect love-making or anything sweet. With Damian, I didn't want hearts and roses. I liked the wild, uninhibited monster who had haunted my dreams for years.

My entire body was numb from a mixture of pain and pleasure. He fucked me with no limits, and I begged him for more with each orgasm he stole from me.

"Look at you, Pet." He removed his fingers from my mouth and pumped into me like a savage. "Completely at my mercy."

His words chilled me to the bone.

"Damian, don't think about doing anything stupid."

He grinned like a psychopath.

Like my psycho.

He tugged on the rope chaining my right wrist to his bedpost, and laughed. "Like what, Pet?"

"I don't know." My chest rose and fell as I studied his face and noted the insanity dancing across his eyes. "But you have that look again. I don't like it."

"I'm giving you what you want." He dropped the rope, a frown in place, and continued fucking me even harder than before. "You asked for this, Pet."

"Quit acting like a lunatic."

He waggled his eyebrows and lifted the knife from the bed. "But I am one. Isn't that right, baby?" Then, grabbing my hip, he shredded my inner walls with his thick cock, slicing into my right breast with the knife. "That's what you think of me."

It was a small cut but still made me gasp. His eyes moved to the blood sliding over my nipple. A wild expression crossed his eyes, and then he leaned forward to suck the tiny bud into his mouth. He dropped the knife on the mattress, and one of his hands closed around my throat. He bit and sucked, tasting my blood as he squeezed my throat, stealing the air from my lungs.

I kicked my legs and struggled against the restraints. But it only hurt more. The ropes burned my skin, a searing hot pain that flooded my body.

Damian slowed his pace, his hand still firmly wrapped around my throat. He tipped his head back, my blood slithering down from his lips to his jaw, looking so peaceful as he came inside me.

My scary monster pulled out of me and dropped onto the mattress as if he had done nothing wrong. Like it was normal to tie up women, choke them, drink their blood, and damn near destroy their pussy.

"Damian, untie me right now!" I wiggled my arms, even though it hurt like hell and was pointless.

"I'm done playing this game with you."

He groaned, giving me a smile that looked more wicked

than cute. Then, despite his hesitation, he begrudgingly freed me from my shackles, one rope at a time. The second he unfastened the last rope, I climbed on top of him, doing my best to hold him down. But it was no use.

He was ten times stronger and bigger than me. Within a second, he had me flat on my back and in control of the situation.

"I'm so mad at you right now." I blinked away the tears threatening to spill down my cheeks. "So fucking mad!"

He ran a hand through his hair and sighed. "I did it again, didn't I?"

"Are you kidding me, Damian?" I shoved my palms into his chest. "How are you so unaware of yourself?"

"Do you always know when you're about to have a disso-ciative episode?" His lips nearly brushed mine. "Hmm, Pet? Are you always in control of your PTSD?"

"No," I admitted. "But I can usually tell when I'm starting to detach from reality."

"Sorry, I tried." He blew out a deep breath and rolled off me. "But I'll never be what you want me to be."

Before I could speak, he slid off the bed, naked and looking so fucking sexy I almost forgot how much I hated him at the moment. Damian wasn't getting off that easily. So I followed him into the bathroom. He turned on the shower and then spun around to face me.

I raised my hand and beckoned him with my finger. "Come here, Damian." He stared through me like he couldn't even hear me. "Get over here and apologize."

A moment of hesitation ensued before he took two steps forward. He scrubbed a hand across his jaw. "I already said I was sorry."

Teeth clenched, I folded my arms over my breasts. "Mean it this time."

He surprised me by lowering to his knees in front of me.

His hands moved to my hips as he pulled me closer, my pussy right in front of his mouth. "I'm sorry."

"Do you know why you're sorry?"

Damian gave me a boyish look and shook his head. "Did I fuck you too hard?" Then he spread my thighs and started kissing my pussy. Soft and slow, he licked me like he should have kissed me. "Did I hurt you, Pet?"

"Yes," I whispered as I fisted his hair and tugged on it, encouraging him to continue.

"Do you want me to kiss it all better?" Damian peeked up at me, his lips glistening with my cum. "Tell me how you want me to make it up to you."

I held his dark hair in a vise. "Do you want to make it up to me? Or are you trying to manipulate me?"

He winked. "A little of both."

And then his mouth was on me again, and I couldn't even focus on my anger, let alone yell at him. We eventually got into the shower, and he fucked me against the wall with my arms above my head as he entered me from behind. The second time, he was still rough, but I was ready for it. I finally understood there was no changing a man like Damian Salvatore. And I realized I wouldn't want him any other way.

Chapter Twelve

ALEX

A few hours after the rough sex with Damian, Marcello stopped by his mother's studio to watch me paint. He sat in the armchair by the easel in complete silence, entranced by each swipe of my brush. His cell phone rang as I finished with the painting of Damian.

Marcello spoke in Italian and then shot up from the chair, extending his hand to help me up from the floor. "We have to go. Luca wants us in his office."

I took his hand, pressing my palm to his chest to regain my bearings. "Why?"

"Your grandfather is here."

He grabbed my hand and led me across the studio, dragging me down the hallway and upstairs to the third floor. Luca occupied most of the west wing. I craned my neck to look at the library as we passed by the double doors. We entered Luca's office, which had high ceilings and a long mahogany desk set between a wall of windows. A patio overlooked the bay.

I was surprised to see Drake Battle and Cole Marshall on the couch beside Damian and Bastian. Everyone gathered around Luca, who lounged in an oversized armchair by the fireplace. It was clear he would become their leader, always at the group's center.

Sonny Cormac and his brothers, Finn and Callum, leaned into each other, their whispers ceasing when I entered the room with Marcello. Luca propped up his dress shoe on his knee, shooting a wicked look in my direction. I hadn't seen him since we got home from The Mansion. As much as I wanted to hate him, I couldn't deny he had an instant effect on my body, stripping me bare with his eyes.

Luca's jaw ticked as he studied the bruises on my neck and arms. "What the fuck happened to you?"

I shook my head. "Not now, Luca."

His eyes shot across the room at Bastian and Damian, and he bared his teeth as he looked at them. Damian gave him an apologetic look while Bastian just shrugged.

"Yes, I would like to know why my granddaughter looks like she's been in a car accident," Pops said with anger, his gaze fixed on the dark marks around my neck.

"I'm fine," I assured him.

I waved to no one in particular and said hello to the group. Some men spoke, while others tipped their heads in greeting. Sonny gave me one of his pretty boy smiles.

"Why are you limping?" Luca asked me, his eyebrows tipped up in question.

I glanced at Damian and shook my head. "Ask your brothers."

Damian smirked.

Bastian laughed.

My entire body ached from my encounter with Damian. It wasn't just from him being rough. I'd also fucked Bastian twice before Damian got a hold of me and destroyed my pussy.

They marked me good.

Luca shook his head, clearly annoyed that his brothers spent quality time with me. He was the only one who refused to fuck me.

"Over here, Alex." Pops flagged me down, a frown making the wrinkles around his mouth look more pronounced. "Come sit beside me." Then he turned to Arlo and said, "I never agreed to let your sons mutilate my granddaughter."

Arlo's eyes shot to me, then to each of his sons. "It won't happen again, Carl." He patted him on the shoulder. "Alexandrea is safe at our estate."

Marcello took his place on the couch next to Damian and Bastian. I rushed over to Pops and threw myself into his arms. He was the reason I was in this situation. But my life would have been much worse if he hadn't saved me from my awful parents.

My eyes swept over the room. "What's going on?"

"You're aware of The Devil's Knights," Pops said. "But I haven't told you much about them."

"Yeah, I know. It's a secret society."

"It's more than a secret society." He set his glass on the table and turned in his chair. "The Knights are a brotherhood. There's a hierarchy in our world. We start as Knights before we can ascend to The Founders Society. You will become the Queen of The Devil's Knights. Which means you need to marry a Salvatore."

"Yes, I know. But I'm not ready to get married," I said, resolute about my decision. "I also don't understand why a group of men need a queen. It doesn't make any sense. They are more than capable of taking care of themselves."

"Because it was the only way to ensure your safety," my grandfather said in a firm tone. "I didn't trust Arlo's boys not to hurt you. But, I also knew that if the Knights had to protect you, it would keep the target off your back."

My eyebrows lifted as I looked at him. "What target?"

"You're a Wellington." He scratched the corner of his jaw and sighed. "Our name holds a lot of power. For years, I have shielded you from the harshness of our world with the help of the Knights. But with power comes a lot of enemies. We owe them, so I agreed to let one of Arlo's sons marry you, with the caveat you would become the first and only queen of The Devil's Knights."

"You came up with the idea to make me their queen?" My eyes narrowed at him. "I wish you would have asked me first. What if I don't want to be their queen?"

"Must you always be so difficult?" Pops fired back.

I flashed a fake smile at him. "I learned from the best."

"Alex," Pops groaned. "This isn't about you or the Salvatores or how you feel about me and this arrangement. The Knights need a queen."

Arlo leaned forward with his elbow rested on the arm of a leather chair. He studied me with his usual impenetrable gaze that sent a chill down my arms. I thought he would speak, but instead, he sat there and waited for my grandfather to finish.

Pops grabbed my shoulder. "Alex, there's something we need to discuss with you." I pressed my lips together, and he continued, "There's a lot of hostility between you and Luca. And something is going on between you and the other boys."

I wanted to say they're not boys anymore. Instead, they had grown into ruthless, sexy men who I let do sinful things to my body.

"You have until the end of the summer to choose who you will marry," he said.

My gaze shifted between Marcello and Luca. "What if I can't choose?"

All business, my grandfather remained expressionless. "Then I will choose for you."

"I already know who you would pick," I shot back.

"Fuck this," Luca snapped, his nostrils flaring, tapping his serpent ring on the arm of his chair. "You promised Alex to me a long time ago, Wellington. No more games."

My grandfather glowered at Luca as he pointed his finger at him. "Boy, you better learn to respect your elders."

"Luca needs to change," I told my grandfather. "Until he does, I won't even consider his proposal."

Leaning back in his chair, Luca folded his arms over his chest. "Not happening."

"Then I guess you'll make this decision easy for me."

He snarled at me, eyes filled with anger. "I should have let them take you."

"I hate you!" I shot up from my chair, my top lip quivering as I glared at him. "Next time, let them take me. Anywhere is better than here with you." I gritted my teeth, fire rolling off my skin. "I'm so done with you."

His top lip quivered. "You're done when I say."

"Marcello is nice to me," I said to torture him, slice open his wounds, and pour salt into them. My eyes moved to Marcello. "We never fight. He does things without me having to ask him. If he asked me to marry him, I would say yes."

Marcello smiled for a second but turned his head to hide it once Luca snapped his head at him. When Marcello looked at me, my heart leaped out of my chest. So many happy emotions raced over me at once.

"Drea," Luca said through clenched teeth. "Don't do this."

The air drained from my lungs as our eyes met. "I can't fight like this for the rest of my life. My childhood was too hard to spend the next thirty years arguing with you."

"You want me to change?" Luca ran a hand through his dark hair and then waved his hand to dismiss me. "Fine. Whatever you want."

"Words have no meaning without action."

Pops grabbed my elbow. "You have people who need you. Men who would fight for you. Kill for you. Even die for you. This isn't about you or Luca."

With the Knights staring at me, my skin flushed with heat. I'd taken this fight with Luca a little too far.

"I planned your wedding for the second week in September," Pops told me.

I cleared my throat, shooting daggers at him. "Excuse me?"

"We don't have time to waste," my grandfather explained. "The Knights can't admit any new members outside of the yearly initiation process until they have a queen. It's in the charter."

"Don't you make the rules? Just break them."

He shook his head. "It doesn't work like that. If I don't follow the rules, why should anyone be under my authority?"

I bit my lip to stifle my nerves.

"The Russians will do anything to steal you from the Knights." My grandfather's expression turned grim. "They will come for you again, and when they do, they will have more men and a better plan. Without a queen, it weakens the Knights' ranks, putting you in a vulnerable situation, Alex."

"I'm not marrying Luca just for the hell of it. You said I have a choice, and I'm not ready to make it."

Arlo's jaw tightened. Luca stared at the wall on the other side of the room. The rest of the Knights nervously shifted in their seats.

"Alex," Pops boomed. "This is a sensitive matter."

"You act like the Salvatores are your enemies when you have been plotting with them behind my back for years."

"We owe them," he said with authority.

"Why did you promise me to them?" I leaned forward and got in his face. "Hmm? Tell me the truth. I accepted this arrangement a long time ago, but I want answers. I'm sick of being the pawn of bored rich men."

"You're not a pawn," Pops assured me, placing his hand on my shoulder to soothe me. "You have more power than you understand."

"Then help me understand because I'm not interested in power or money. Tell me what you did," I demanded. "If you want me to be part of your billionaire boys' club, I want to know your secret. Why do you owe Arlo a debt?"

He shoved a hand through his white hair and sighed. "Because your mother murdered Eva."

My heart nearly stopped at his confession. I clutched my chest, eyes wide as I stared at his withered face for any signs of malice.

It was the truth.

Fuck.

Cold waves rushed up and down my arms, slithering down my back. "What? Are you...?" The words were on the tip of my tongue. "No, she wouldn't... She didn't..." I shook my head, unable to think clearly over the ringing in my ears. "Why would she do that?"

"Your mother poisoned Eva with a drug produced by Wellington Pharmaceuticals." He leaned closer and put his hand on my knee to stop it from trembling, but even his touch did little to quell the anxiety coursing through my veins. "The FDA took it off the market because of its side effects. Even in small doses, it causes death."

I couldn't stop blinking as I stared at my grandfather. My mother killed my idol. She took Luca and Marcello's mother from them.

"She tried to poison me when I was a child," I whispered in disbelief, tears wetting my cheeks. "I was sick for weeks. Was it the same drug?"

Pops nodded. "Your father took you to the hospital before you overdosed. But unfortunately, Eva wasn't as lucky. Luca found his mother on the floor in her studio."

I covered my mouth to stifle my gasp. "But the newspapers said she died in a car accident." My eyes widened as I glanced over at Luca. "You've always known about this?"

Luca nodded.

"The day we met?"

Another nod.

"Now I understand," I muttered, still in shock. "It makes sense why you've been so…" I swiped at the tears leaking from my eyes. "I didn't know… Why didn't anyone tell me?"

"I hated you at first sight," Luca admitted, his arms crossed over his chest, a dress shoe propped up on his knee. "I knew you weren't your bitch mother. But I still didn't like you. So I merely tolerated your existence."

I looked at Marcello, who stared back at me with his sad, lonely eyes. Everyone in the room knew but me.

"Why would she do that?" I asked Pops.

He sipped from the snifter of scotch in his hand. "She regretted leaving Arlo after I took away her trust fund. Your parents have no life skills. Between the two of them, they couldn't even pay the cable bill."

I knew that story all too well.

When we had food, my parents never gave it to Aiden and me. I was lucky to get the crust from my mother's sandwich. Of course, that was on a good day. We always had used dirty clothes that were disgusting and an embarrassment to wear to school.

After my grandfather had given us his last name, I realized most people didn't live like us. But most people didn't live like the Founders either. I went from one extreme to the other overnight, a real-life Cinderella story.

My top lip trembled as I thought about my mother and the past.

"But why did she do it?"

"Your mother was jealous of Eva," Arlo confessed.

Pops sat back in the leather chair and drank from his glass. "Your mother doesn't have enough talent to accomplish what Eva did in her short life. She believed Eva was in her way. Savanna saw her as competition, though anyone with any vision could see that was not true." He shifted in his chair to set the glass on the table in front of him. "Your mother hated you for the same reason."

"What?" I shook my head. "No. I didn't start painting until I was in high school. It was my doctor's idea to deal with the stress."

"That's not true," Pops said with a sincere look. "You started sketching when you were only two years old."

"No, I don't remember that."

"It's true," Arlo interjected. "Your mother sent the sketches to Carl, thinking he would see your talent and want to be part of your life. She tried to use you and Aiden to bribe him."

"Why didn't you come for us sooner?" I whispered the words as tears stained my cheeks. "Did you know how she treated us?"

"No, I didn't know she was abusing you and your brother." He removed the silk handkerchief from his jacket pocket and handed it to me. It probably cost a fortune, but I didn't give a shit and wiped my eyes with it. "If I had known, I would have adopted you sooner." He swiped at my cheek and smiled. "Listen, Alex, I know this is hard to hear, but it's the truth. You needed to understand why this marriage is so important."

"I feel ridiculous!" I threw the handkerchief at him. "You let me think the Salvatores were the bad guys for years when it's us. We're killers!"

"I'm not," Pops said in his defense. "Neither are you."

"She's my mother," I snapped. "Your daughter! Don't tell me our blood isn't tainted. I'm not stupid. You can pretend your secret society is nothing more than rich men making deals behind closed doors, but you're a liar. You didn't get rich from selling pharmaceuticals. Aiden was right to want out of this family."

"Alex, please control your emotions." He held out his palm as a peace offering. "You're getting upset. And you know what happens when you can't control yourself."

"Fuck off!" I hopped up from the chair so fast my head spun. "I should have run away with Aiden. He begged me to leave and never return. But I always felt like I owed you for saving me from my mother." I tipped my head back and laughed like a fucking lunatic, feeling like I was completely losing my mind. "Except you didn't save me. You're no better than her. Another liar. Manipulative. I'm only here because you have something to lose."

"I'm sorry, Alex," Pops said as I turned to walk away. "But this is the least we owe them."

He was right.

I stopped dead in my tracks, my back to him. We owed them for what my mother did to theirs. Their horrible, abusive life with their father resulted from my mother's actions. No amount of money would ever satisfy Arlo Salvatore. Nothing could repay him for taking the life of his wife.

Marcello rose from the couch and crossed the room, holding me in his strong arms. "Just hear him out, princess." He kissed the top of my head, the delicious scent of his cologne wafting off him. "Just breathe." His hands glided over my arms as he bent down and looked into my eyes. "It's going to be okay."

"How can you stand to look at me?" I muttered, now crying again, tears sliding down my face.

He wiped them away with the pad of his thumb. "Because I can't imagine a life that doesn't include you. What happened in the past is over. You are not your mother. I don't blame you for what she did."

I wrapped my arms around his neck and cried on his chest for five minutes before I stopped shaking. This was the last thing I had expected. My mother was a lot of things, but I didn't think she could kill. Sure, she was cruel and could give the Wicked Witch a run for her money, but I never thought she would stoop so low.

Marcello helped me back into my chair beside my grand-father and stood behind me with his hand on my shoulder. We sat in silence for a moment, everyone in the room staring at me. None of the Knights had spoken. I wasn't even sure why they had to attend this shit show.

I always felt safe with Marcello. With Luca, I felt like every nerve ending in my body was on fire. Like I was losing control. It was an out-of-body experience I'd never had with anyone else.

Luca made me feel alive, but maybe it was just the adrenaline rushing through my veins. The fear and desire laced together.

My grandfather placed his hand on my knee. "The Devil's Knights charter says the current Grand Master has to transfer his power to his oldest son within one month of his twenty-fifth birthday. Luca turns twenty-five on July thirty-first. I expect your decision by then."

"Okay," I said, still deflated by the news about my mother, not the least bit thrilled about the shotgun wedding. "But I don't think I can choose."

His eyebrows raised an inch as he looked at me. "Why not?"

"Because I'm with all four of them."

A gasp slipped past his lips, but he quickly slapped a stern expression on his face. "You can't marry four men, Alex. Choose one of them, or I will choose for you."

Because I was angry with him, I pointed at the dark handprint around my neck. "This is from Damian choking me during sex." Then I showed him the black and blue marks on my shoulders. "Bastian gave me these right before Damian tied me to his bed." Next, I lifted my skirt a few inches to show him the dark fingerprints on my thigh. "These are from Marcello when I fucked him in the car." Then I shoved my hair off my neck so he could see the bite marks on the right side. "And these are from Luca's teeth."

My grandfather's nostrils flared. He aimed a nasty glare at each of the Salvatore boys and then finally at Arlo. "Damian and Bastian were not part of the deal. We agreed Alex would choose between Marcello and Luca."

Arlo raised his hands in surrender. "Carl, I assure you, I didn't know. But it doesn't look like they forced themselves on her."

"She's been living under your roof. How do you not know what your boys are doing to her?"

He shrugged. "I haven't seen your granddaughter in weeks. This is a big house."

"They didn't force me," I said to ease his anger, though it did little to help our cause. "I wanted them to fuck me. I saved my virginity just for them."

I thought I heard Sonny laugh on the other side of the room.

Pops flew out of his chair like it was on fire, hands clenched at his sides. "Don't speak to me with that dirty mouth."

"Are we done here, Wellington?" Luca asked my grandfather with a cocky grin. "I have another meeting in ten minutes."

He pointed his finger at Luca. "You're on thin ice, boy. Watch how you speak to me, or your family will lose their standing with The Founders Society. This marriage is only in play because I have allowed it. I don't have to make this right between the Wellingtons and Salvatores."

Arlo joined my grandfather and set his hand on his shoulder. "Carl, how about we discuss this in my office? A shipment of the Macallan Red Collection just arrived. Your favorite."

Pops nodded, never one to refuse expensive scotch. As he left the room with Arlo, he didn't look at me.

The second the door slammed shut, Sonny burst into a fit of laughter. "Holy shit! I've never seen Wellington lose his cool before." He raised his hand for me to slap. "That was some gangster shit, Little Wellington. You showed him."

Luca rose from the armchair and moved behind his desk,

flinging his arm. "All of you, get out of my office! This meeting is over."

I approached him with caution because he looked slightly unhinged. "We should talk."

Eyes on the computer monitor, he clicked a few buttons and shook his head. "Not now, Drea. I have to prepare for a conference call."

"Come find me later."

He ignored me and typed feverishly, his fingers gliding across the keys.

"I'm starving," Bastian groaned. "Who's staying for lunch?"

The Knights grunted in agreement.

Chapter Thirteen

ALEX

After the meeting ended, I sat on the veranda that overlooked the bay with the Knights. I felt like their queen with how each of them showed their admiration. It was subtle for some, all in the way they watched over me. Whereas with others like Sonny, it was apparent.

Marcello sat on my right, his fingers burrowed into my hip like he wanted everyone to know I was his. Sonny sat on my left and flirted with me throughout lunch, doing his best to steal my attention from Marcello.

Bastian and Damian sat directly across from us. They stared at me with their usual hunter's eyes. It was as if they were afraid someone would take me away from them if they didn't keep their sole focus on me. Luca stayed in his office for another meeting unrelated to the Knights. He rarely joined us, always busy with work, and it was seriously getting on my nerves.

After my grandfather dropped that bomb on me, I wanted to talk to him. To all of them. But not with the Knights here.

We ate family-style, gourmet Kobe beef sliders to skewered steak and lobster rolls. I reached across the table to grab a plate. When I looked up, the Knights on the other side of the table stared at me.

Drake licked his lips, his eyes traveling between my mouth and my cleavage. He shoved his hand through his dark hair, sweeping it off his forehead. The tech billionaire always dressed in expensive suits like armor clung to his body.

I had to laugh when I noticed a blue T-shirt beneath his oxford. It had the Superman logo on it. His eyes followed mine, and then he rolled his shoulders.

Cole sat beside Drake, holding my gaze with a look that made my skin sizzle. You could tell Cole had spent his entire life in military school. Arms corded with muscle, he had bands of dark tattoos wrapped around his biceps. He never wore suits, not unless required. Dressed in black cargo pants and a tight T-shirt, he was drool-worthy.

"What are you two staring at?" I asked them.

Drake grinned like an idiot while Cole stared at me with fascination. I clutched the plate of burgers and pulled it toward me. I had the attention of every man at the table.

The Knights were good-looking, blue-blooded men. It was like their parents had filled out a form, checked off all the right boxes, and maybe even offered sacrifices to their gilded gods.

"Why are you all staring at me like I'm your lunch?"

"Might want to fix your shirt, queenie," Finn Cormac said with a wink.

Sonny's younger brother looked like him in every way. He was tall, handsome, and with sun-kissed skin. The same wide green eyes and surfer blond hair. Except Finn had a little more muscle, broader in the shoulders.

"Or don't," Sonny added with laughter in his voice. "I prefer this view."

"Your nipple is showing," Drake said.

"Oh, my God." I stuffed my boob back into my bikini top.

Marcello reached over and squeezed my boob playfully. "I'm hungry." He tipped his head at the burgers. "Feed me."

I laughed. "You're a grown man. Feed yourself."

"C'mon, princess." He wet his full, sexy lips with his tongue. "I'm starved."

"For attention," I shot back as I lifted a slider from the plate.

As I bent over to put the burger between Marcello's teeth, Sonny's hand glided down my backside, all the way down my thigh.

"Sonny," I groaned. "Control yourself."

"That's impossible with your ass in my face," he quipped. "Consider yourself lucky I didn't take a bite out of this sexy ass."

"Get your hands off our woman, Cormac," Bastian fired back with venom in his tone.

My heart pounded as I looked across the table and into his eyes. I felt like I would spontaneously combust whenever he looked at me. Of course, it didn't help Sonny was invading my personal space with his delicious scent, trailing his fingers up my leg like he'd done it hundreds of times.

I shoved his hand off my leg. "You better watch yourself, Sonny Mac. My men are protective psychos."

He leaned forward and breathed so close to my mouth I felt his breath on my face. "So are your Knights."

I grabbed another burger and fed Marcello. He bit into the burger, and I ate the other half, staring into his adorable blue eyes as we chewed our food.

"Feed me next," Sonny begged.

I laughed. "Not a chance in hell."

"I got a thousand dollars on them fucking by the end of lunch," Callum said as he dropped a stack of hundred-dollar bills on the table.

"I got five on it," Cole chimed. He removed his ATM card from his wallet and added it to the pile.

Sonny threw his Black Amex card on the table on top of Cole's card. "I'll take that bet."

"Nah," Drake said as he reached into his pocket. "I have a better bet. Ten thousand says she picks Marcello over Luca."

"Cheap asshole," Bastian growled with dissatisfaction. "Pony up a hundred grand if you want to make it a gentleman's bet."

"I'm not cheap," Drake said in his defense, removing the checkbook from the inner pocket of his suit jacket. "Double it, and we got a deal."

"Done," Bastian said without hesitation.

"Count me in." Damian pulled out his wallet. "My money is on Luca."

"Me too," Bastian said with an apologetic look at Marcello.

"Fuck both of you," Marcello shot back.

Bastian shrugged while Damian gave him a seriously bone-chilling smirk that screamed, *I eat souls for breakfast.*

I glanced over at them, still leaning on the arm of Marcello's chair. "Why are you guys betting on who I marry? This is ridiculous."

"We bet on everything," Finn said. "We even bet on their chances of getting you back to Devil's Creek."

"I had no choice," I told him. "They tied my brother to a chair and forced me to leave with them."

"I said you'd at least kick one of them in the balls before they got you on the plane." Sonny shook his head, laughing. "You disappointed me, Little Wellington."

"You guys are morons with too much time on your hands," I countered. "And for the record, I'm not fucking Marcello by the end of lunch."

"How about after lunch?" Drake joked.

"I got ten on that," Finn said between bites of his burger.

"All of you are pigs," I muttered. "Stop taking bets on me."

"Look," Sonny said with a cheeky smile. "I'd gladly take a bullet for you if it means getting hand-fed by your fine ass."

"I second that." Cole winked. "Make it a flesh wound, okay?"

"Pussy." Sonny howled with laughter. "Fucking flesh wound? Take it like a grown-up, Marshall."

The rest of the guys echoed their agreement.

I raised my hand to silence them. "No one is shooting anyone."

Sonny slid his arm behind my back and pulled me closer to him. "You better get used to us all up in your business. We know everything about you, Little Wellington."

"So I guess my grandfather's announcement wasn't all that shocking to you guys."

"Not really," Sonny admitted.

"We saw it coming," Drake said. "Luca's fucked this up for years. It was only a matter of time before Arlo or Carl enforced the Charter."

I glanced at Marcello. "What about you? Did you know my grandfather had the wedding planned?"

Marcello shrugged his broad shoulders against the chair. "I don't think Luca has ever considered the possibility of losing control. You have to choose at *Legare*."

I angled my body to look at him. "What is *Legare*?"

"It's a ceremony that simultaneously crowns the new Grand Master of The Devil's Knights and the queen. We've never done it before. You will be our first queen."

"What happens during this ceremony?"

"You have to claim each of the Knights," Sonny interjected. "And then we watch you claim the Grand Master."

I turned in my seat to face him. "You mean I have sex with him?"

His eyes lowered to my cleavage and then back to my face. "Yes. And I, for one, am looking forward to seeing our queen in action."

I slapped him on the arm and chuckled. "You're sick."

After letting his words sink in, I looked at Marcello and then across the table at Damian and Bastian. "What about the three of you?"

"We'll be there," Bastian said.

"But what if I want all of you to participate in the ceremony?"

Bastian rolled his shoulders. "Take that up with Luca."

They'd made it clear that they wanted me to marry Luca from the start. No one seemed to think otherwise, not even the other Knights. So why did everyone discount Marcello? He was the best choice for a husband and father. I could see myself with him. But it wasn't just him anymore.

I had all four of them.

If I ever said yes to Luca's proposal, I would not be marrying Luca alone. They would all, in some ways, be my husband—the father of my children. I wanted a life with each of them.

After lunch, I shot up from the chair and stripped off my shirt. I had a red bikini beneath my tank top and skirt.

Marcello put his fingers between his lips and whistled as his eyes wandered up and down my body. "Damn, princess."

A few of the Knights echoed his sentiment.

"I think he meant to say fuck-hot." Sonny drank from his beer as he eyed me up. He licked his lips and tapped his thigh. "Come sit on my lap, Little Wellington."

I shook my head. "Stop flirting with me, Sonny."

Sonny shot up from the chair with lightning speed and hooked his arm around my middle. Before I could stop him, he lifted my feet off the ground. He threw me over his shoulder, dragging me toward the pool.

I smacked his back, my boobs practically falling out of the top. "Put me down!"

He laughed as he inched closer to the water. "I can't wait for another second to see this gorgeous body soaking wet."

"I'm going to kill you, Sonny!" I pounded my first against his back. "Put. Me. Down. Now."

"She's gonna make you pay for that, bro," Callum warned his older brother.

"I'll be ready and waiting to take my punishment," Sonny said before dropping me into the pool's deep end.

I sank like a stone, my feet touching the bottom of the pool. When I resurfaced, I had a cluster of wet curls stuck to my cheek and in my eyes. I spit water out of my mouth, shoving my hair behind my ears.

"Sonny! I'm going to kill you."

He stood at the pool's edge, his hands on his narrow hips. "You look mad, Little Wellington."

I glared at him, ready to rip out his throat. "You bastard. I can't get my hair wet. I'll look like a poodle that got electrocuted."

"Hmm..." He shoved a hand through his perfectly styled blond hair and gave me one of his boyish smiles. "Not exactly how I'd pictured you handing out my punishment, but I can work with that."

"I have other ideas for your punishment," I shot back.

He licked his lips and bent down at the pool's edge, running his long fingers across the top of the water. I swam into the shallow end and waded through the infinity pool that overlooked the bay. Annoyed, I rushed over to Sonny, shoved my palm into his chest, and pushed him down on the lounge chair.

I jumped on top of him and rubbed my wet body over his Tom Ford suit.

Sonny waggled his eyebrows, a smirk tugging at the right corner of his mouth. "This is some punishment."

"You're not supposed to like this."

He laughed. "I don't give a shit about this suit." His hands fell to my hips, and he rolled his tongue across his bottom lip. "The sight of you on top of me is priceless."

Before I could escape his firm grip, I heard Luca's deep voice from a distance. I glanced over my shoulder at the back of the house. He leaned out the window on the third floor, dressed in a black suit and armed with a nasty look that could kill.

"What the fuck do you think you're doing?" Luca shouted. "Drea, get your ass up here. Now! Bash, Marcello, Damian. You too!"

He slammed the window before we could tell him to fuck off.

Marcello smacked my ass. "Let's go. My brother doesn't like to wait."

Chapter Fourteen

ALEX

Wrapped in a beach towel, I walked down the hallway beside Marcello, Bastian, and Damian. They joked about Luca being a jealous, possessive prick who ruined the fun for everyone else.

We still hadn't talked about my mother's role in Evangeline Franco's death. I knew that conversation would come eventually and dreaded having it. In so many ways, I felt like I owed him. Like I owed all of them for my mother's reckless actions.

Luca sat behind a long mahogany desk, dressed in a three-piece suit. My handsome devil focused on the computer screen before him, looking so severe and intimidating.

His eyes shot up from the screen as we walked into the open room with high ceilings and tons of furniture. The room was large enough to have a bar, sitting area, and a conference table accommodating at least twenty people.

Luca tapped his thigh, staring through me with those piercing blue eyes. "Get over here, Drea."

I stopped midway into the room and shoved my hands onto my hips. "What did I do now?"

"It's time for your punishment." He clenched his jaw. "You've been a very bad girl."

I scoffed at his comment. "Because Sonny threw me into the pool?"

He shook his head. "Have you forgotten what you did on our way home from The Mansion? We risked our lives to get you to safety, and you defied me." Luca patted his thigh. "Get over here. I won't ask you again."

I dropped my towel on his floor and gave him a nice view of my tits falling out of the red bikini top. Bastian grabbed my ass from behind. Marcello massaged my boob with his big hand. And, of course, Damian couldn't stand to be left out. He tilted my head back and bit my neck like a fucking vampire going in for the kill.

I moaned as they touched me.

"Now," Luca demanded. "I don't have all day. Stop fucking around."

They let their hands fall from my body, and then Marcello smacked my ass to push me toward his older brother. I stopped beside his chair, and his eyes bore into mine, cutting through me like knives.

Luca leaned back, arms crossed over his chest.

I pushed my breasts out to tease him. "What's my punishment, sir?"

I had only called him that a few times, but he seemed to like it. He needed to feel in control, powerful.

Luca cocked his head to the side and scratched his jaw. "Bend over my desk."

I licked my lips. "And then what?"

An evil smirk tugged at the corner of his mouth. "Try not to scream."

His desk phone rang, interrupting our staring contest. Luca hit the speakerphone button and muttered words in another language. Then, rambling in rapid succession, Luca fired back comments at the man talking to him.

Luca grabbed my hips and pushed me onto his desk, shoving my cheek to the wood. He hit the mute button on the speakerphone, and then his hand came down hard on my ass cheek. It hurt at first, but as he continued to punish me, the pain turned to pure pleasure.

My gaze often traveled over to his brothers, who stood a few feet from the desk. Their big cocks tented their dress pants, all of them enjoying their brother spanking me like a rotten child.

I moaned with each whack of his palm, soaked through my bikini bottoms when he finished with me. He stopped to unmute the call, then mumbled something I couldn't understand to his business associate.

After a minute of discussion, he hit a button on the phone again. His fingers slipped beneath the straps of my bikini bottoms. He had them off in a split second, throwing them at his brothers.

He wanted them to watch us.

Did he find enjoyment in this?

Was it about me and the punishment he thought I deserved? Or was this a punishment for them?

Luca flipped me over and pulled down his zipper. Then, he whipped out of his big cock, stroking his length. My sexy devil pressed his palm to my stomach, and I leaned back on my elbows, giving him the full view.

Marcello came behind me and untied my bikini top. The straps fell from my neck, the fabric dropping onto my stomach. He peeled it from my body, and then his hand covered my right breast. Bastian appeared at his side and massaged the other one. Damian just watched us, staring down at me like he wanted to devour me.

But it was Luca's turn.

All three of them had gotten a turn with me. So why did Luca want to share this moment with them when he could have me all to himself? I never understood him or his motivations. Luca Salvatore was a mystery I couldn't solve.

A man's voice blared through the speaker, drowning out the rapid beating of my racing heart. Luca spoke to him for a second, and then he went back to carefully appraising my body. He set my skin on fire with one look, heat rolling off me in waves.

When he looked at me like this, I wanted to tear off his clothes and beg him to claim me. And judging by the look on his face, he was about to do just that. He branded me with his fingers that slowly inched up my thigh.

A crazed look flickered in his blue eyes before he bent forward and licked his lips. "Can you be quiet, baby?" Luca whispered with his mouth inches from my pussy.

His breath fanned across my skin, driving me fucking crazy. How could I say no?

"Yes," I muttered.

He raised his finger to his mouth. "Shh…"

His tongue rolled over my aching clit, and a whimper slipped from my lips. Luca stopped licking me and shook his head, warning me to stay quiet. Then he went back to licking me straight down the middle.

I gripped the edge of the desk and arched my back, needing more of his tongue. His tongue drove inside me, and like a hungry animal, he devoured me, taking turns between sucking on my clit and lapping up my juices. He lifted my thigh, dropped it over his shoulder, and thrust two fingers inside me. Marcello clamped his hand over my mouth to stifle my screams, even though I was trying my best to keep the men on the phone from hearing me.

"Mr. Salvatore," one man said, and Luca tortured me by pulling his head back.

He spoke again, and another man joined the call, giving Luca a reprieve. He glanced up at me with my cum coating his full lips, giving me one of the sickest smiles I'd ever seen.

Then he ravaged me again, licking me from front to back, tasting every inch of me. I moaned right as I hit the peak of my climax. Marcello clamped his hand over my nose and mouth to silence me. I screamed against his skin, my teeth scraping his flesh.

Bastian bent down to suck my nipple into his mouth while Damian bit the other one. The four of them worked as a team, giving me equal love and attention. On the verge of another orgasm, my entire body trembled when Luca shoved two fingers inside me, spreading me open. I tugged on his short black hair as I rode out my high, chasing my pleasure to the finish line.

After my body stopped convulsing, Luca sat back and lowered my thigh to the desk. The others dropped their hands and mouths from my body. They knew how to worship a woman and make me feel like a queen.

Luca stared at me with carnal hunger in his eyes. Then it was his turn to speak on the call, and he muttered words in a foreign language for a solid minute before turning his focus back to me.

I slid off the desk and dropped to my knees between his spread thighs. His chest rose and fell as I took his cock in my hand, stroking his long length. He tilted his head back against the chair, his fingers massaging my scalp as he pulled my head closer. I stuck out my tongue to lick the tip. His lips parted as our eyes met, and then he forced me to take all of him.

I sucked his cock, and he fisted my hair like a savage, grabbing my curls so hard my scalp burned as I hummed on his cock.

"Fuck, baby girl," he grunted.

He entered the conversation again, leaning over to talk into the speaker, which forced more of him down my throat. Luca was too long and thick for me to handle him without gagging. Thankfully, he didn't talk for long, which helped loosen his hold on me.

He bent down and whispered against the shell of my ear. "Keep this up, and I'm going to tear up your pussy."

I moaned in response.

"You like that, my dirty girl?" Luca yanked on my curls. "Hmm? You want me to punish you some more for disobeying me?"

Luca slid my hair off my forehead so he could watch me choke on his length. Then he pulled out of my mouth and helped me up from the floor so that he could bend me over his desk. I palmed the wood and looked at his brothers. All three of them grabbed their big cocks over the front of their pants, aiming their sinful gazes at me.

Luca's fingers skated down my back and over my ass cheek. He leaned forward and sucked my earlobe into his mouth. "Isn't this what you've always wanted, Drea? An audience to admire you while I fuck you."

I glanced at him over my shoulder. "Yes."

Luca forced me to watch him with other girls back in high school. He would bend them over the sink in the boys' bathroom and fuck them as he watched me in the mirror. His brothers would hold me down, touch me, and rile me until I felt like I would combust. Each time, I'd leave the bathroom angry, aroused, and confused about why I liked it so much. I wanted to be one of those girls, and he damn well knew it.

Luca's thick cock pushed between my wet folds, stretching me open with each inch. He was so damn big. I closed my eyes and pressed my lips together as he fully seated himself inside me. I breathed deep, my fingers sliding across the desk as he thrust his hips. A moan slipped past my lips, one after the other, and I didn't care if he punished me for it.

This time, Marcello didn't put his hand over my mouth. None of them moved from their places a few feet from the desk. It was as if they knew this was Luca's plan all along. To dominate me in front of them. Make them watch how much pleasure I derived from this sick, demented psycho.

With one hand, he squeezed my shoulder and fucked me hard, shaking the drawer each time he pumped into me like a wild animal. Papers flew to the floor. Shit dropped from his desk like it was raining stationary. The desk drawers banged as if they were about to come off the hinges.

I screamed his name over and over until my throat was dry. He eventually tired of me disobeying his command to remain quiet and ripped off his tie. Then, without warning, he put it over my mouth and pulled hard, securing it behind my head.

It was degrading to have him do this to me in front of his brothers. But this was what I'd wanted from him. For years, I had imagined him embarrassing me like those other girls. Fucking me so hard I couldn't speak. So many times, I would wake up to dreams of him, my hand shoved down my panties, rubbing my clit.

I slid my hand down my stomach and massaged the aching bud, staring into the eyes of my other men as Luca owned every inch of my body.

As I came for the second time in a row, a man on the phone said, "Mr. Salvatore, are you still there?"

He reached over me to hit the button on the phone, not breaking stride for one second. There was no doubt you could hear our skin slapping together and my muffled moans as he spoke to the man.

Luca had some serious stamina. Not once did he slow down to give me a second to adjust to his size. He pounded into me like he was trying to imprint his cock.

Luca muted the call again, and then he yanked on my hair, pulling my head back so I could look into his eyes. I came again, and I could see him losing all control this time, trembling from his orgasm. He came inside me, filling me up as he removed his tie from my mouth and kissed my lips.

We rarely kissed. But this time, it felt natural, like he didn't hate me. Like he enjoyed this moment of intimacy.

After he pulled out of me, Luca tucked himself back into his pants. His arms wrapped around me, and he set me on his lap.

"Lift your hips, baby girl." He spoke against the shell of my ear. "You better not spill a drop of my cum."

His brothers readjusted their cocks, staring at me like they wanted to rip me apart.

Luca turned my head and sucked my lip into his mouth, then tugged with his teeth. "Do you like being treated like a dirty little slut?"

I nodded and kissed him again, unhooking his tie around my neck. "Luca, that was…"

"I know, baby girl."

Clutching my hip, Luca leaned forward and answered the man on the phone. A heated discussion ensued for a few minutes before he looked at me again. "I need to focus." He tapped my thigh with his fingers and lowered his voice. "My mother's paintings just arrived. You only have one week to study them before they go back on loan to another gallery."

I slipped my fingers between his. "Come with me."

"I'm on all-day conference calls." He tipped his head at his brother. "Marcello will sit with you in my mother's studio."

"Thanks for the orgasms." I kissed his lips as I hooked the tie around his neck and slid off his lap. "I'm guessing I won't see you for the rest of the day."

"The rest of the week." He lifted my hand and kissed my skin, causing me to shiver from his touch. "My brothers will keep you company until your showcase at the Blackwell Gallery."

Chapter Fifteen

DAMIAN

The New York crime families came through on their promise to Luca. It was worth every cent of the ten million dollars we paid them, pocket change for men like us. I owned watches that cost more.

Despite our hesitation to work with the Mafia again, they were valuable. They had more men than The Devil's Knights and quickly located a few of the top-ranking leaders of the Volkov Bratva.

Bastian drove us to the safe house in Beacon Bay. My brother hated when I handled jobs like this one for our family. He hated those moments when I turned into a monster that even he feared. I wasn't like other people and didn't want to be like them. But, for as long as I could remember, I wasn't right in the head.

I was different.

I'd always had these dark desires that claimed hold of me. Even Bastian couldn't stop me most of the time. My father never even tried. He had encouraged me to hone my craft and taught me how to torture, maim, and kill my victims. Meeting Arlo Salvatore was the best thing that ever happened to me. So was being part of his family.

And my family needed me.

Bastian parked in front of the abandoned apartment complex and stared up at the building. "I'm only okay with this because it will protect Alex." Then, he snapped his head to me, his jaw set hard. "It's a means to an end."

I nodded.

"I'm not spending all night here." He turned off the engine and unbuckled his seatbelt. "Marcello has to leave for a few hours to work with Alpha Command." He pushed open the car door, his eyes on me. "We can't leave Alex with the guards."

Luca was waiting for us in the apartment. Beforehand, he had met with the Mafia families who dragged the men back to Beacon Bay for us.

"We trained the guards to protect her," I pointed out. "That's why we pay them so well."

He shoved a hand through his dark brown hair and sighed. "Make it quick. Okay? I'm fucking tired and want to pass out when we get home. And I want to do that with Alex naked and riding my dick."

The thought of her on top of Bash, with those big tits bouncing in his face, made my cock hard. I loved watching her with my brothers. It was such a fucking turn-on to see her gain pleasure from other men. Each of them gave her something different, something the other couldn't. That was the reason our arrangement worked so well.

"Yeah, whatever." I opened the door, one foot out of the car. "This won't take long."

We hopped out of Bastian's Porsche and headed into the building. No one had lived here in years. It was on the lower class side of Beacon Bay, where gangs like The Serpents ran crews. There was a lot of crime in this part of the town, making our criminal activities seem less prevalent.

The four of us chose this place because it was close to home and easy to access in an emergency. We hadn't intended to use the safe house to torture and kill people. But it served its purpose.

As I walked up the stairs beside Bastian, I breathed in the scent of bleach that lingered in the air. The whole place smelled sterile and clean. If these walls could talk, you would hear the screams of hundreds of men. Their ghosts probably lingered within these halls, trapped here for all of eternity.

I smiled at the thought.

I didn't kill good people. No, I chose men who deserved to die. Men who raped women, hurt children, and killed people. They did terrible things, earning them a special place in Hell. And I was more than happy to send them on their merry way.

We ascended the stairs in silence. Bastian's demeanor shifted every time we walked into this building. He couldn't comprehend why I had to do this. Why the need to kill surged through my veins, the nagging voice in my mind telling me to scratch the itch.

Even as children, I felt this bond with Bastian and him with me. I'd never felt that with another person until we became Salvatores. My brothers didn't understand my urges, but they still accepted me.

As I opened the last door on the left, my nose tipped up at the delicious scent of their fear. That was the best part about taking a life. It wasn't the stench of their blood I craved most. I enjoyed putting the fear of the Devil in them. Taking a life gave me power, and control, something I needed to survive.

Inside what used to be the apartment's living room, Luca had four men strapped to the tables. Luca sat in the chair by the window and smoked a cigar. He grinned at me as the smoke billowed around his head. Just as sadistic as me, Luca enjoyed watching me in action. We were both monsters, each with a sick desire to hurt people.

The men were conscious, struggling against the restraints binding them to the tables. It excited me but also annoyed me to see them awake. I enjoyed the look in a man's eyes when he realized there was no escape.

Luca rested his Ferragamo boot on his knee, fixing his eyes on me. "We'll have more trash to dispose of by the week's end. The Five Families are locating the rest of these scumbags." He tapped the ash of his cigar on the tray beside him. "Unfortunately, some of the higher-ups have fled to Russia. We'll have to bide our time and see if they return to the States."

"This should be enough to send a message to the bosses," Bastian commented, moving across the room past the tables to stand beside Luca's chair.

Luca's blue eyes flickered with the same madness as mine. "I look forward to sending their heads back in boxes." He took a puff from the cigar and blew out a cloud of smoke. "I had new boxes made for the occasion."

Bastian shook his head, disgusted by the idea. He didn't enjoy it the same as Luca and me. But, for him, murder was a necessary evil.

"The boxes say *Property of the Salvatores* on the top." Luca tipped his head back and laughed, the smoke gathering in front of his face. "Silk lined, too. Very nice. I think Konstantin Volkov will like them. They'll make a nice souvenir."

"You need fucking help." Bastian dropped into the chair beside Luca. He leaned forward to grab a cigar from the humidor, unable to look at us. "Both of you are sick."

I rubbed my hands together, drooling over my next kill. The walls, floor, and ceiling had plastic tarps taped down to make it easier to clean up later. Bastian often joked that the place looked like Dexter's kill room. But Dexter had nothing on me.

I got to work organizing the collection of weapons Luca had laid out for me on the kitchen island.

Should I start with the pliers?

Maybe a scalpel?

All of them had a hand in Alex almost getting raped.

They helped plan the attack at The Mansion that could have gotten all of us killed. Alex wouldn't be on the Il Circo website if they hadn't put her up for auction. And since we couldn't get to the boss of the family, we had to take it out on his men.

I lifted the pliers from the counter, pocketed the scalpel, and walked over to the first table with a clamp in my hand. Disgusted by my method of torture, Bastian shook his head. But when did he ever approve? He merely accepted the fact he couldn't change me. But it didn't stop him from trying to get me help.

He was the reason I had agreed to see Dr. Lansing. Not like the old man could help me. I was beyond saving.

I stared at the man on the table, my mind slowly drifting to my special place. A sly grin stretched the corners of my mouth as I leaned over the table and studied the curves of his face, the rapid beat of his heart as he tried to scream against the bandana covering his mouth.

Luca got up from the chair and pointed at the man. "That one is Nikolay Petrov. He ordered his men to find and rape Alex. If you hadn't killed the man, they would have taken turns with our girl. I want you to think about that, Damian. Think about what they would have done to her. This is your duty to the family. Protect our queen."

That was all I needed to hear before cutting off his cock with the scalpel and shoving it into his mouth. He bit down on it, screaming and choking on his flesh as the life drained from his eyes.

Chapter Sixteen

BASTIAN

Why did Luca have to encourage Damian?

If he hadn't been at the safe house, detailing each of the Russian's crimes, Damian wouldn't have been out of his mind. He fucking lost it and went full-blown ripper, covering every inch of the space in blood. We had it all over our clothes, even on our faces.

He was out of his mind.

So fucking gone.

Physically, he sat in the chair beside me with a vacant stare in his eyes. Mentally, he was somewhere only I could reach him. I knew what I had to do once we got inside my bedroom. It wouldn't have been the first time I had to calm him down. Damian couldn't soothe himself, so I had to be the one to do it.

Luca parked his Aston Martin next to mine and headed into the house without a word. He liked when Damian was all riled up and out of control, and the bastard knew I was fucking pissed at him for turning him into a monster. The Russians got what they deserved. They would have hurt Alex repeatedly until she was nothing more than the shell of the girl we loved.

I didn't hate that Damian disposed of them. I hated I was left to clean up the mess, to deal with snapping him back to reality.

Once inside the house, I looked at Damian's face, completely covered in blood. He reminded me of a demon that crawled straight out of the depths of Hell. Damian had a dead look in his green eyes like he wasn't even in his body. Top lip quivering, he looked at me, his hands balled into fists at his sides. He clenched his teeth, staring right through me.

Fuck.

I knew what I had to do.

Pushing on his back, I steered him up the staircase at the front of the house and followed him into my bedroom. His room adjoined to the bathroom he shared with Alex, so I intentionally avoided that direction. I slammed my palm into his back and forced him into my room.

"Take off your clothes, D."

He seemed to snap out of his head for a second at the sound of my voice. Just long enough to give me a once over, then went back to nothing. Back to the fucking dark place in his sick brain.

"Damian, now!" I yanked on his tie and pulled him closer to me, choking him a little. He liked when it hurt, and there was some level of pain involved. "Strip."

After my second request, his fingers moved to the top button of his dress shirt. I slid the jacket over his shoulders and then removed mine. Blood stained our suits, so there was no point in having them dry-cleaned. I studied all the blood on our skin and shook my head. This was excessive, too fucking out of hand this time.

I slid my fingers beneath the waistband of his briefs. "These too, D." Then I shoved him toward the bathroom.

I kicked off my boxers and threw them near my closet door before walking into the bathroom with Damian. He hadn't spoken a word since before he took the life of his first victim.

His eyes widened when he looked at his blood-stained body in the mirror, his cock rock fucking hard. Doctors called it erotophonophilia, sexual arousal from murder.

He rolled his thumb over the tip of his cock, and pre-cum dripped onto his hand. Our eyes met in the mirror as he stroked his cock.

I reached into the glass shower and turned on the water, feeling the temperature with my hand. "Shower." I pointed my finger. "Now, D."

After a kill, he didn't want to wash off the blood. Instead, he wanted to savor the moment. But this was necessary. The only way to bring him back to life was to help him forget about it.

I gripped his shoulder when he didn't move and forced him into the shower with me. He turned to move past me, and I slammed his back into the wall. It was the same process every time. Damian wanted to go back out and hunt. But I feared he would go right for Alex like he did last time.

I pinned him against the wall by his throat, jerking his shaft so hard his eyes rolled into the back of his head. His hand came up to my throat. He wanted to choke me as he did to Alex.

But I was in control this time.

The room fogged with steam. Damian grunted with each rough tug on his cock, begging me with his eyes for more.

I heard the bathroom door creak open behind me. The scent of her vanilla body wash filled the room. Damian stared at Alex over my shoulder, and then his eyes shifted to me. I didn't bother to break stride and continued jerking his cock so he could rid himself of the demons. So he wouldn't take this shit out on our girl. I knew what he wanted when he looked at her.

Not fucking happening.

Chapter Seventeen

ALEX

M arcello sat beside me on the balcony while my other men were dealing with business. I had a sketch pad rested on my thigh and a charcoal pencil in my hand. We sat in silence, listening to the waves crash below on the beach.

I liked this about Marcello.

The silence was oddly comforting and felt so natural, like we'd known each other our entire lives and didn't need words to communicate.

He'd taken me down to his spy shed earlier, so he could monitor some of the security feeds around Devil's Creek. I never had time alone, and I was okay with that. But, after the attack at The Mansion, I didn't feel safe without one of them by my side.

Around ten o'clock, I heard two sets of shoes slap the floor in the hallway. I dropped the sketch pad and pencil onto the table beside me.

Marcello placed his hand on my back. "That's my cue, princess. You're spending the night with Bash."

I wrapped my arms around his middle and laid my head on his muscular chest.

"I'll be home in the morning." He kissed my forehead and

released me from his grasp. "If you need anything, call me, okay?"

I nodded.

He tapped my ass lightly, a playful smile on his lips. "Go see Bash. He'll help you get to sleep."

Then he left my room in a hurry.

He was the head of security at Salvatore Global and the leader of Alpha Command, a team of mercenaries for hire. I wasn't sure what that side of his business entailed.

I poked my head into the hallway and saw Roman posted up at the end of the corridor. Then I walked past Damian's bedroom and into Bastian's. The room was empty, which was odd because I heard them come home. Even Marcello seemed to think they were here.

A pile of clothes trailed across the floor and went straight to the ensuite bathroom. Then I heard the water running behind the closed door.

I stripped off my clothes as I moved toward the bathroom and pushed the door open. My eyes widened at the feral grunts.

And then I saw them.

Bastian and Damian were naked and in the shower together. I watched them through the foggy glass doors, and my lips parted in surprise. Now I understood why they were so close. Because they were into each other.

Oh. My. God.

Bastian held Damian against the wall with one hand wrapped around his throat and the other stroking his enormous cock. But Damian wasn't submitting to him. Instead, he squeezed his hand around Bastian's throat, his eyes rolling into the back of his head with each groan.

I leaned against the door frame, peeking into the steamy room like some creepy stalker. Once I laid eyes on them, I couldn't stop staring. My skin heated as flames danced up and down my arms and legs. Already naked, I cupped my breast and massaged my painfully sore nipple while rubbing my thumb over my clit.

Skin slapped, their grunts filling the air. As I stood in the doorway, my nipples pebbled. Liquid heat pooled between my legs. Even though I couldn't see them clearly, the sounds alone were enough to spark something inside me.

What the hell is wrong with me?

A hand snaked around my middle, and then another covered my mouth. "Shh," he whispered against the shell of my ear.

I leaned back against his muscular chest and felt his cock digging into my ass. His hand slid up my stomach and over my breasts. Slow and steady, he took his sweet ass time exploring my body. My skin scorched from his touch.

A moan slipped from my throat as he rolled his thumb over the aching bud. He bent me forward with force. Breathing hard, I pressed my palm to the wall in front of me. A rough hand slid down my stomach and rubbed my clit.

His tongue glided across the back of my neck, his teeth grazing my hot flesh as he plunged two fingers inside me. I rocked my hips to meet his thrusts as he stretched me out.

I licked his hand, and he groaned in my ear. Heat spread down my arms, igniting a fire inside me, bringing me back to life. I closed my eyes and listened to the groans in the room, riding out my high as I came on his fingers.

Luca unzipped his pants, pressing the tip of his cock at my entrance. "Don't say a word," he said before sucking my earlobe into his mouth and plunging his cock inside me. "Don't scream. It's better if they don't know we're here."

"How did you know where to find me?" I whispered.

"I was stalking you on the security feeds." Luca pulled out and slammed back into me, moving his hand over my mouth to silence my moans. "Quiet, baby. My brothers don't like people knowing about their dirty little secret." His fingers closed around my throat, his cock so deep inside me from this angle I'd never felt this full. "Be quiet and let me fuck you, baby girl. We all have demons to feed."

I knew the three of them had gone somewhere together tonight. Marcello said it had something to do with capturing a few of the Russians. By the look of it, they killed people. That was the only time Damian lost control.

Luca fucked me so hard that the shelves on the wall rattled. He ignored his own rule about being quiet, stripping away my sanity with each thrust of his thick cock. Choking me with one hand, he silenced each of my screams with his other hand, drowning me in the scent of sandalwood that lifted off his skin.

As my legs shook, I palmed the wall for support and rode out the waves of pleasure. Luca was so close I could feel his cock pulse inside me. I tightened my grip on him, and he groaned in my ear. That simple movement drove him insane, and he fucked me harder, squeezing my throat until I gasped for air.

I watched Damian come in Bastian's hand, and then he leaned his head back against the wall. Damian let his hand drop from Bastian's throat and to his side. Luca's pace never faltered. He wasn't paying attention to them, anyway. With his face buried in the crook of my neck, he pounded into me.

Something fell off the shelf to my right and crashed onto the floor. Bastian's head snapped to me, and his eyes widened as he stared back. He washed Damian's cum off his hand and then hopped out of the shower.

Luca finished inside me a few seconds later, exhausted and out of breath, peppering kisses along my jaw. "Fuck, baby girl." He massaged my breast, pinching my nipple between his fingers. "You can feed my demons anytime."

Bastian wrapped a towel around his waist and approached the door. "What the fuck are you two doing?"

"We could ask you the same," I shot back with a smile.

"Look, Cherry." Bastian scrubbed a hand across his jaw. "It's not what you think."

I licked my lips. "I was kind of hoping it was like that. Because I have never been so hot in my life."

Bastian waggled his eyebrows and smirked. "Oh, yeah?"

I reached out for his hand, and he pulled me out of Luca's arms. His hand slid up my stomach, his fingers brushing my nipple.

"I want more. I want all of you."

Bastian glanced over his shoulder. "Damian can't play with us tonight, baby."

I folded my arms under my breasts and frowned. "Why not?"

"Because he's not…"

Before finishing his thought, Damian said, "I'm fine, Bash."

Damian stood at the bathroom's center, his naked body like a work of art, sculpted to perfection. Water dripped onto the tiled floor and pooled at his feet. He didn't notice or care as his eyes seared my skin like lasers.

"The fuck you are," Bastian hissed.

"No, it's okay." I moved toward him. "I need to see him when he's like this."

"Like what?" Damian snapped with venom in his tone.

"You know what, Damian!" I pushed past Bastian. "This isn't the first time I've seen that crazy look in your eyes. The first time you fucked me, you scared the shit out of me. But I still let you fuck me again." I stopped in front of him and looked up. "I'm not afraid of you anymore."

His green eyes flashed with excitement, and before I knew what was happening, he lifted me onto the counter. He didn't waste a second, thrusting his cock into me like he wanted to tear me apart. My head hit the mirror, but I didn't give a damn.

The pain came with the territory.

131

I gripped the counter's edge and rocked my hips to meet his. He was like a feral animal, out of control with his need for release.

"Damian," Bastian warned, clutching his shoulder. "If you hurt her again…"

Damian's lips parted, but he didn't speak.

"He won't," I said, sure of my response. "Let him go, Bash."

Bastian didn't ease his grip on Damian's shoulder. I looked over at the door, where Luca tucked his cock into his pants and zipped up.

"Luca, don't leave. Watch me."

Luca's eyes snapped to me as Damian choked me. Bastian stood behind Damian, digging his fingers into his flesh to control him, while Luca gripped the doorframe and watched his brother claim me, his eyes wild with desire.

"Damian." I wet my lips with my tongue and moaned. "Tear my pussy up. Mark me." My eyes slammed shut from the sheer pain of his cock ripping through my inner walls. My fingers slid through his hair, and I brought his mouth to mine. "You're such a good boy, Damian. Come for me."

Heat glided down my skin as Damian shattered my world. He stole several orgasms from me, making me come so hard I struggled to catch my breath.

Not long after I found my release, Damian crashed on top of me, holding me against the mirror as he came inside me. His entire body trembled, and I ran my hands up and down his muscular arms.

I shoved my fingers through his wet hair and forced him to look at me. "How many people did you kill tonight?"

His lips thinned into a straight line. "Four."

"Did you do it for me?"

He nodded.

I sucked his bottom lip into my mouth with him still inside me. He tugged on mine with his teeth.

"It's okay, Damian."

And when he was hard again, I pressed my heel into his ass. I slid my thumb across his lips and smiled.

"Lose yourself with me. You don't have to hold back."

I wanted him to be himself, not some other version he repressed. Bastian's hand lowered to his side, and he stepped back to give Damian some room. He propped himself up against the wall and stroked his cock, his eyes never leaving mine.

Luca hadn't moved from the doorway. His cock tented his pants, but he made no move to scratch the itch. Not like Bastian, who jerked his shaft as hard as Damian fucked me, watching me with a predatory gaze.

After all three of us came, Luca kissed me goodnight and left the bathroom, promising to see me for breakfast.

Damian carried me into Bastian's room and set me on the mattress. He kneeled at my side before he lit the candles on the nightstand. Bastian turned on my playlist and got into bed with me.

As Damian rose from the floor, I stretched out my fingers to touch him. "Stay with us."

He turned away but hesitated for a second.

"Please, Damian."

His eyes flicked back to me. He studied me for a moment, his jaw set hard.

I patted the space beside me. "Please."

In an instant, his resolve faded, and he got under the covers with us. Bastian clutched my hip from behind and held my back to his chest. Whenever we slept together, we always passed out like this.

Damian's hand moved to my inner thigh. "Are you sure about this?"

"I'm sure about you." I covered his hand with mine. "You won't hurt me."

What could have passed for a smile graced his blood-red lips.

"Can we talk about what I saw you and Bash doing in the shower?"

Bastian buried his face in the crook of my neck. "Not tonight. Go to sleep, Cherry."

"I'm okay with it," I told them. "If you're into each other—"

"We're not," Bastian bit out.

Bastian's words said one thing, but the look on Damian's face said another.

I clutched his arm, digging my nails into his skin. "Damian, tell me the truth."

He looked over my shoulder at Bastian.

"Why are you being so secretive?" I shoved Bastian's hand off my hip and rolled onto my back. "I know what I saw earlier."

"We don't like men," Bastian said after a long pause.

"But you like each other?"

Bastian slid his fingers through his hair and looked up at the ceiling. "We have a special bond. I don't know what to tell you, baby. But it's not what you're thinking."

"Then tell me." I turned my head to each side to look at them. "I'm not going to judge you."

"It started when we were sixteen," Bastian said in a hushed tone. "I only did it to help Damian with his bloodlust."

"What happened?"

Damian's long fingers dipped beneath my panties. "I killed someone who tried to hurt our father. The sight of his blood on my skin..." He groaned at the memory. "I couldn't control myself. No matter how hard I tried to cum, I couldn't... And then Bash walked into the bathroom and fixed me."

I glanced at him. "By fixed, you mean he got you off?"

He nodded.

"Have you ever kissed each other?"

Bastian sighed. "Not on the lips."

My eyebrows raised a half-inch. The idea of them together was too fucking exciting, but I was trying to play it cool. "But you've kissed other places?"

"Yes, Pet." Damian breathed on my earlobe and tested my slit with his finger, groaning with satisfaction. "Look at how wet you are thinking about us."

I rocked my hips to push his finger inside me. "Have you ever fucked?"

"No," Bastian said in an instant.

Damian worked my inner walls with two fingers while he sucked my earlobe into his mouth. Then Bastian wrapped his hand around my throat as Damian bit my earlobe and fucked me with his fingers. He pumped into me fast, pulling out to add a third finger, and then slammed back into me.

They were trying to distract me from asking more questions. It was working, but I was determined to know more about them.

I moaned Damian's name, which only encouraged him to go deeper, his movements rougher with each thrust. "I want both of you," I whispered as Bastian tightened his grip on my throat. "In every way. Don't hide from me anymore."

"It's time to cum, Cherry." Bastian pressed his lips to mine and sucked on my bottom lip. "Cum all over my brother's fingers, dirty girl."

My entire body went numb from the waves of pleasure shooting down my arms and legs as if on command. Damian held me tighter as he pumped his fingers into me, shredding my inner walls as I found my release.

He sucked my cum from his fingers and then tilted my head to the side, his teeth grazing my neck. Damian was ravenous. My sexy hunter never seemed to get enough of me.

I ran my fingers over the scar on Bastian's chest. An X made with a knife right over his heart. "Are you ever going to tell me how you got this one?"

He smirked. "Ask Damian. He's the one who gave it to me."

My lips parted in shock. "You let him mark you?"

Bastian tipped his head back and laughed. "I let him do a lot worse than that."

Damian's lips lifted from my neck, his breath ghosting my skin. "Story time is over for tonight, Pet."

"Seriously?" I shook my head. "You confessed to having a thing for each other. But you won't tell me about a stupid scar."

"It's a long story," Damian said. "We don't have time tonight."

"It's almost midnight." Bastian pointed at the clock on his bedside table. "Time for bed."

I stretched my fingers out to slip them between Damian's on the mattress. He let me hold his hand. Who would have thought a simple gesture would mean so much?

Bastian turned me so my back faced him. His arm snaked around me, and he kissed my cheek. "Sweet dreams, Cherry."

"Night," I muttered to my guys, and I was dead to the world within minutes.

Chapter Eighteen

ALEX

On the night of my first art exhibition, I wore a sleek black camisole dress with a slit down my left thigh. I paired it with black Valentino pumps that brought me to Luca's shoulder. He was an entire foot taller than me, towering over me at six foot three inches.

Luca slid his arm behind my back, clutching my hip as we moved through the Blackwell Gallery. Marcello walked with us on his right, Bastian and Damian on my left.

Bastian wore a navy blue suit and a smile that could damage the hearts of women across the city. But, of course, Damian dressed in all black, including his dress shirt and tie. He rarely added color to his wardrobe.

As Luca led me around the gallery, I wiped my sweaty palms down the front of my dress to still my nerves. Everyone stared at us. Some offered polite smiles, some tipped their heads, while others watched us.

I was one of the youngest artists to have a solo showcase at the Blackwell Gallery. Evangeline Franco was the first.

I was the talk of the town, thanks to an article about my pieces in *The New Yorker*. Luca had arranged the interview. He was making my dreams a reality, and I knew there were strings attached. But now that we were finally coming together, acting like a couple, I reconsidered his proposal. Slowly, Luca was becoming not only the man I wanted him to be but the man I needed in my life.

"You deserve this, Drea." Luca's fingers trailed down my trembling arm, his soft touch helping to soothe my nerves. "I predict you'll sell out the entire gallery."

I swallowed hard to clear my throat. "I hope so."

"The staff had to turn people away at the door," Bastian added in a deep tone that crawled down my spine. "Everyone wants a piece of you, Cherry."

"What if everyone hates my paintings and I don't sell one?"

He swept his arm out at the massive crowd. "Look around you. How many artists garner a fanbase like this on their first showing?"

My stomach churned from the stress. I hadn't had an opportunity like this one since art school. This was the big leagues, a legit show in SoHo that could make my career.

"I have to give my speech soon." My throat tightened in anticipation of standing in front of so many strangers. "How bad would it be if I vomited on my guests?"

Bastian laughed. "You won't."

"Stop worrying about everything that can go wrong," Luca ordered with fire behind his words. "Focus on what will go right. Tonight is already a success."

I bit my bottom lip and stared into the expanse of the crowded room. "I'm afraid to read the reviews tomorrow. What if the art critics hate my pieces?"

Luca tugged on one of my curls and pulled my mouth closer to his. "Stop overthinking everything, Queen D. The Many Faces of the Devil series is a hit."

Marcello yanked me out of his brother's arms, his palm on my back as he pressed my chest into his. His fingers wove through my curls. "This is a moment you will never want to forget. Calm down, princess. Just relax and take it all in. We'll be right by your side."

I expelled a deep breath, clearing my lungs. "I'm nervous." I waved my hand in front of my face, growing redder by the second. "I don't want to screw this up."

"I'm right here." Marcello cradled me in his arms. "Shh, princess. Let your heart rate slow down. Breathe, baby."

In his arms, I always felt safe, comforted. Marcello was the most loving and could instantly calm me down when I was on the verge of a panic attack.

Then it was Bastian's turn to steal me away, wrapping me in his strong embrace. "We got you, girl. As long as we're here, nothing bad will happen. Everything will be okay." His hand lifted to point at the room. "Look at these people who came here to see you."

"That's not entirely true." I drew a breath from between my teeth. "Luca had a lot to do with this."

"I only showed the owner your portfolio," Luca clarified, though I wasn't so sure I believed him. "He's the one who asked where I found you and if you would be interested in a showing."

I slipped out of Bastian's grip and moved between my men, who circled me. "I'm glad all of you are here with me."

I reached out to touch Damian's arm since he was the only one who hadn't tried to comfort me. It wasn't in his nature, and I understood that.

My grandfather and Blair appeared a few minutes later with Arlo. I ignored my grandmother and smiled at Pops, who pulled me into his arms and smacked a kiss on my cheek. The overwhelming scent of his Jean Patou aftershave floated into my nostrils. My stomach churned, but I ignored the dizzy feeling that only could have come from my nerves.

"Thank you for coming," I said to the group.

Arlo closed the distance and leaned in to kiss me on each cheek. "Congratulations, Alexandrea."

When did Arlo ever greet me with a kiss?

Arlo ran a hand over the dark stubble on his jaw. "My late wife was the same age as you when she had her first showing at this gallery."

I bet he crushed as many hearts as skulls when he was younger. His sons inherited his good looks and the same deep, sexy voice.

Arlo pointed to my left, his finger aimed at the new addition to my collection. "This piece reminds me of something Eva painted for me. She called it Master of Mystery."

I nodded. "I'm calling that one Devil in Disguise."

Arlo gave me a closed-mouth grin. "The board at the Franco Foundation chose well. We all have faith in you, Alexandrea."

I smiled at his words. "Thank you. That means a lot to me."

Luca replaced his father a few seconds later. The soft fabric of his suit jacket brushed my arm. The saltiness of the sea mixed with sandalwood clung to his skin. We stared at the wall in front of us, our eyes moving between two of my devil-themed paintings.

Luca's fingers grazed mine as we stared at his canvas. A painting of a man with dark spiky hair, red eyes, and a golden crown on his head. Surrounded by ash and smoke, it was clear he was the Devil. "This painting captures our past well. But let's forget about the past for tonight. I'm no longer your devil, baby girl."

I rolled my tongue across my chapped bottom lip. "Why are you being nice to me? This is so unlike you, Luca."

"Because I don't hate you."

Luca hated the idea of love and intimacy. He'd never learned how to process his emotions after his mother's death, and after years of abuse, he thought he was incapable of love. Instead, his father showed his love through power and possession.

He slipped his fingers between mine, holding my hand in public, which shocked me. "Tonight, everyone is here for you."

Luca wasn't always a shit human being. Sometimes, I saw a man with a heart and soul untainted by violence and corruption. I craved those brief moments with him, savoring them long afterward.

Too bad they never lasted.

A dozen of The Devil's Knights posted up around the gallery. Sonny and Drake hung out in front of the painting of Marcello.

When I first painted Luca, I gave his piece a name that suited how I felt about him.

The Devil I Hate.

I had already named the paintings before we had our heart to heart.

Marcello looked like a Greek warrior fighting his way out of Hell with a golden crown atop his dark head. He didn't have the demon eyes like Luca. No, my handsome protector was my savior, the one I turned to the most.

The Devil I Crave.

Bastian's painting was to my right, over where Cole stood with two dark-haired Knights I hadn't met until tonight. Hunter Banks, the son of a weapons manufacturer, and Braxton Cade, the son of a senator. They were from Devil's Creek and went to York Military Academy with Cole. And both just as handsome and muscled.

I stared over at Bastian's image and smiled.

You could tell it was Bastian with those big gray eyes and the sexy smirk that graced his lips whenever he looked at me. He also wore a golden crown that floated above his dark, messy hair that had ash falling into it.

The Devil I Love.

Finn and Callum Cormac drank from glasses beside Damian's painting. I had saved him for last and didn't get the urge to paint him until after he exposed me to his other side. So I went into my studio after our first time and painted what felt right, natural.

He was even more devious looking than Luca, with flames in his eyes, the fire illuminating his skin. His golden crown tipped to the side, just crooked enough to make him look even more mischievous.

The Devil I Fear.

It was the truth, and I could only paint what I saw inside a person. Though fear was a strong word. I let him tie me up, cut my skin, and pound my pussy until I couldn't walk out of his bedroom. But there was still the lingering fear at the back of my mind, and I wondered what would happen if he ever snapped.

Mark Blackwell, the gallery owner, appeared on my right side. "You're on in ten minutes, Alex." He patted my shoulder. "This is an incredible turnout for a debut artist." His gaze drifted to Luca, and he lowered his head in greeting. "Mr. Salvatore, nice to see you again. Any chance you will reconsider showing your mother's work here in the spring?"

"Let's see how tonight goes, shall we?"

I knew Luca had some trick up his sleeve and sighed as Mark walked away.

Luca noticed my irritation with him and raised my hand to his mouth to kiss. "It's not what you think, Drea. I didn't bribe him or blackmail him into this showing."

"Do you promise?"

He kissed my lips. "Promise, baby. You worked hard for this opportunity. I only showed him what he was missing."

"Okay, I believe you." I slipped out of his grasp. "I need to use the ladies' room. I had too much champagne."

Needing a minute alone to gather my thoughts, I walked away from my men. Marcello called out for me to wait up for him, but I bolted through the crowded room. I wanted some space to think about my speech with no one hovering over me.

I headed down the long hallway toward the back of the gallery. It was empty on this side of the building, with only a few people lingering with drinks in their hands. I rounded the corner, searching for the bathroom, and hit a dead end.

And when I spun around to head in the other direction, someone clutched my shoulder from behind. Then they opened the exit door and shoved me outside.

Chapter Nineteen

ALEX

W ith a hand on my back, someone pushed me out the exit door and into the dark, empty alleyway. Nerves coursed through my veins, my heart clambering out of my chest as the adrenaline rushed over me.

"Calm down, princess," Marcello whispered in my ear. "It's just me."

Seconds later, tires screeched, and then Luca drove down the alleyway in his Aston Martin Vantage.

Marcello opened the passenger door and helped me inside the car. "We'll deal with the threat," he told Luca. "Go!"

Then, he slammed the door and ran inside the building with a gun in his hand.

"What's going on?" I asked Luca as he peeled off down the dark street.

"I have to get you to safety."

"But it's my first gallery showing," I said with tears in my ears.

"You'll have another showing." He made a hard right onto a busy street and floored the gas pedal. "We spotted two men with the Volkov Bratva in the gallery. Damian and Bastian kept them busy while Marcello got you outside."

"I need more, Luca. Tell me why they're hunting me."

He patted the top of my head. "Head down, baby girl."

I ducked down to keep my head out of view. "You're the most confusing man I have ever met."

"Other men would bore you."

Nerves stirred in my belly as Luca whipped through the streets, dodging cars until we were on the highway. My back molded to the leather seat when the speedometer went over one hundred and twenty miles per hour. Luca drove like a psycho, making hard turns in and out of lanes.

I gripped the door handle, fear shaking through me. "What the hell is going on, Luca? Stop keeping secrets from me."

He kept his eyes on the road and ignored me, gripping the steering wheel with his jaw clenched. Luca was so closed off, a mystery even after all these years. And I was sick of being kept in the dark.

"Stop driving like a lunatic and tell me why I'm in so much danger."

He glanced over at me, his knuckles white from wrapping them so tightly around the steering wheel. "Okay, fine. You want the truth?"

I leaned closer to him. "Yes."

"Someone listed you on an auction site right before we left for The Mansion. We took you there to get you out of Devil's Creek. There's a bounty on your head, and many people want it."

I rested my elbow on the armrest and looked over at him, mouth hanging open in surprise. "Auction? Like the one we watched at The Founders Club?"

He shook his head. "No, this kind of auction is different. There are almost no rules, no limits to how much you can spend. But there is one rule they enforce. If you list a person for sale at an auction, you must produce them."

I covered my face with my hands and gasped. "I can't believe this. How could you let someone list me for sale?"

"I'm sorry, baby." He reached over and squeezed my thigh. "I didn't mean for this to happen. I kept you away from Devil's Creek to protect you. To shield you from this side of our lives. That's why I let you go for five years. It was easier that way."

"Why do they want me? And please don't say it's because you have enemies. I'm getting sick of hearing that!"

A dark chuckle escaped past his full lips. "You are worth more than you realize, Drea." He looked at me out of the corner of his eye. "Has your grandfather mentioned the Wellington dowry to you?"

I bit my lip and considered his question. "I don't think so. He's mentioned his legacy and that he wants Aiden to take over for him when he retires."

"Your grandfather is the third richest man in the world. But the dowry is about more than the money. It's about the power. If one of my enemies were to get their hands on you, make you their wife, they would get the dowry. So Carl would have no choice but to hand it over."

My eyes widened. "Exactly how much am I worth?"

"Billions," Luca said as if it were ten dollars. "But as I said, it's not about the money." Luca looked in the rearview mirror at Marcello's blue Maserati behind us. "Generations of Wellingtons have collected secrets on presidents, heads of state, bankers, Fortune 500 companies, secret societies... You name it, and your grandfather probably knows about it."

"Where does my grandfather keep his secrets?"

"In a vault would be my guess." He rolled his broad shoulders. "No one, not even my father, knows where he keeps the black book."

I lifted an eyebrow at him. "That's why you want to marry me? To get access to a book?"

"Initially, yes. That was my motivation." His lips pressed

into a thin line as he glanced over at me. "But now... I have other reasons for wanting to marry you."

"Such as?"

"Do I need to spell it out for you, Drea?" He sighed. "I think it's obvious why I want you."

"Not to me."

"Because the thought of losing you fucks with my head. I've never been afraid of anything in my life. Not until they listed you for sale at Il Circo."

"What's Il Circo?"

"A club where anything goes. It's by invitation only. They hold monthly auctions on the Dark Web. Men from the depths of the criminal underworld bet on anything from women to the outcomes of death matches."

My stomach churned at his confession, and I was almost afraid to ask, but I had to know the truth about our situation. I turned in my chair. "Have you ever placed a bet?"

He shook his head. "I have a lot of vices, but there are some lines I don't cross." Then he placed his hand on my thigh, his fingers inching up to my core. "I've been doing everything in my power to stop the auction. I won't rest until I get you off that fucking site. But, unfortunately, the Volkov Bratva has a long-standing relationship with the owners of Il Circo."

"What happens if they succeed?"

"I won't stop until I have eliminated the threat." He tapped his fingers on my leg to the beat of the rap song on the radio. "The Knights are working around the clock to ensure your safety. We won't let anyone hurt you, Drea. I promise."

"I know you will protect me, but I'm still scared."

"It's okay, baby." He smoothed a hand over my thigh. "We will get through this together. You have the Knights at your disposal, which means you have an army of men willing to die for you."

"I don't want anyone to die for me."

"Knights defend their queen at all costs. It's one of our most sacred laws."

"Luca, you're not dying for me. I can't lose you."

He gave me one of his sly grins that made my heart race. "You saying you'd miss me, baby?"

"Of course, I would."

"We're at war," he said with zero emotion. "Anything can happen to me. I accepted my fate a long time ago. If I have to die protecting you, I will. You are all I care about, Drea."

I could hardly catch my breath. "Luca, please be careful. It would break me to lose one of you."

He patted my hand. "My life doesn't matter without yours."

"Luca," I groaned. "Don't say things like that."

"It's true." He grabbed my hand and pressed a soft kiss to my skin. "If you die, I'm going with you."

"No one is dying," I said with tears in my eyes. "Stop talking about death. It's making my stomach hurt."

"If anything happens to me, you will marry Marcello. He will protect you."

We drove the rest of the way in silence.

After Luca parked, he ushered me into the house with his hand on my back. Marcello joined us a few seconds later. Bastian and Damian were at least thirty minutes behind us.

My handsome devil's eyes raked over my face, and my heart crashed into my chest. I hoped for more intimacy from Luca. But as usual, he did the opposite of what I expected.

"Take her upstairs," Luca said to Marcello before taking off down the hallway. "Don't let her out of your sight."

"Luca," I shouted. "Get back here."

He didn't bother to glance over his shoulder. "Don't worry about me, baby girl. I have a party to plan. You'll see me soon."

I begged him to come back, but he raised his cell phone to his ear and kept walking.

I looked at Marcello. "What party?"

"We're inviting all of our allies to Devil's Creek to meet our new queen."

"Luca told me about the auction." I walked beside him upstairs and down the long hallway toward my bedroom. "Don't you think it's reckless to have a party when men want to kidnap me? Luca said they will force me to marry them to steal my family's money and some stupid black book."

"He told you about the book?" Surprise tipped up Marcello's eyebrows an inch. "So you know everything, then?"

I nodded. "Yeah. He didn't hold back."

He ushered me into the bathroom and drew me a bath. It helped me sleep, and after the night we had, I needed my soothing bath beads.

Marcello tapped the edge of the tub. I sat, and he got down on one knee in front of me. He looked so handsome, but not perfect. His hair was always out of place and falling onto his forehead like he didn't give a damn.

I slid my fingers through his dark hair. "I'm scared, Marcello."

"You have nothing to fear, princess." He moved between my thighs as the bathtub slowly filled with water. "No one is going to touch you. This party isn't a social gathering."

I climbed onto his lap and hooked my legs around his back, covering his heart with my palm. "Whatever it takes, Marcello. I can't lose you."

He shoved a loose curl behind my ear and licked his lips. "I'm not worried about me, princess."

Chapter Twenty

ALEX

On Saturday night, Marcello walked into my bedroom without speaking a word. He went into the closet and grabbed a red bikini that looked like strings dangling from his fingers.

"Luca wants you to wear this one." He dropped it onto the bed beside me, eyeing my body as if I were already naked. "Our guests are arriving soon."

"How many Knights are there?" I shifted my stance to look up at him. "I mean in total."

He scratched the corner of his jaw, eyes on the wall as he considered my question. "Active? Close to three hundred across the country."

My eyes widened at his confession. "You invited three hundred people here?" I shook my head in disbelief. "This house is big, but not that big."

He sat on the bed beside me and lifted me onto his lap. "We invited the Knights. They wanted to meet their future queen."

I smiled at his words. "When will I become their queen?"

"After you accept Luca's proposal."

"What if I want to marry you instead?"

He sighed, his eyes lowered to the floor. Marcello insisted I marry Luca. So even though my grandfather said I had a choice, I didn't have one. Not when Marcello and his brothers were so loyal to Luca.

"We've gone over this, princess." He squeezed his big hand around my thigh. "Marry Luca. That's the way it's supposed to be."

"I'm serious, Marcello." I stroked my thumb across his cheek and stared into his pretty blue eyes. "I would rather marry you."

He released a deep breath, turning his head toward the window. "I know you think I'm the better choice."

"You are," I said without hesitation.

"Not true." His eyes met mine once more. "My brother is the reason you're still alive. When the rest of us failed you, Luca succeeded."

"They drugged you. None of you could control that."

"Still," he groaned. "I failed you. I should have anticipated the attack at The Mansion."

"Even the all-knowing Luca hadn't expected it. Don't blame yourself, Marcello. You did nothing wrong."

"Luca saved you." He pursed his lips. "In his way, he cares about you."

"This is what you want?"

He nodded.

"Okay." I slid off his lap and clutched his shoulder. "I will consider his proposal. But I'd much rather it be you."

"You'll change your mind about him," he said with certainty in his tone. "Give it time."

Marcello shot up from the bed and closed the distance between us, the bikini hanging from his finger. "Put this on."

I bit my lip as I looked at the skimpy ass fabric. "Luca wants me to wear that in front of his friends?"

"My cousins are coming tonight, too."

"Which cousins? The Serpents?"

He nodded. "They'll be here. But I was talking about the Luciano brothers."

"Right." I bobbed my head. "Your Mafioso side of the family."

"We were the only ones with enough sense to get out."

"I thought you can't leave the Mafia once you're in."

Marcello rolled his shoulders as if it were an easy task to walk away from the Mafia. "My father has his ways. He's the reason we didn't become Made men."

"How did he get out of it?"

"The Founders Society."

My eyebrows raised. "They're that powerful?"

"You don't even know the half of it. The Founders run this country. Even the Mafia relies on their connections."

"Really?" My voice reached a higher octave. "The Founders are in bed with gangsters?"

"Not quite. The Founders are the only reason most of my family members aren't in jail."

"Your family has so many secrets." I took the bikini from his hand. "I expect to learn all of them once I become a Salvatore."

His grin mirrored mine. "That will be soon, princess." He clutched my wrist and made slow circles over the top of my hand. "When you say yes to Luca, you're saying yes to all of us."

At least a hundred people crowded around the Olympic size pool at the Salvatore Estate. Strings of fairy lights floated above us, dangling from the trees like stars in the dark sky. A rap song cranked through the outdoor speakers. Then, as if the beat made everyone lose their minds, a group of women in skimpy bikinis jumped up on a table where Sonny sat with a few of the Knights.

Luca's eyes traveled up and down my bikini-clad body. The red triangles of fabric barely covered my nipples, and the stringy bottoms did little to hide my ass. It surprised me that Luca wanted me to wear this in front of his friends.

The bathing suit left pretty much nothing to the imagination.

I sipped from my martini glass, shaking my hips to the beat. As I walked by Luca's chair, he hooked his arm around my thigh and tugged me onto his lap.

"You've been chatty tonight," he whispered into my ear. "Getting to know your loyal subjects, Queen D?"

I smiled at his nickname for me. "I guess you can say that."

"I want you to meet my cousins." He tipped his head at the men sitting on the other side of the table. Luca rose from his chair, bringing me with him, and pointed at a tall, dark-haired man who was probably in his mid-thirties. It wasn't hard to miss the family resemblance. "This is Dante Luciano."

The Don of the Luciano crime family. They ran Atlantic City and most of the casinos in the town. I hadn't realized the Salvatores were so Mafia-connected until Marcello had explained their family's past.

Dante rose from the chair. He was tall and solid beneath the black designer suit. I offered him my hand, and he raised it to his mouth and kissed my skin.

"Such a beauty," he said in a thick South Jersey accent. "Welcome to the family, Alexandrea."

A shiver rolled down my arm, and I forced a smile. He reminded me of a younger version of Arlo Salvatore. Cold, calculated, but also somewhat charming. Dante Luciano had a magnetism that surrounded him. He had that extra something that made you melt into a puddle at his feet.

His three brothers stood beside him. It was a pool party,

yet they were the only people on the property wearing suits. Even my guys had dressed down for the special occasion.

Stefan and Angelo had the same dark hair, except they were maybe five years younger than Dante and identical twins. The only difference between them was a scar on Angelo's right cheek. It looked like it came from a knife, which made me wonder about the story behind how he got it.

The last Luciano brother was probably around thirty, give or take, and unlike his brothers, he had blond hair and blue eyes. They didn't even look related.

"This is Nicodemus," Dante said in a deep tone that made my arms' hair stand at attention. "He's the bastard of the family."

My eyebrows lifted at his confession.

Nicodemus shot a sideways glance at his older brother and shook his head. "Thanks for the fucking introduction, brother."

"What?" Dante smirked, shoving his hands onto his hips to reveal the guns strapped to his chest. "Are you not our father's bastard?"

"Get over it," Nicodemus snapped at Dante.

I could feel the tension between them, their anger toward each other radiating off them in waves. Nicodemus must have looked like his mother, with blond hair and blue eyes, opposite his half-brothers.

Dante narrowed his stance as he glared at his brother. "Sit down and show some fucking respect."

I looked at Nicodemus, unsure of what to say, and then extended my hand to break the tension. "Nice to meet you."

"Ignore my brother. I'm Nico." He flashed a charming smile that reached his stunning blue eyes. A cute dimple popped in his right cheek. "It's a pleasure to meet you, *regina.*"

Queen.

Luca snaked his arm around my middle and pulled me down onto his lap. Dante spoke to Luca about the family business, while Marcello, Bastian, and Damian talked to the twins, leaving Nico out of the discussion. I studied him from across the table, wondering how he ended up with his brothers.

They left Nico out of the discussions, but he didn't care. His eyes moved around the backyard with curiosity as he sipped from the glass of scotch in his hand. I wanted to know his story.

After an hour of conversation and many drinks, the Luciano brothers excused themselves from the table to deal with a business matter. Some Knights had cleared out from the backyard, taking women with them.

Luca rubbed his hard cock against my ass, so I rocked my hips to the beat, grinding on him. He dug his fingers into my hips with his usual rough possession. My nipples hardened as I rubbed my pussy against his hard cock, drenching my bikini bottoms. Marcello watched me from across the table, his eyes on my breasts, ready to fall out of the top. A sly grin tipped up the corners of his gorgeous mouth.

Damian curled his hand into a fist on the table, studying me like he wanted to peel back each layer of my skin. Knowing that sicko, he probably did. Beside him, Bastian reached down to fix himself over his shorts. Shirtless, all three showed off their muscles and dark tattoos.

Damian had the most ink. His tattoos started beneath his collarbone, down his arms and chest, dipping beneath the waistband of his shorts.

Bastian had tons of scars, but the X over his heart interested me most. He had a few black tattoos that looked like the markings on the wall I'd seen in The Devil's Knights' temple.

This was the first time I'd ever seen Luca completely shirtless. He had the most scars, which made sense after everything Marcello had told me about their childhood. He only had one black tattoo with The Devil's Knights crest—a knight's helmet with crossed swords.

I jiggled my tits in front of Luca's face and straddled his

thighs. Riding his cock over his shorts, I threw my arms around his neck as we took turns singing different parts of the song. My lips brushed his, and he sucked my lip into his mouth.

Luca groaned, his fingers piercing the skin on my thigh. "If you don't calm down, Queen D, I will whip out my dick and come all over your tits."

I grinned. "Maybe I want you to do that."

A wave of heat rushed over my skin as I continued dancing, losing myself to the music, unable to ignore his massive cock digging into my thigh. He was so big I felt him everywhere.

Luca lifted me onto the table and moved between my legs. His brothers leaned forward as Luca kissed my stomach, slipping his finger beneath the thin piece of fabric covering my soaking wet pussy.

"Luca," I moaned. "Not here. Not in front of everyone."

He looked over his shoulder at those who remained at the party. They were all busy drinking and hooking up, not interested in what we were doing over here. But I didn't want to expose myself in front of strangers.

"The Knights will see you in more compromising positions during Legare."

"They can wait until then," I fired back, attempting to sit up, but he pushed me back down on the table. "Take me somewhere more private."

Luca turned his head to look at the pool house at the back of the property. An evil grin stretched across his face. Then he scooped me into his arms, barking orders at his brothers to follow him.

Chapter Twenty-One

ALEX

L uca set my feet on the ground once we were inside the pool house. The space was decorated to look like an old ship and had high-end furniture and decor. It was stunning, with exposed wooden beams on the ceiling and walls.

I heard loud musing blaring from a distance, the sounds of women moaning and people fucking. The Knights were not shy. But I wasn't ready to let them see me with my guys. Not until I had to let them watch us during Legare.

I wanted to know more about the ceremony, so I asked Luca if we could do a trial run of what I could expect. I still hadn't accepted his proposal, but I was close to giving in to him. It was only a piece of paper, a marriage that would make me a Salvatore.

Make me one of them.

I wanted so badly to be part of their family. For the first time in my life, I had a home and people who cared about me. Men who would give their lives to defend mine.

Luca moved behind me and gathered my curls in his hands, dipping his head down to kiss my neck. "What do you want, my queen?"

"You," I whispered. "All four of you."

Luca's fingers trailed down my hot skin, his sinful touch leaving fire in his wake. I leaned back against his chest, reveling in the pleasure of his lips on my neck, his tongue gliding across my skin. Marcello, Bastian, and Damian dropped to their knees in front of me. They would dress in their ceremonial robes for the actual ceremony and bow their hooded heads to their queen.

"Do you want to claim your Knights?" Luca asked between kisses, his fingers branding my flesh.

I looked up at my handsome devil. "Yes."

Luca clutched my chin. "Choose your Knights."

I stood before them completely naked, my nipples hard from the chill in the air. Luca's long fingers brushed my right arm, and my skin pebbled with tiny bumps from his delicate touch. He continued his slow perusal of my body, his hands moving to my breasts. I moaned as his thumbs brushed my nipples.

I let him touch me for a few seconds longer before running my fingers through Marcello's thick, dark hair. He tilted his head back so I could stare into his sad blue eyes. My sexy prince made my heart leap out of my chest with one look.

Marcello's eyes raked over every inch of my body. I held out my hands, and he slipped his fingers between mine. His skin was warm and rough, and I loved how electricity skated up my arm from his touch.

I moved his big hand to my inner thigh and guided his hand. He licked his lips, staring at me with desire in his eyes. Luca dug his fingers into my hips from behind and pressed his chest to my back. He resumed his gentle kisses along my neck and jaw, his hand sliding down my stomach.

Marcello knew what I wanted and took charge, gripping my thighs as he licked my clit. A flush of heat rushed through my body.

"Choose the next Knight," Luca said with authority.

Of course, he was taking our fake ceremony seriously. So I

moved back from Marcello and stepped in front of Bastian. He looked up at me, his dark hair falling onto his forehead, a wicked smirk turning up the right corner of his delicious mouth. I slid my fingers through his hair and repeated the same process with Damian.

All mine.

Luca lifted me onto the dining room table. His fingers burrowed into my hips, his rough touch branding my skin like hot pokers. He stood between my spread thighs, and my guys lined up beside him.

Luca kissed me with so much passion my head spun. He devoured me with a savage hunger, claiming his queen. As our lips separated, I struggled to catch my breath, desperate for more of his skilled tongue.

Luca's fingers wove through my curls as he tilted my head to the side, his teeth grazing my hot skin. He grabbed my hip, bending down to suck on my nipple, taking turns sucking and biting me. Intense waves of pleasure heated my skin as my handsome devil pinned me down with his hand on my stomach, and then his head dipped between my legs.

I tilted my head to the side to look at my guys. Marcello wet his lips as he watched his brother lick my pussy. Damian's chest rose and fell with each breath. Bastian ran a hand through my hair, giving me a look that seared my skin.

Luca worked his magic on my clit, sucking so hard my legs trembled. I screamed his name, my gaze shifting between them.

I raised my hand and beckoned Bastian with my index finger. He moved to the other side of the table from Luca and held down my arms when my body wouldn't stop trembling. And then his lips were on mine, his tongue invading my mouth.

Luca made me come two more times before I tugged on the waistband of Bastian's shorts.

"I want all of you naked."

Luca gave me a wicked grin and made a show of pulling on the strings of his shorts. The others didn't waste a second, stripped-down within seconds.

Naked and with his olive skin glistening with sweat, Luca stepped back, allowing his brothers to approach. All of them were naked and toned, so damn delicious my insides practically combusted.

As part of Legare, the ceremony that would bind me to the Knights, Luca had to claim me in front of the Knights. But since our arrangement was unusual, his brothers would get a taste before they crowned me queen.

I got on my knees on the table and turned to face Bastian. As I kissed my way down his ripped stomach, I gave him a few strokes. Marcello and Damian moved behind me. As I leaned forward to taste Bastian, one of them licked my pussy, his tongue slipping between my folds. Like the night they took my virginity, it was thrilling not to know who was touching me.

Another pair of hands gripped my right thigh, and then two long fingers spread me open. Bastian pulled my hair, grunting as I hummed on his cock, practically choking on him as my men worked together to make me come. After he came into my mouth, he traced the length of my bottom lip with his thumb.

With Marcello and Damian working together, my body shook uncontrollably. Then, like a hurricane sweeping over the land, ripping apart everything in its wake, I came hard on one of their tongues.

After I came, I clutched Bastian's wrist and pushed his fingers inside me.

"Harder," I groaned.

He gripped my shoulder and added another finger, thrusting into me like he was fucking me with his big cock. Marcello appeared beside him. I put a hand on each of their shoulders. Bastian continued his quick thrusts that tore moans from my lips while I guided Marcello's hand to my stomach, encouraging him to touch me.

Without instruction, he did what I wanted and rolled his thumb over my clit. I held onto their strong shoulders and kissed Marcello. My loyal protector, my friend, the one constant.

"Marcello," I whispered.

"Tell me what you want, my queen," he said in a deep, sexy voice that did sinful things to my body.

I traced the length of his lip with my thumb. "You."

Marcello took control and flipped me onto my back. Like his brothers, he was a hunter. And I loved this side of him.

Damian pounced on me like he was laying claim to his next victim. With Marcello between my thighs, Damian rubbed my clit with his thumb, gesturing for Bastian to come forward. Bastian wrapped his hand around my throat, and then his lips were on mine.

Consumed by all of their delicious scents, I drank them in, loving the feel of their hands, tongues, and mouths on my body. After I came on Marcello's tongue, he looked up at me and wiped his mouth with the back of his hand. Damian and Bastian still had their hands all over me. I was on the verge of another orgasm, so close as Damian bit my nipple and Bastian pinched my clit.

Then Damian was between my thighs, giving me a satisfied smile before his tongue glided over my hot flesh. Bastian went back to rubbing my clit, while Marcello switched between massaging my breast and sucking on my nipple. I took Marcello's hand, and he plunged two fingers inside my wetness.

I could feel Marcello's fingers matching the rhythm of Damian's tongue. Then Marcello's lips were on mine again as Bastian sucked on my nipples. All of their names slipped from my mouth, one after the other.

They made room for Luca, parting to his sides as if this

were the actual ceremony. My men looked so sexy, covered in sweat, their hair messy and wild from me tugging on it.

On the night of Legare, I would share this part of myself with the Knights, bound to them forever. The ceremony meant more to my guys than a marriage. Legare was the ultimate joining of the five of us, removing all the barriers.

Luca spread my thighs with his big hands and stood between them. His hands roamed through my hair, tugging on my curls right before kissing me. Each kiss was rough and aggressive like he wanted to take out all of his frustration on me. Seeing me with his brothers must have riled him up and forced the monster to come out and play.

Luca kissed me like he wanted to suck the air from my lungs. And with each kiss, we fought a war with our tongues, conquering one another. Then, as our lips separated, he grabbed my hair, tilting my head up as I wrapped my hand around his thick shaft. He grunted with each stroke and tightened his grip on my hair.

Luca squeezed my throat, kissing me so hard and fast I moaned into his mouth. He drove me wild, teasing me, taking his sweet ass time. Then, in one quick thrust, he filled me, trailing his fingers up and down my thigh as he fucked me as if possessed. When Luca lost himself in me, there was no turning back. He had to work through his inner demons while I let him play with mine.

He lifted my legs over his shoulders, pumping into me so hard he shattered my existence. It was a high unlike any other, a sensation that made my skin tingle. Luca looked insane when our eyes met. Fire raced down my arms and legs, my heart pounding in my chest.

I came once, twice, three times until I lost count. He was wild and out of control, a man on a mission to ruin his queen. Before he came, he pulled out of me and lifted me off the table, carrying me in his arms across the room.

"Luca, where are we going?"

"Shh, baby." He rubbed my back with his palm. "You'll like this." Then he set me down and glanced over his shoulder at Bastian. "Grab the rope."

My eyes widened at his words. "Rope. For what?"

He grinned like an evil mastermind. "You'll see."

Bastian gathered a handful of rope from a pirate's chest on the opposite side of the room. A shiver of fear and excitement rushed down my arms, all the way to my toes. I knew Bastian liked bondage, and Damian was definitely into rough, kinky shit. But I hadn't experienced all of their dark desires simultaneously.

Bastian threw the long rope over a wooden ceiling beam and tied knots to secure it in place. I stared at him, my mouth hung open, slightly terrified of what would come next. Before I could get out a word, Damian scooped me into his arms and raised me so Bastian could tie each of my wrists above my head.

"Guys, seriously, I don't know about this." I glanced down at them, biting my bottom lip. "I don't know if I'm ready for whatever you have planned for me."

"Don't knock it before you try it, Cherry." Bastian lifted my right thigh and pressed hot kisses to my skin. His eyes met mine for a split second, and then he licked me straight down the center, ripping a moan from my throat. "You'll like the dark side. It's more fun."

Damian clutched my other thigh to hold me in place. He stroked my slit with his long finger, staring up at me as he licked his blood-red lips. "It's not too late to run, Pet. But just know, we will always find you."

Marcello moved between them, his hair unruly and falling onto his tanned forehead. He looked at me with hunger in his eyes. "I won't let them hurt you, princess." His hand slid up my thigh. "Do you trust me?"

I nodded. "Always."

"Good." He kissed my pussy like he was making love to it,

sweet and slow and so damn sensual I almost forgot I was hanging from a ceiling beam. "Relax, princess. We're gonna make you feel good." Marcello's eyes met mine. "Can you do that for me?"

I would have done anything for him.

"Yes," I whispered.

Since Marcello was the one to calm me down, he got me first. He wrapped my legs around his back, breaching my folds with his big cock. I figured he was easing up on me since he knew his brothers would be rough.

His cock worked my inner walls, making me feel so good I moaned his name as a mind-blowing orgasm shattered me.

"Fuck, princess," he groaned with each thrust. "Cum on my cock."

He drove into me, deeper and deeper, his teeth grazing my nipple as he fucked me so good the beam creaked above me. Marcello filled me with his cum, some of which slid down my thigh after he pulled out. His eyes lowered between my thighs, and a smile graced his full lips. Out of breath, he leaned forward to kiss each of my breasts.

Luca shoved him out of the way and stole me away like a hungry lion dragging his prey back to his cave. He gripped the backs of my thighs and pounded into me so hard the beam sounded like it would crash to the floor. I looked up to double-check check the wood wasn't about to snap in half.

When my eyes met Luca's once more, he smirked. "Don't worry, baby girl. It will hold you."

"I sure hope so," I whispered between moans, my eyes slamming shut from his big cock splitting me open.

My sexy devil curled his fingers around my throat, pumping into me so fast that I struggled to catch my breath. I'd learned with them that pain wasn't always bad. Not even when they choked me, bit me, or marked my skin until I had black and blue marks all over my body. I loved the sensual side of each of my men. And I especially loved it when Luca dominated me, worshiped me like a queen.

Like his queen.

He would never be a good man. None of them would ever be good, not even for me. But I wouldn't have wanted them any other way. Sent to me straight from Hell, my devils were right where they belonged—with their queen.

"Luca," I screamed as he tightened his grip on my windpipe, taking me to new heights. "Harder, harder…" A whimper escaped past my lips. "Oh, my God."

His lips hovered over mine. "Yeah, baby. I am your God." He fisted my hair in his hand, pulling my mouth closer to his. "Now, come on my cock like a good girl."

My orgasms exploded around me, one after the other, in a delicious succession that made my legs weak and my gums go numb. I came several times before his legs trembled.

He grunted my name between curses and rested his sweaty forehead against mine, breathing through his nose. "Fuck, Drea. You drive me crazy, woman."

Seconds after Luca pulled out of me, Bastian moved him aside, claiming me with his usual possessiveness. It was a miracle all four of them could share me without killing each other. They worked well as a unit and needed each other in different ways. Maybe that was why this relationship felt so natural for all of us.

Bastian squeezed my throat, and my eyes slammed shut as he thrust his cock into me. He pulled out and then slammed into me, marking me with a predatory look in his gray eyes. His fingers burrowed into my ass cheeks, his balls slapping my skin with how hard he drove into me.

"That's it, Cherry." He grunted the words, sweat sliding down his forehead and onto his toned chest. "Fuck, your pussy is so tight." Bastian rocked his hips so he could fill me. "Squeeze my cock, baby." His eyes closed the second I complied with his request, and when he opened them again, a sadistic smile stretched across his face. "Good girl."

Hooking my arms around his neck, I leaned forward and sucked his bottom lip into my mouth. His grip on my throat relaxed as he kissed me back. He massaged my clit with the pad of his thumb, making small, circular motions that had me writhing with pleasure.

Damian moved behind me, the scent of his woodsy cologne filling my nostrils. He must have been too impatient to wait any longer because he buried his fingers in my hips and sank his teeth into my neck.

My sexy vampire prince.

"Oh, God," I moaned. "Damian... Bash. I want both of you... at the same time."

Bastian's face illuminated from the crooked grin pulling at his handsome features. Then he glanced over my shoulder at Damian. "Help me get her down, D."

Damian held me up so Bastian could untie the knots around my wrists.

Bastian lifted me over his shoulder as if I weighed nothing and plopped down on the couch, moving me on top of him. He rubbed the tip of his cock against my entrance and smirked. "We've waited a long time for this, Cherry. You sure you can handle both of us?"

I nodded. "I want both of you."

He grinned as Damian moved behind me on the couch and straddled Bastian's thighs. "Relax, Cherry. It will hurt less if you do."

Damian clutched my shoulder as he shoved his fingers inside me, soaking his fingers with a mixture of Marcello, Luca, and my cum. He massaged my inner walls for a second, and then he plunged his wet fingers into my ass. My eyes snapped shut from the initial shock. He was rougher than when Bastian had done it a while back. But Bastian was always more gentle than Damian. Even Luca went easier on me than my dark prince.

When I opened my eyes, Luca and Marcello stood naked beside each other, their cocks hard again and their devious stares aimed at me.

Damian pulled my arms behind my back and tied my wrists together with a silky fabric.

My top lip quivered. "What are you doing, Damian?"

"Shh." His hand covered my mouth. "No more talking, Pet."

I shot Bastian a worried glance, but he just laughed.

"We got you, Cherry."

He sucked my nipple into his mouth, biting my skin hard enough to leave marks, and slid his cock inside me. Damian slapped my ass a few times, helping me ride Bastian's cock.

Luca walked over to the dining server and opened a drawer. He pulled out condoms and sex toys before he tossed a bottle of lube at Damian. I didn't bother to ask why they kept that shit in the pool house.

Damian put some lube on his finger and massaged me. It hurt but felt good. I pressed my palms to Bastian's chest as Damian replaced his finger with his cock and inched inside me. Eyes closed, I blew out a deep breath through my nose and focused on breathing.

"Relax," Bastian ordered as his hand grazed my back. "It will get worse before it gets better. Just focus on riding my cock, baby. "

I opened my eyes and looked at him, my chest rising and falling. "Have you had many dicks in your ass, Bash?"

He snorted with laughter. "Nah, baby. But if I'd let any man near my ass, it would be Damian."

"I would be down for watching that," I moaned, no longer thinking about Damian and Bastian moving inside me at the same time.

His silly banter snapped me out of my head. And now I

was riding the waves of pleasure along with them. Like Marcello, he always knew the right thing to say to me. They both had a special gift.

Damian's hand closed over my throat, just enough to make me gasp. "Good, Pet." He tilted my head back as he matched each of Bastian's thrusts. "Open up. Make room for both of us."

"Jesus," Luca hissed as he moved to the other side of the couch, hovering over us. "Baby girl, you don't want to know what I want to do to you right now."

I tipped my head at his monster cock, which he stroked as he stared at my lips. "I think I have an idea."

He rounded the couch so he was at my side, and then he grabbed the back of my head. It wasn't easy to suck his cock into my mouth with two men fucking me. But I did my best to lick his skin. Then Marcello tugged on my head and put his dick in my mouth.

They took turns popping their dicks in and out of my mouth, yanking on my hair, and rubbing their thumbs across my swollen lips. Bastian came first and then lifted me off him. He nodded at Damian as if they had a secret code. And then Damian pulled out of my ass, quickly shoving his cock into my pussy.

He held me down on Bastian's chest and fucked me without mercy. Bastian tilted my chin up to look into his eyes, kissing me hard and fast as his brother's cock pulsed inside me.

After Damian came, he didn't make any move to pull out of me. We stayed like that for a solid minute, laying on top of Bastian, breathing as one. Damian eventually sat back on the couch between Bastian's legs. I was so exhausted I could barely keep my eyes open.

But Luca and Marcello had other plans for me. They each tugged on my curls with one hand, stroking their thick cocks. I looked up at them, so fucking spent, I just opened my mouth, knowing what they wanted from me. Luca came first, coating my lips and tongue with his cum right as Marcello finished on my tits.

I collapsed on Bastian's chest, coated with his brother's cum. He didn't give a shit and hugged me back.

"Now I know what it's like to be in a porno," I joked. "Holy shit! That was… I feel like I'm high."

"Yeah. But you didn't have to fake all those orgasms." Bastian laughed as he kissed my forehead. "Fuck, baby. I can die happy after that." He shook his head. "Now that's how a queen claims her Knights."

Luca sat on the floor beside the couch and rubbed my ass. "She's ready for Legare. Isn't that right, my queen?"

I bobbed my head in agreement. "I'm ready to become your queen."

"Our queen," Marcello clarified as he dropped to the floor next to Luca. He lifted my hand and kissed my skin, bowing his head. "Long live the motherfucking queen."

Chapter Twenty-Two

LUCA

I sat in a chair by the fireplace with the local members of The Devil's Knights surrounding me. Marcello was the only one missing. He was with Alex in our mother's studio, distracting her so I could discuss business with the Knights.

The Luciano brothers and two dozen Knights were in Devil's Creek to help us with the Russians. The Five Families had already located members of the Volkov Bratva, but we were no closer to getting Alex off the Il Circo website.

After the auction lapsed, the bounty on her head doubled to four million dollars—twice the amount. Alex was for sale at the next auction, the one scheduled for right before the wedding her grandfather had planned.

"Where are Arlo and Carl?" Sonny tipped a glass of Irish whiskey to his lips. "I got shit to do."

It was nine o'clock in the fucking morning. I had a lot of vices, but even I didn't drink this early.

"Yeah, looks like it," I shot back. "Busy day on the yacht, Cormac?"

Sonny rolled his eyes and sipped his drink.

What the hell did he know about real responsibilities? The shipping heir spent most days fucking women and drinking.

Occasionally, he worked when we needed his help to move containers with illegal shit between ports. Not like he needed the money. None of us did.

"My father is coming." I pushed up my jacket sleeve and checked my watch. "So is Wellington. They should be here any minute."

As one of The Founders Society Elders, Carl Wellington could speak on their behalf. He was a high-ranking member of the organization that overlooked the secret societies in the United States. Every group beneath The Founders Society had a specific purpose.

There was a hierarchy.

The Devil's Knights answered directly to the Founders. Smaller groups like The Serpents worked for us, handling corporate espionage and fixing scandals.

I glanced over at Damian, who had dark circles beneath his eyes. Bastian looked equally tired. Alex must have kept them up late again.

Drake Battle leaned forward, propping his elbows on his thighs as he pinched the bridge of his nose between his fingers.

I tapped the ash of my cigar on the tray. "Rough night, Battle?"

"Yeah." He sighed as our eyes met. "I was up all night doing coding sprints. The board wants to see a working demo of my AI software on Monday."

"Tell them to fuck off." I leaned back in my chair and blew out a puff of smoke. "It's your tech."

He snorted. "I'm not a dick like you. Battle Industries is spending close to a billion dollars to develop the technology."

I shrugged. "I just threaten our board if they get out of hand."

"The shit you get away with, Salvatore." He shook his head and smirked. "No, it doesn't work like that at my company. I respect my board."

"Fuck them." I took another puff of my cigar, and the smoke gathered above his head. "My last name is on the fucking building. Not theirs. And I remind them every day."

Drake howled with laughter. "Asshole."

"Hold their secrets over their heads," Bastian chimed. "That's what Damian and I do with the Atlantic Airlines board."

"Because you learned from the master," Drake quipped with his eyes on me.

We had a saying in Devil's Creek. Secrets are commodities. I collected secrets as if they were money because they were more valuable.

My father cleared his throat and entered the room with Carl Wellington in tow. Carl looked like a Founder, dressed in a six thousand dollars suit, his white hair styled and the air of entitlement surrounding him like fog.

"Gentleman." He tipped his head to the group and sat in the chair beside me. "I have no time to waste. So let's make this fast."

"We have a problem," my dad said as he dropped into the armchair on my right. "Someone intercepted one of the Mac Corp shipping containers before reaching the port."

Carl's eyes narrowed. "Which one?"

My father ran a hand across the dark stubble on his jaw with his cold, hard stare fixed on Carl. "One of the Basiles' orders."

I stamped out my cigar, breathing through my nose to contain my rage. "What about the other containers?"

"Untouched," my father said. "As far as we can tell. We'll know more in the next few hours after a full inventory."

"What is The F Society doing about it?" Drake asked Carl.

"Let us handle them," Carl said with authority. "Worry about keeping my granddaughter safe. Alex is my primary focus."

"No one will touch her," I assured him. "You have my word."

His expression darkened. "If anything were to happen to Alex, things will worsen for The Devil's Knights."

I nodded. "Understood."

"And for your family," Carl added with a bite to his tone.

"No harm will come to Alexandrea," my father cut in. "We have guards watching her twenty-four hours a day. Marcello is with her right now."

Carl rose from his chair, straightened his lapels, and glanced at my father. "Arlo, I'll speak with the Elders about the Sicilians."

As Carl walked toward the door, a loud boom sounded. The silent alarm on the wall flashed red, illuminating the wood panels in my office. Then all of our cell phones dinged at once.

The Knights checked their phones as I shot up from the armchair to scan the security feeds. The men at the front of the estate took heavy fire from a small army dressed in camouflage from head to toe.

We were also getting hit from the back, a sniper taking out the guards posted at the cliff's edge. A few men hopped out of a helicopter, jumping down from the cargo net as they shot at our foot soldiers. Our men dropped to the ground, one after the other, gone before they even knew what hit them.

"How the fuck did this happen?" I asked my father. "We tripled our guards, and we're using Drake's AI software to detect threats by air."

"Fuck," Drake bit out, staring down at his phone. "I didn't get a notification because the system is down. They fucking hacked us."

I reached for my gun with one hand and my phone with the other. Armed and ready to fight, the Knights approached the door, awaiting my orders.

My father stood at my side, his hand on my shoulder.

"Every war has casualties, son." He tapped his fingers on my upper back. "Go protect our legacy."

I dialed Marcello and raised the phone to my ear. He answered on the first ring. "Put Roman and Dom on Alex and meet us downstairs."

I hung up and shoved the phone into my pocket. Another loud bang followed by a ripple of gunfire rang through the air.

"Let's go," I told the Knights.

I led the pack out of my office and down the hallway, leaving Carl and my father behind. With our guns raised, we kept our backs against the wall and crept downstairs to the second floor.

Marcello met us on the landing and took control, guiding the group downstairs. My younger brother was better at tactical planning. He was the muscle, and I was the brains.

We ascended the stairs to the first floor. In his element, Marcello issued orders under his breath. He tipped his head, telling Sonny and Drake to head toward the back of the house.

It sounded like our men were doing their best to eliminate the threat. Everyone in Devil's Creek would hear the gunshots. It was a good thing the cops were in our pockets.

We moved down the main hallway as a unit, and as we passed one of the smaller formal dining rooms, glass shattered. Entering with caution, we surveyed the room. Shards of glass and burning scraps of fabric scattered across the hardwood floor. Dark smoke clung to the air, sweeping across the room like fog.

Marcello turned to me. "Looks like a homemade bomb."

"Our enemies haven't brought the fight to us in a long time," Damian said with an evil grin.

I could see the wheels turning in his sick head. He was looking forward to making these assholes bleed. But so was I. There was something magical about taking a life, holding it in your hands. It gave me the power of a fucking god.

Why would they attack us at home, where we should have seen them coming? We had the advantage on our turf. This distraction was a ruse to get us away from the real prize. My heart thudded in my chest, racing so fast my pulse clawed at my neck.

I grabbed Marcello's shoulder, and he turned to face me. A shiver rolled down my spine. "We played right into their hands."

Chapter Twenty-Three

LUCA

As we ran toward my mother's studio, Alex screamed for help. Chills spread down my arms like spiders crawling over me. I thought about the horrible shit my enemies would do to Alex. My heart pounded like a drum because I knew what I would do.

Roman wasn't standing guard. None of our men were anywhere in sight. That was unusual. We had guards posted on every floor as a precaution.

The walnut floor shone from a distance with a thick substance. As I stopped in front of the studio doors, I realized it was blood. I stood in the doorway with Marcello by my side and stared in horror.

Roman was on his knees with his head hung low, blood dripping onto the floor. He was one of our best guys, trained by my brother. Dom was dead and lay face down next to a canvas. Another one of Marcello's most loyal men.

A skinny man with dark sleeves of tattoos pointed a gun at Roman's head. A muscular man held Alex with a blade to her throat. One wrong move, and he could filet her like a fish. Another man stood behind them with his gun aimed at the back of Alex's head. They dressed in dark blue camouflage, half of their faces obscured by matching bandanas.

"Marcello," Alex cried out, tears spilling down her cheeks. "Marcello, shoot him."

Not me.

My brother.

What the fuck?

She thought he could protect her better. Maybe he could. He was better trained and more skilled with weapons. It was my fault they had grown closer in my absence. I allowed my responsibilities to Salvatore Global and The Devil's Knights to put even more distance between us.

Marcello's jaw ticked. "It's okay, Alex."

Alex whimpered, her chest heaving.

I held out my hand. "Hey, baby. Look at me. Okay, can you do that?"

Her eyes found mine, and she swallowed hard.

"You're not worth anything to them if you're dead," I told her.

"Don't fucking move," the dark-haired man said with a thick Russian accent. "Because I will kill her."

No, you won't.

He didn't have the authority to kill Alex. Viktor Romanov worked with the Volkov Bratva and knew the Knights were keeping his daughter from him. He wanted her back alive. So I knew Alex would be safe for now.

Capturing the queen of the Knights would give them temporary power over us, but killing her would fuck up his boss's plan.

My eyes swept over the room, attempting to piece it all together. Ripped canvases, tarps, and various colors of paint littered the floor. The balcony doors were wide open, the breeze from the bay blowing the curtains. So that was how they got past the guards on the first floor. And that was exactly how they planned to steal our queen from us.

JILLIAN FROST

I raised my gun and aimed at the piece of shit's head. My brothers followed suit. We had to be smart about this. One slip of his hand, and he would hit Alex's carotid artery. She would bleed out on the floor within seconds.

"Take one more step, and your queen dies," he warned.

I didn't recognize the man. But based on his accent, I assumed he worked for the Volkov Bratva. Another goon they sent to do their bidding. When would Konstantin Volkov realize he had to show his face before I would reveal my hand? I wasn't about to waste my best moves on his backup squad.

"Let her go," I ordered. "She's not the one your boss wants."

"Your queen is fair compensation for our troubles," he said in broken English.

"We have Viktor's daughter. If he ever wants to see her alive, you will make the call."

I had promised Cole Marshall we would spare his girl. But I didn't give a damn about Grace.

We'd kept her alive for the past ten years for one purpose—to trade her for a meeting with Viktor Romanov. He was the leader of The Lucaya Group. The man who ordered the deaths of Damian and Bastian's parents. And he was the one who sent these scumbags to my house to steal Alex.

The man inched backward, toward the open balcony doors, with the blade digging into Alex's flesh. She looked at me for help, a plea in her watery eyes.

"Drop your guns on the floor," the man growled.

Alex squealed as he sliced into her skin. A droplet of blood slid down her pale neck. I wanted to shoot this motherfucker in the head, but I couldn't take the risk. With his blade already cutting into her flesh, I had one move.

The man behind Alex kept a gun to her head, and a second one pointed at us. I could dodge a bullet, but that blade was too close to her throat.

178

"Do it," I told my brothers as I bent down to set my gun on the floor.

My brothers followed suit.

"Get on your knees," the Russian in charge ordered.

Teeth gritted, I snarled at him before sinking to one knee.

"Slide the guns to me."

I pushed our guns to the center of the room. The life drained from Alex's eyes as she stared at me. She thought we had given up on her.

Not a chance.

We had sworn an oath to protect our queen. No way were they leaving our house with her.

"Viktor's daughter is alive," I said, which gained the leader's attention. "She looks just like her mother. I have proof of life if your boss wants to make a deal."

He reached into his pocket and raised his cell phone to his ear. We only needed one slip-up. A small window of opportunity to get her away from him.

I watched the rise and fall of his chest and noted the doubt in his eyes. He handed the phone to the man behind him, and they exchanged a few words. His hand slipped on the knife, and as he lowered his guard, I drew my gun from the holster and shot at his elbow.

It was enough to loosen his grip on Alex without hurting her. He staggered backward, grabbing his arm and howling in pain. As I rushed across the room, Marcello shot the man behind Roman. I launched myself at Alex, clutching the back of her head as I tackled her to the ground to shield her from the gunfire.

Her life was worth more than mine.

I would gladly die for my queen.

Bullets rang out, and I waited a few seconds before I rolled off Alex. I brushed my thumb across her cheek. "You okay, baby?"

Chest rising and falling, she nodded.

I helped her up from the floor and surveyed the destruction. The man who held Alex at knifepoint was on the floor on his back, gasping for air. Blood dripped from his mouth as he attempted to speak.

He looked up at me, eyes wide. "Is Viktor's daughter alive?"

I tipped my head back and laughed. "Fuck no, that stupid cunt is dead."

A lie.

I wanted him to leave this world thinking he'd failed his boss. Viktor's daughter was Bastian's cousin on his mother's side of the family. The only living granddaughter of Fitzgerald Archibald Adams IV, the highest-ranking Elder and the Grand Master of The Founders Society.

Old Fitzy had promised both Damian and Bastian revenge for their parents' deaths. Even his flesh and blood weren't safe. That old bastard only cared about money and power, and he had more to gain from my brothers than the girl.

"Call Wellington!" Damian hunched over a body on the floor. "We need a fucking doctor. Now!"

I moved to the center of the room with Alex clinging to my side, stepping over their bodies to get to my younger brother. Marcello laid on his back beside Roman, his hand on his stomach. Blood stained his white dress shirt, leaking onto his fingers. He had one eye open, taking shallow breaths as he struggled to speak.

My chest tightened as fear rushed over me.

"Marcello." Alex dropped to her knees beside him. "No, no, no... Keep your eyes open." She wiped the hair off his forehead and shrieked. "You're not allowed to die on me."

He stared at her, the life slowly draining from his eyes. She unbuttoned his dress shirt and studied the bullet wound. There was so much blood it stained her skin.

Alex looked up at me. "Luca, go get help."

Carl stayed in my office with my dad. Alex's grandfather

was a skilled surgeon and didn't become the CEO of Wellington Pharmaceuticals until after he retired.

I removed my phone from my pocket and dialed Carl, who answered on the second ring. I explained the situation, and he said, "I'm on my way. Assemble the mobile triage in the ballroom. Collect the Knights, get them to help you move Marcello's body, but be careful."

"Is that Pops?" Alex looked up at me with tears streaming down her cheeks. She wiggled her fingers for me to hand her the phone. "Pops, he doesn't have much time. He's losing too much blood." Wiping blood away with the bottom of her shirt, she appraised the wound. "I think the bullet hit his liver. He can't die. Just tell me what to do."

I ordered Bastian and Damian to ensure the medical staff made it onto the premises. They ran out of the room without a word. Then I wrote a group text message to the Knights, telling them to get upstairs with a stretcher.

After several attempts on his life, my father had spent millions on a mobile triage unit. Within minutes, we'd have medical staff on-site if they could get past the armed men still firing shots outside.

I hovered over my brother and Alex, my eyes flicking between them. "Stop touching him. Your grandfather said we have to be careful."

"Just sit down and shut up." She pointed at the floor. "Let me take care of Marcello until we can move him."

This girl would be the death of us.

She held my brother's hand. "I'm here, Marcello." Thick tears fell from her eyes. "Don't leave me, okay? Help is on the way. Stay awake. Can you do that for me?"

As my brother's eyes snapped shut, Alex screamed his name. She tried again and again, but he was dead.

Chapter Twenty-Four

ALEX

I made a deal with the Devil. And not with the handsome one standing beside me, watching his brother's life dangle from a string. No, I prayed to the evil lurking within the halls, the monster that lived inside all of us. I'd never believed in a higher power, but I would have gladly signed a contract in blood.

Sold my soul to the Devil.

Anything to keep Marcello alive.

The thought of losing him sliced into my chest, gripping my heart so fiercely that I begged for the pain to stop. I leaned against the wall in the ballroom, tears streaming down my cheeks. My legs shook so severely that Luca had to hold me up.

But I pushed him away.

I didn't want to be touched.

He'd done everything in his power to save me from his enemies. My devil protected me from the demons on our doorstep. But when I was this upset, I craved silence and isolation. Marcello gave me those moments.

He has to live.

We followed them downstairs after the medical response team lifted Marcello onto a stretcher. The Devil's Knights were already in the ballroom, helping a group of nurses and doctors assemble a mobile operating room.

Within minutes, they transformed the elaborate room into a hospital ward. A plastic curtain hung from poles around the operating table, creating a clean environment. Well, clean enough, given the situation.

They moved Marcello to an operating table surrounded by beeping monitors and medical equipment. A nurse ran lines to his arms and placed sensors on his chest. Dressed in scrubs, my grandfather stood beside the table, his hand outstretched as a man handed him a scalpel, and then he went to work.

A gunshot to the liver gave him about thirty percent of survival, but Marcello was in good hands with Pops. Before his retirement, my grandfather was one of the top surgeons in the country. But even with his skills, the mortality rate was high. So I prayed to the Devil again and begged him to let Marcello live.

I can't lose him.

Leaning forward, I cupped my knees with my hands and blew out a deep breath. In and out, I tried to steady my nerves. My heart raced so fast that I thought it would break right through my chest.

Luca cupped my shoulder and whispered, "Calm down."

"That's the last thing you say to someone when they have a panic attack," I snapped.

He tried to hug me, and I knocked his hand away. Luca had never been there for me when I needed him. He was usually the reason for my pain and suffering.

"Drea," he groaned with a pissed-off expression scrolling across his tired face. "I'm just trying to help."

I closed my eyes and breathed through my nose. Sweat slid down my forehead, dripping onto my eyelids, forcing me to blink a few times to clear my vision. "I have to work through this on my own."

"If I were Marcello, you'd let me touch you."

He was right.

I would have flung myself into Marcello's arms and allowed him to run his fingers through my hair. When I was with Marcello, I truly felt at peace.

We had a special connection.

My emotions were so out of whack I needed someone to blame, someone to hate. Luca was the perfect scapegoat. He'd caused some of the worst moments in my life, but there were a few times when he'd shown me so much pleasure and joy.

Luca crossed his suit-clad arms over his chest and snarled at me. "I almost lost you today. My enemies won't stop until they pry you from my dead hands. We need to be united."

"I'm still here," I pointed out. "Those men are dead and rotting upstairs and are no longer our concern. You should worry about Marcello's life, not me."

"That's where you're wrong, baby girl." His fingers slipped beneath my chin, tilting my head until our eyes met. "I always worry about you. You are my one constant. My number one priority."

"Yeah, right?" I snorted. "When have you ever put me first?"

"Always," he challenged with heat behind his words. "I may not be there physically, but I'm always watching you."

"Because you're a psychopath. Not because you care about me."

He studied my face for a moment. Then he shook his head and stormed across the room toward his father.

I stayed with Bastian and Damian.

"He'll calm down." Bastian slid his arm behind my back and pulled me into his chest. "He's upset, too, baby."

Damian tapped his fingers on my hipbone, and I melted

into his warm embrace. "Marcello is indestructible. Even the Devil himself couldn't kill him."

"I hope so," I muttered.

"He's right." Bastian forced one of his adorable smirks that made the dimple in his cheek pop. "Marcello is like a real-life GI Joe. He can withstand just about anything."

I laughed at his reference because I often thought of Marcello as my hero. Whenever I needed him, he was always there to save the day.

I laid my head on Bastian's chest, and tears spilled from my eyes and onto his shirt. He massaged my scalp, so gentle and loving.

"I need him," I choked out with tears streaming down my cheeks. "He can't die... Marcello promised me before he left the studio that he would be careful. He said he would come back for me."

"It's okay." Bastian cradled the back of my head. "Just let it out. I got you, Cherry."

"Luca doesn't get it," I whispered. "He doesn't understand why I need Marcello."

"He's under a lot of pressure... and you still haven't accepted his proposal."

Before I could respond, the monitors screeched at the opposite end of the room. We drifted toward the operating table. The Devil's Knights gathered about ten feet away from the plastic curtain, watching my grandfather operate.

I gulped down my fear, knowing this could be it. Every second was precious at this point. I thought of our final moments together, right before Marcello left his mother's studio to defend this castle on the sea.

I couldn't lose him.

I needed Marcello.

Bastian led me by the hand toward the curtain. My head pounded right at the base of my skull, blurring my vision. The room spun in front of me into a mess of colors and sounds.

That constant beeping reminded me of what little time Marcello had left.

My grandfather shouted at someone, his words muffled.

Why can't I hear him?

His voice sounded so far away.

Five, four, three, two, one…

Just breathe, Alex.

As we stopped beside Luca, I clutched my chest to stop the pain. The sobs ripped from my throat and stung my lips.

"He's dying," I whispered. "It's all my fault…" I lowered my head and focused on breathing, attempting to control the swirl of emotions tearing through my insides. "It should have been me."

"Breathe." Luca ran his fingers up my arm in a soothing motion. "Breathe, baby. We got you."

Bastian stood beside me, his hand on my hip to steady me as Luca grabbed my arm. Pressing my thumbs to my eyelids, I forced back the tears and let them comfort me.

I needed them.

"Marcello will pull through," Luca assured me.

My eyes met his cold blue ones that looked sadder than usual. "If he dies… I can't do this anymore. It's too much, Luca."

Luca curved his arm around me and rested my head on his hard chest. "It's okay, baby. Close your eyes. It will all be over soon."

"No, it won't. Those men will come back for me. This is only the beginning. Isn't it?"

He nodded. "They will return. Next time, they'll have more resources." Luca swiped a tear from beneath my eye. "We'll be ready."

I glanced around the room. A worried Sonny shoved a hand through his blond hair, biting the inside of his cheek. Drake had tears in his eyes as he watched Pops operate. He turned his head and wiped at his eyes when he caught me looking.

Arlo waited outside the plastic curtain, his arms crossed with his back to us. His gaze hadn't shifted from Marcello, not once. Bastian and Damian leaned into each other, speaking in hushed tones. Their faces were as cold and emotionless as marble. Like Luca, I couldn't get a read on them. None of the Salvatores wore their emotions. They had learned from an early age how to bottle them up.

I recognized a few of The Devil's Knights sitting at a table pushed into the corner of the room. The tallest, Cole Marshall, had white-blond hair styled off his forehead. He wore hunter-green fatigues and a fitted shirt that made his big biceps look more prominent.

Callum Cormac sat beside Cole, his head lowered to his lap as he loosened his tie. Finn was on his right, the youngest of the Cormac boys. He had the same blond hair and sun-kissed skin as his brothers.

I closed my eyes, attempting to block out the beeping monitor. To forget about the man who held me at knifepoint. The bullet lodged into Marcello's liver.

My grandfather yelled, "We're losing him."

With those words, I moved toward the curtain, following the sound of his voice. Luca shouted my name, but I couldn't make out the rest of the words over the ringing in my ears. My pulse thumped in my neck, pounding hard and fast.

I stopped beside Arlo, who stood painfully still, his eyes on his son. Lights flashed before my eyes, Marcello's name a whisper on my lips. More sounds penetrated the air, voices reaching a higher octave.

Machines screeched. Pops yelled something, and as his face came into focus, someone moved behind me, crushing me against a hard chest.

Then someone jammed a needle into my arm. "No," I slurred.

"He's gone," someone said from a distance.

Gone.

Gone.

Gone.

Before I could process the words, I lost my footing. And the room spun around me.

.

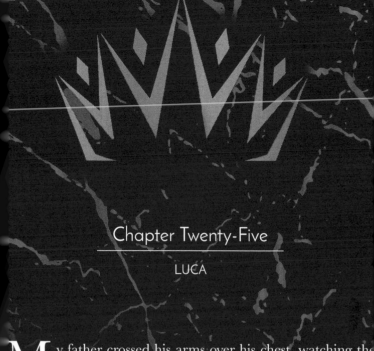

Chapter Twenty-Five

LUCA

My father crossed his arms over his chest, watching the medical team work on my brother. We were the same height, six foot three inches, and had the same black hair and rugged features. In so many ways, we were the same.

He hadn't spoken a word since Carl started operating on Marcello. Cold and calculated, Arlo Salvatore was a man with no emotions. I learned everything from him. How to fight, how to lead, how to kill, and how to shut out the world.

Most people hated my father because he was ruthless, fearless, and downright terrifying, but they also respected him. I'd known from an early age he was preparing me for the world's harshness. Every scar was a lesson, a reminder of how tough I needed to become to survive.

The scar on my shoulder was from his belt buckle and served as a lesson in obedience. I had a long, jagged scar that was a lesson for selfishness on my back. I remembered each one when I looked in the mirror.

When Marcello was born, I was eighteen months old. I didn't remember holding him, but I had seen the pictures of my mom placing Marcello in my arms. I sat on the couch beside my parents with that crazed look

Even back then, I knew I wasn't normal.

My cold blue eyes had a hollow look to them. And if you stared for too long, they turned a shade of blue so dark they appeared black. My mother's friends would tell me I was adorable and would be as handsome as my father.

But I knew what hid inside me.

The darkness.

The anger.

Marcello was different, untainted by evil. When we were kids, he stole all of my parents' attention. I'd hated him so much I wanted him gone. I had dreamed of how I would kill him to have my parents to myself. And when I was five years old, I tried to get rid of him.

I slipped through the halls of my estate, careful not to make a sound. Gripping the Spider-Man pillow in my tiny hands, I held it against my chest. There wasn't a single bit of hesitation in my footsteps. My breathing was even and controlled. I committed to my mission, and nothing would stop me.

Marcello's bedroom was down the hall from mine. I pushed open his door and stood in the entryway with a grin plastered on my lips. He was napping in his bed, snoring as I approached him. A humidifier blew a mist across the room.

I smelled the saltiness of the sea in the air. The scent of the bay permeated every inch of this house. I could always catch the faintest hint and loved it. When I gazed at the bay, I felt a sense of calm wash over me. It helped quell the rage inside me.

I stood beside my brother's bed with the pillow in my hand. "Wake up, Marcello."

He was sound asleep, dead to the world.

I flicked his cheek with my finger. "Time to wake up."

He groaned, then his eyes fluttered as they met mine.

"She's not your mom." I hovered over him with the pillow. "She's mine."

Marcello squirmed as he tried to get up from the mattress, but I pushed him down, holding him with all my strength.

"Luca," he cried, swatting at my hands.

I lowered the pillow over his face. "Shut up."

He screamed for my parents.

"Brother," he whined in that stupid childish voice. "Brother…"

For a moment, I hesitated, as if hearing the word brother triggered something inside me. And that brief pause saved his life.

My mother shouted behind me. Something hit the floor with a thud, and I dropped the pillow. I spun around, staring at my mom. She was beautiful, with long black hair like silk and the same blue eyes she'd passed down to her children.

With tears in her eyes, her body trembled with fear. "Luca, what are you doing to Marcello?"

"I was…"

I was going to kill him.

Juice spilled on the floor and splashed her expensive heels. She yelled for my dad, her shrill voice sounding like nails running down a chalkboard.

"Figlio del diavolo," my mother whispered, her eyes widening as they landed on me.

I started learning Italian when I was two years old and understood her. She was the daughter of immigrants and mostly spoke in her native tongue. My mother called me the son of the devil. Marcello, her precious angel, sat on his bed while I stared at her with my usual dead expression.

I loved my mother more than anything in this world. But sometimes, I felt it. I knew I scared her, too.

My father's dress shoes pounded the floor. He stopped in the doorway, his intense gaze sweeping over the room. His eyes fell to the juice on the floor, then to me.

Dad's jaw tightened as he burned a hole through me with his eyes. "What did you do, Luca?"

I shrugged, giving him a bored look.

"He tried to suffocate Marcello with his pillow," my mother shouted, tears streaming down her cheeks.

"It's okay, Eva." My dad pulled her into his arms and kissed the top of her head. "The boy will learn his lesson and take it like a man."

A typical child would have trembled in fear. But not me. The thought of punishment almost excited me. When I did terrible shit, my parents paid attention to me. They stopped making a big deal over Marcello and had to address my behavior.

My dad released his grip on my mom and snarled as he approached me. "Is this true? Did you try to kill your brother?"

I nodded, not the least bit sorry.

He smacked me so hard across the cheek my knees hit the floor, and an intense pain crawled up my legs and back. Then, standing over me, he kicked me with his shoe. It didn't hurt as much as the fall, but it still fucking hurt.

"Look at me, boy," Dad growled.

I did as he instructed.

"You are my heir, Luca, but you are rotten. And if you touch Marcello again, I will beat the sickness out of you."

"I'm sorry," I lied.

I wasn't sorry for shit.

When I looked up at my mother, who hugged herself as she cried, I knew I'd fucked up. Because her love meant more to me than anyone. Only a mother could love someone like me.

My father shook his head. "You're not sorry."

He always saw right through me. Our souls were so similar he knew what I was thinking. I was his son in every way.

Mom grabbed Marcello from his bed and cradled him in her arms, planting kisses on his cheeks. She rocked him, and I hated him for it because I wanted to take his place.

"It's okay, Marcello," she whispered and stroked his dark hair. "Mommy's here now."

I never wanted to see that look in her eyes, never to feel whatever this was again. My mom was the only person who made me feel something. I felt dead on the inside with other people, like there was a hole in place of my heart.

Dad bent down on one knee and slid his fingers beneath my chin. "One day, this kind of brutality will serve you well. But, until then, you better not defy me. Do you understand me?"

I blew out a deep breath. "Yes, Father."

"Step out of line again, and you will suffer."

I rubbed my knees, wincing at the pain still shooting up my thighs.

He glanced down at my deliberate movements. Then his focus was back on my face. "Pain is weakness leaving the body. Once you understand that, Luca, it doesn't hurt as much. Toughen up. I can't have a baby as my heir. There is no room for weakness in our world."

"I'm not weak."

"No, you're not," he said with the same vacant look. "One day, my son will rule the world. And I will make sure you understand the consequences of having weaknesses."

I cupped my father's shoulder as we watched Carl Wellington perform his magic on Marcello. If my brother didn't survive, it wouldn't just break Alex. It would crush all of us. Thankfully, my father had taught me how to take the pain and use it for good. He showed me how to wield it like a weapon.

I never had a single weakness.

Not until I met Alex.

Despite our past differences, I was like my father in every way. Years of his cruelty had hardened me into a man forged from steel. I embraced the pain and believed I needed to atone for all of my horrible thoughts and actions.

We were both sick fucks.

I enjoyed receiving his punishments as much as he enjoyed giving them. And as an adult, I enjoyed handing out the same misery to others.

Marcello was nothing like me.

I'd spared him years of pain because of my mother. I took the beatings when my father was at his worst. Then, two days before my mother's death, I made her a promise, one I would never forget.

My mother stood on a scaffolding ladder in her studio, with her long, black hair piled on top of her head, with two paintbrushes holding it up. She always wore her hair like that when she was painting. It was like she couldn't waste a second looking for a hairband. When she was in her element, nothing could deter her. We were a lot alike in that regard.

Marcello was eight years old and slowly following in her footsteps. He sat on the floor in front of an easel, his paintbrush sweeping across the canvas. He was a natural artist who had our mother's talents.

I tried to paint, but I was my dad in every way. My book smarts would make me a powerful man one day, and I followed my father's carefully laid plans. But I often appeased my mother by trying to paint. She was happy to see Marcello and me in her studio, acting like a family.

After the time I tried to kill him, I never attempted it again. We still weren't on the best terms, but I tolerated him for my mom. I liked making her happy and never wanted to hear her call me the devil's son again. She loved me more when I was good, and my father loved me more when I was bad, like him. So I learned how to share different parts of myself with my parents.

I strolled toward my mother, the stupid boat shoes she insisted I wear slapping the floor. Her head snapped in my direction, a smile gracing her red lips. She wore a shade of lipstick that was so vibrant it looked like blood.

I liked that color.

That morning, she laid out a pair of black cargo shorts and a navy blue-and-white-striped polo shirt on my bed. She insisted I wear more casual clothes since I preferred suits like my father. He had Brioni make custom suits, so we looked like twins.

"Luca." My mom smiled. "Where have you been hiding?"

"I was helping Dad with something."

I left out the part where I stuffed a wet cloth into a man's mouth before my father beat the shit out of him for information. He never hid the violence from me. It had started when I was around five years old, not long after I tried to kill Marcello.

I think he knew back then I was ready for this lifestyle.

When I was older, he involved me in the corrupt side of his business, and I never looked back.

My mother climbed down from the ladder and patted the top of my head. "Have you been a good boy today?"

"No," I admitted.

"Luca," she sighed. "What did your father make you do?"

"Nothing I couldn't handle."

"You're a child." She bit her cheek as she looked down at me. "Go play with Drake Battle. He's your age, sweetie."

I sneered at her suggestion. "He's boring and plays video games all day."

Mom ran her fingers through my hair, which I would have hated if it were anyone else. No one but my mother could touch me. "He's a nice boy. You should ask him to come over and go swimming."

I was well beyond sleepovers and play dates with the neighborhood kids. Mentally, I was already in my twenties, while kids like Drake still slept in Superman pajamas and played with fake guns. So why pretend when my dad let me shoot the real thing?

I shook my head. "No, I'd rather play with Dad. I don't want to swim."

She sighed and bent down to my height. "Your dad isn't playing. That's real." Her red nails brushed my cheek. "Luca, you need to make some friends. Have a life outside of this house that doesn't involve your father."

"I don't need friends. I have you and Dad."

"And Marcello." Her lips pressed into a thin line. "Il sangue non e acqua."

"Blood or not, I don't want him," I fired back.

She blew out an irritated breath. "The two of you don't always get along, but you are brothers. Blood is thicker than water. Promise me, mio principe, that you will take care of Marcello."

"I promise."

I found her two days later on the floor of her studio with her head turned to the side. Her lips were so blue I'd never forgotten the color of death. The stench of a rotting corpse.

At that moment, I knew I had to honor her dying wish to protect Marcello. It was the least I could do for the only person who ever made me feel normal.

My father gripped my bicep, pulling me out of my memories. I turned to look at him, my eyebrows lifted in question.

He leaned closer and lowered his voice. "If Marcello doesn't make it, you need to marry Alexandrea immediately. Do you understand me?"

I nodded.

"We can't afford a moment of weakness. Everyone will want blood."

Chapter Twenty-Six

ALEX

D rifting between sleep and consciousness, I fought against the nightmares commanding control of my body. I tried so hard, telling myself it was time to wake up.

As I opened my eyes, I rolled over onto a soft surface, curled my arms around a pillow, and stretched my legs across a bed. For a moment, I'd forgotten about everything.

The attack at the estate.

The sound of the monitors.

Marcello's heart stopped beating.

Tears coated my bottom lids, my chest heaving from crying so hard.

"She's awake," a male voice boomed.

I could sense his presence before he ran his fingers down my arm. "I'm here, Drea."

I blinked away the hazy image of my handsome devil, and he blew out a relieved breath. Luca hovered over me, his spiky dark hair all over the place. He was usually so perfect and manicured.

"He's dead." I covered my heart with my hand to still my rapid breathing. "Isn't he?"

Luca took my hand, his fingers soft and warm against

mine. "No, baby. He pulled through. Your grandfather saved Marcello."

I had the sudden desire to climb out of bed, but Luca held me down when I tried.

"You need to rest."

"No." I shoved his hand away. "I want to see Marcello."

"He's out cold, Drea." His knuckles brushed my cheek. "Just stay in bed and let me take care of you."

Take care of me? When the hell did Luca ever comfort me? If I wanted to feel better, I went to Marcello. He always knew the right thing to do and say.

"I'm fine." I rubbed the sleep from my eyes and sat up. "Let me see him."

Luca stepped to the side, and Marcello's bed came into focus. He was in the hospital bed beside mine with his eyes closed. I could see his chest rise and fall, and let out a sigh of relief.

He survived.

I slid my legs off the side of the bed. My head spun from a wave of nausea that caused me to stagger to the right. Luca grabbed my bicep to hold me up. "You've been sleeping for close to twenty-four hours. The drugs are still in your system. You need your rest."

I clutched his shoulder, fighting the dizziness sweeping over me. "What the hell did you give me? I feel like shit."

He shrugged. "A cocktail from your psychiatrist."

I pressed my palm against his chest to regain my balance. "Dr. Porter gave it to you?"

He hooked his arm around me and nodded. "You need to take it easy until the drugs wear off. It was a heavy dose."

My mouth hung open in shock. "Why did you drug me?"

"Because I didn't want you to see what was happening to Marcello."

"He's alive," I breathed, saying the words aloud to comfort myself.

"Yes." He stroked my arm with his fingers to soothe me. "And he'll stay that way if you let him sleep."

I looked up at him, eyes narrowed. "I've been out for a day, and he still hasn't woken up?"

He shook his head. "We have to wait and see. Marcello could wake up a minute from now or never. It's too early to tell. But, at least he's breathing, and his brain function looks good."

"His heart stopped, didn't it?"

"Yeah, baby. He died on the table twice before your grandfather revived him."

"But he promised me," I sobbed, resting my head on his chest. "He said he would come back."

"Shh," Luca whispered as he held me tighter. "It's going to be okay."

"No, it's not," I muttered between crying fits. "Not if he dies."

He's just sleeping, I told myself. He will wake up.

Luca stood behind me as I swept the dark strands off Marcello's clammy forehead. Even in sleep, he was beautiful. He looked so peaceful. I felt a flicker of heat spread down my arm as I touched his skin. That connection was always present. The same energy I'd felt every time he touched me.

I traced the length of his jaw with my fingers and whispered, "Come back to me, Marcello. I need you."

I checked each dip in the heart monitor, studying it like a hawk. Then, gripping the bed rail, I leaned forward to kiss his forehead. "Wake up, Marcello. Your queen demands it."

"Let him sleep," Luca said over my shoulder.

"Shut up, Luca," I snapped, anger surging through me as I spun around to face him. "Stop telling me what to do."

My heart thudded as his teeth clenched, and I realized I was out of line. Marcello was his brother, not mine.

"I'm sorry." I closed the distance between us and brushed my fingers against his. "I didn't mean to yell at you. It's just…" My words died off in my throat as I glanced over at Marcello.

"I know," Luca muttered, his eyes downcast.

I slid my hands up his chest, wrapping my arms around his neck. Our eyes met for a moment. He looked so sad and beautiful that I wanted to kiss his lips. Luca held me like he was afraid I would disappear if he let go.

"I'm sorry," I whispered again, my head foggy from the drugs. "I can't lose him."

He tensed at my words. "I know. Try to relax, okay?"

"He has to live."

"He will, baby." Luca bent down and kissed my forehead. "Stop worrying about Marcello. He's a fighter."

Someone cleared their throat behind us.

Until then, I hadn't noticed we were still in the ballroom. My eyes traveled around the room and landed on Arlo and Pops. Damian and Bastian sat at a dining table beside a few of the Knights who were there before I'd passed out. They lounged on elaborate dining chairs with the Salvatore snake crest emblazoned into the wood.

Drinks in hand, they studied me with curiosity. Arlo sat beside Pops in a new suit. My grandfather looked as if he'd aged ten years within days. Sonny and Drake wore suits from the day before. Dark circles ringed their eyes, their hair messy and without its usual polish.

The golden boy of Devil's Creek always looked like a billion bucks. But seeing Sonny so disheveled and heartbroken made my stomach hurt. This had to be killing him. He'd been Marcello's best friend since they were in diapers. When Marcello couldn't count on Luca, he had Sonny. They had each other.

Arlo's gaze drifted to Luca's hand on my hip. His intense stare unsettled me. Luca often looked at me the same way. Like he was staring through me, digging deep into my soul, attempting to extract my secrets.

Pops ran a hand through his white hair, forcing a smile as our eyes met. The stress of Marcello's operation must have taken a toll on him.

I slipped out of Luca's grasp and walked over to the table. Pops slid out of his chair and stood to his full height.

I launched myself into his arms. "You saved him," I said as he hugged me. "Thank you."

"This is a tough situation." He patted my back with his palm. "Marcello has to wake up on his own."

I peeked up at him. "Do you think he will?"

"I'm optimistic." He held me at arm's length, a severe expression crossing his withered face. "But you need to prepare yourself for him never waking up."

"Pops, I can't do this if he doesn't..." I wouldn't even allow myself to finish the thought.

It was all five of us or none of us. That much I had made clear to each of the guys now that we were in this together. And if Marcello didn't live, I was finding my brother and getting as far away from Devil's Creek as possible.

Before Pops could respond, I heard a familiar voice whisper my name, and my pulse raced.

Chapter Twenty-Seven

LUCA

The world stopped at the sound of his voice. Chairs scraped across the tiled floor, and the Knights stepped forward in unison. They stood in a straight line several feet from Marcello's bed. That was how we moved, how we operated. We were a team, a unit, and nothing could break our bond.

When I was younger, I didn't want to be friends with them. Even when my mother had insisted, I wasn't fond of the idea of friendship. I didn't like needing people. My father had instilled the importance of trusting and relying on myself. And so I'd distanced myself from everyone but my family.

After my initiation into The Devil's Knights, I realized I needed them as much as they needed me. The shit we had endured together bonded us in ways that surpassed the bonds of friendship. We were closer than blood, like brothers in every way. Sure, we still had our disagreements, but we would kill for each other, die for each other.

And we all agreed on one thing.

We had to protect our queen at all costs.

My father blew past them and stood beside Marcello's bed with his hands shoved into his pockets. His usual vacant stare scrolled across his tired face, though I could tell he was pleased. My father rarely showed emotion. By observing him, I'd learned how to conceal my own. So did my brothers.

Carl Wellington snapped his fingers to gain the nurse's attention and then moved toward the side of the bed with the monitors.

"Alex," Marcello whispered, his eyes still closed. His voice was raw and even scratchier when he repeated her name.

After the nurses checked his vitals, Carl waved Alex forward. She leaned over the side of Marcello's bed and held his hand on top of the mattress.

"I thought I lost you." Alex rubbed her thumb over his cheek, a big smile on her beautiful face. "You scared me to death." She blew out a deep breath. "How do you feel?"

"Like I got shot."

He attempted a smile, but he looked like he was in a shit ton of pain. Marcello winced, then turned his head away from Alex. My brother didn't want us to see him as weak. Alex thought of him as indestructible, her hero.

She sat on the bed beside him and smiled, leaning over to whisper something in his ear. My brother attempted to smile and grimaced in pain.

My dad moved to my side, his jacket sleeve brushing my arm. "What's going on with Marcello and Alexandrea?"

"Nothing," I lied.

He shook his head in disapproval. "You're losing your grip on her. Need I remind you of the importance of this union?"

"No. She's mine."

"She has feelings for Marcello," my dad insisted.

It was a statement, not a question.

Anyone could see how much she cared about him. Marcello had always admired his queen and would have treated her better than me, showing her real love. I'd shielded him from the brunt of my father's rage, and he wasn't as cold and cruel. His heart wasn't black and tainted like mine.

"Alex won't choose Marcello over me," I said to assure him, though my voice lacked confidence.

Would she?

"She can only marry one of you. So you better get your head back in the game."

"Alex is marrying me," I fired back.

I would kill Marcello before letting him walk down the aisle with my girl. Maybe I didn't deserve her. I'd fucked up more times than I could count, but no one would ever care for her like me. No one could fulfill her desires or satisfy the darkness in her soul the way I did. She would always come back to me, no matter what.

I was sure of it.

My dad shoved his hands into his pockets, his eyes on Alex as she kissed Marcello's forehead. "I don't care which one of you marries her as long as she produces an heir. If we don't fulfill the terms of The Founders Society deal, we're in trouble."

"Dad," I groaned. "I got this. Trust me."

"You could have locked down this arrangement years ago." Disappointment scrolled across his face as he lowered his voice. "Marcello would have married her already. Instead, we are in an impossible situation because of your inability to put the past behind you."

"I will ask her again." I lowered my voice and leaned into his side. "We had a rocky start. It took Alex a while to readjust to Devil's Creek."

"And whose fault is that?" Dad turned his scary dark brown eyes on me, giving me a look that burned my skin. "You haven't spent much time with Alexandrea since she arrived in Devil's Creek."

"I was trying to keep psychopaths from kidnapping her." My nostrils flared, annoyed with his intrusion into my life. "She understands that."

He released a dark chuckle as he gazed at Marcello and

Alex. "You threatened to break her finger to put a ring on it. I expect you to know better than to handle her like that. She's a lot like your mother, Luca."

"I apologized. Alex knows I didn't mean it."

"A queen demands respect," he said in a matter-of-fact tone. "Alexandrea doesn't know it yet, but she is queen material. You almost had her. She was right there within your grasp before you played games with her. You have screwed up everything for this family with your petty bullshit."

"Her mom killed mine. That's not something I could get over."

"No?" Dad cocked an eyebrow at me. "Because I disagree. Put your ego and pride aside. She is nothing like her mother, Luca." He snickered. "I can assure you of that. Alex may look like Savanna, but that's where their similarities end."

"I know that now. It took me a long time to see it."

"Alex is your second chance to become part of The Founders Society someday. If you had done what I had asked of you five years ago, you would have already married her. We would have an heir from a Founding Family. And we wouldn't be standing here right now."

"She's a means to an end," I whispered with a nod, repeating the words he'd said to me for years. "I know, Dad. You've told me a few hundred times."

"Without this union, we will lose everything. You have seen firsthand what happens to men banished by The Founders Society. Do you want that to happen to us?"

I sighed. "Of course not."

"If she favors your brother, then he will marry her."

"She's not marrying Marcello."

He rolled his shoulders. "Doesn't matter to me."

"Well, it matters to me."

I looked over at Carl Wellington, who was talking to Sonny on the other side of the room. My father's gaze followed mine.

"Carl's vote with The Founders Society carries a lot of weight. We don't have the same connections or status as the Wellingtons. But we have money and the Knights. As long as you stick to the plan, we will have everything we want. I have spent years working toward a future for my sons. So don't fuck this up."

"I have the situation under control."

I watched Alex fawn over my brother like he was a newborn baby. The same anger and rage I'd felt as a child toward him bubbled up, simmering right at the surface. When I hated Alex, I didn't care if my brothers fucked her. They could have killed her for all I cared.

But things were different now.

Hands balled into fists at my sides, I gritted my teeth and pushed down my unwanted feelings. I could deal with hurtful emotions, but I could never process intimacy and love.

Marcello often told me I needed to learn to deal with my emotions. But it was easier to trap them inside a box and throw away the key.

"You have one job to do," my father said harshly. "Do you understand me?"

Alex held my brother's hand on top of her knee with a smile that illuminated her face. He said something to her, and her laughter floated through the air. They had a natural ease in their interactions. Unlike Alex and me, they just clicked. She needed him in her life.

"I will fix this," I told him.

Chapter Twenty-Eight

ALEX

L uca got into bed beside me and brushed the curls off my cheek.

I fell asleep in Marcello's hospital bed after he passed out from the pain meds. My grandfather had assured me Marcello's vitals looked good and that he would likely make a full recovery. But I was too afraid to leave his side until Luca swaddled me like a baby and took me upstairs.

"Luca," I whispered as I laid my head on the pillow. "Will you stay with me?"

Without a word, he shot up from the bed.

My handsome devil unzipped his slacks and slid them down his toned thighs. "Mmm…"

"I thought you were tired," he said with a mischievous look.

"I can look, can't I?"

He smirked as he unbuttoned his shirt and slid it over his shoulders, revealing his scarred, muscled stomach. "Go ahead."

He got back into bed and hooked his strong arm around me. I traced my thumb along his jaw, stopping at his lips.

His eyes flickered with madness. "My little devil," he whispered against my lips. "Do you need me to feed your demons?"

I wet my lips with my tongue. "Kiss me until I fall asleep."

Luca crushed my lips with a kiss, sweeping his tongue into my mouth as his fingers wove through my curls. His touch was soft and loving, an unusual side to Luca.

I wrapped my leg around him and rocked my hips. He grabbed my hand, moving it over top of his rock-hard cock that poked through the slit on his black Dolce & Gabbana boxer briefs.

"You drive me crazy, baby," he whispered between kisses.

"Luca," I moaned. "What happened to just kissing?"

He laughed, then dipped his hand between my thighs. "I am just kissing you."

"No, you're not." I sucked his bottom lip into my mouth as he shoved his hand down my shorts and rolled his thumb over my clit. "Oh, God, Luca. Mmm…"

"I know you need to come, baby," he said in a husky voice that made my skin burn. "Let me take care of you."

My resolve faded as he rubbed my clit, ripping another moan from my throat. I kicked off my shorts and flipped onto my back. Luca didn't waste a second, quickly moving between my spread thighs with a greedy look in his eyes.

He caged me against the mattress and pushed up my shirt. A cool breeze blew in from the open French doors. The chill in the air and his mouth on my skin caused my nipples to harden into points. Luca bit my lip as he teased my wetness with his finger.

I arched my back, and Luca groaned, kissing me harder as he deepened the kiss.

Luca was never sweet or gentle with me, but he wasn't his rough and possessive self. Something had shifted between us.

As our lips separated, he pulled my shirt over my head and threw it across the room. He watched his fingers move inside me, his eyes widening with each thrust.

Gentle, soft, loving.

Was he capable of this?

His tongue glided across my hot skin, bringing me seconds away from an orgasm. I could feel it building with each flick, heat coiling in my belly as he massaged my inner walls with care. Luca's tongue rolled over my throbbing clit, and then he spread me open with his tongue, igniting every pleasure point in my body at once.

He held me down and licked me aggressively, his tongue taking me to new heights. With his hand on my breast and his tongue licking my pussy, I came so damn hard I saw stars.

I reached between us and grabbed his cock, his shaft long and hard and growing even harder in my hand. He removed his boxers and positioned himself between my thighs.

"Go slow."

"Whatever my queen wants," he whispered.

As he inched inside me, he ran his fingers up and down my thigh, taking his time. I didn't think a man like Luca could make love to me, so I soaked up every second of this moment.

"Luca," I whimpered as he kissed my lips.

"You feel so good, baby." He sucked on my lip as he rocked his hips. "Fuck, I missed you."

"It's only been a few days."

He kissed me again. "I'll never get enough of you, Drea."

My body melted into his, and I slowly unraveled beneath him. It was so easy to lose myself with this gorgeous man. He bit my lip playfully, a sexy smile teasing his lips. I looked up at my powerful prince with his strong jawline, high cheekbones, and those pretty blue eyes that sliced right through me.

I dug my heel into his ass and arched my hips, needing more of him. "Come for me, Luca."

A feral look danced across his face. "Oh, I'm coming, baby."

He pumped into me a few more times, the tremor shaking

through him vibrating my body. Lips parted, he stilled on top of me, his cock pulsing inside me, and looked into my eyes.

"That was perfect," I breathed.

He kissed me. "I knew you needed that."

"Luca, I need to know something."

His thumb grazed my cheek. "Anything."

"Do you think you'll ever love me?"

He blew out a deep breath, his expression darkening. Luca attempted to roll off me, but I grabbed his bicep.

"Don't withdraw from me, Luca. Please give me something."

His eyes snapped shut. "I don't know how to love you. What does that word even mean?"

"Love isn't a word," I insisted. "Love is emotion. Actions. Intention. That was love when you protected me from your enemies and risked your life for mine."

He shook his head, and a strand of his dark hair dropped in front of his eyes. "You're my queen, Drea. I will always put your life before mine. So will the rest of the Knights."

"It's been years. You must feel something for me."

Luca pulled out of me, withdrawing from me as he moved to the mattress beside me. He propped himself up on his elbow, unable to meet my gaze. "Why are you ruining this?"

"Why does the thought of loving me make you sick?" I forced down the tears stinging my eyes. "Is the idea that horrible?"

"No," he admitted. "But that word has no meaning to me. There are no words to describe how I feel about you. What binds us will destroy us. You may call it love, but I call it something else. The darkness inside us and the demons that want to claim our souls bind us. We all have that in common. You, me, the Knights. Forever and always, bound to one another."

"What binds us will destroy us," I repeated. "Where have I heard that before?"

"It's the motto of the Knights. And as our queen, we are all bound to you."

Even though his words should have comforted me, I felt nothing but anger and frustration. "And here, I thought you were capable of real feelings."

"Legare means to bind in Italian. What binds us will destroy us," he repeated. "And what will destroy us unites us."

Anger coursing through my veins like hot lava, I slid across the mattress and covered myself with a sheet. "Get out."

He groaned as he sat up, reaching out for me. Luca attempted to touch my arm, and I recoiled from him.

"You should go."

I rushed into the bathroom and locked the door behind me.

Luca banged on the door. "C'mon, Drea." He jiggled the handle as I backed into the room, bumping into the counter as the first tear fell. "Open this door, baby."

"Go away, Luca!"

"No," he growled. "Open this fucking door before I break it down."

I put my face in my hands and sobbed. "Just leave me alone!"

"What are you doing in there, baby?" Luca threw his weight into the door like he was trying to break it down. "You better not be hurting yourself."

"Luca, I'm not suicidal. Please, give me some space."

"*Mi dispiace bellissima*," he said in Italian before muttering several curses. He punched the door and grunted, "Fine. Have it your way. But I'm not giving up on you."

Chapter Twenty-Nine

ALEX

That night I dreamed of The Devil's Knights. We were in their temple, hidden in the catacombs beneath Devil's Creek. An eery silence fell over the room, lit by dozens of candles. It was intimate and romantic, but what we were about to do together was far from romance.

Luca stood behind me with his hands on my shoulders. He pressed his lips to my earlobe, sending a shiver down my spine. "The queen must accept her Knights."

The Knights circled me and dropped to the ground on their knees with the hoods of their cloaks covering their lowered heads.

I stood in front of the Knights. With my naked body on display, I moved toward the man in front of me. Even with his head down, I knew it was Marcello. I could sense him anywhere. Like Luca, he was a part of me.

I shoved the hood off Marcello's head, and his eyes met mine. He looked so damn sexy I licked my lips, and he returned the gesture as he studied my body with care.

"I choose you, Marcello Salvatore." I moved my hand to his cheek and smiled.

I woke up in a cold sweat, screaming his name.

Marcello.

I needed to see him, so I headed toward the door. Roman hadn't survived the attack. His replacement was a twenty-something guy named Benji. He stood outside of my bedroom with his back to the wall.

Benji stared at me, arms crossed over his chest. Dressed in a black suit, he had dark hair, olive skin, and a scar that ran down his neck. He looked dangerous and kind of scared me. But he was here for my protection. Supposedly, he was one of Marcello's best men.

He pushed himself off the wall and slowly approached me. "Everything okay, Miss Wellington?"

"Yes." I stepped into the hallway, closing the distance. "I need to see Marcello."

He pointed at the door across from mine. "Mr. Salvatore moved him closer to you."

I thanked him, then headed toward Marcello's temporary bedroom. It was dark inside, the only light coming from the moonlight filtering through the curtains. The room mirrored mine and had a balcony overlooking the bay and an ensuite bathroom.

Leaving the door open a crack, I used the light from the hallway sconces to lead the way. Marcello slept in a four-poster bed under a mound of blankets. There was a hospital bed beside it. I assumed the medical staff left it there in case shit went south and they needed to move him.

The monitor beside his bed beeped in a steady rhythm. He had IVs and a bunch of shit attached to his body. I hopped onto the mattress and rested my head on the pillow beside his head. Just being next to him made me feel safe. Like I could finally breathe.

I slipped my fingers between his and watched him sleep, staring at his chest rising and falling beneath the covers. So fucking thankful he survived the attack. He breathed softly and moved a little when I stroked his skin with my fingers.

After a while, I stopped fighting sleep. My eyelids grew heavy, and I closed my eyes, consumed by the sound of Marcello's breathing.

He was alive.

A hand slipped beneath my shirt, and fingers traveled up my stomach, inching toward my breasts. Eyes closed, I laid my head on the pillow and let him touch me. Let him roll his thumb over my painfully sore nipple. This was a nice dream, the perfect escape from reality. He felt so good, his hands warm and rough as he claimed me.

I opened my eyes. Marcello was asleep beside me, touching me without even knowing it. At least I thought he was sleeping. I still craved him, but I didn't want him like this. Not when he was unconscious.

I grabbed his hand and moved it to the mattress. Heart pounding in my chest, I lay on my side and watched him. I sighed in relief. I had never been so scared when he was on the operating table.

"Morning, princess," Marcello said, his voice hoarse.

"Morning." I smiled so wide my cheeks hurt. "How are you feeling?"

"I'll live," he muttered. "Did you have a nightmare?"

"Yeah. I couldn't get back to sleep without knowing you were okay." I brushed the sweat-matted black hair off his forehead. "Do you need a nurse? You look pale."

He closed his eyes and breathed through his nose. "Pain is weakness leaving the body."

"I can ask the nurse to give you more morphine."

I attempted to slide off the bed, and he said, "No, don't

leave." He held out his hand and wiggled his fingers. "Come here."

"I thought you were dead," I choked out, fighting tears. "Marcello, I can't lose you."

"I'm not going anywhere." He patted the top of my hand with his fingers. "Don't worry about me, beautiful."

I lifted the blanket to inspect the bandage over his wound, exposing his scarred but muscled chest. "Did you get all of these scars from your father?"

A mess of scars covered his olive skin. Luca's scars were so bad they looked like spiderwebs that spanned most of his chest and back. But Marcello's scattered from his hip to his shoulder.

"A few of them, yeah. Luca took most of the punishments. My dad rarely hit me, but when he did, Luca always stepped in front of me."

"I'm surprised he would sacrifice himself for anyone else."

"He made a promise to our mother before she died."

"To protect you?"

He nodded. "When I was a kid, I didn't know any better. My mom treated me like a baby, while my dad let Luca shadow him everywhere. I was more like my mother, and my dad knew it. So did Luca. After she died, I realized I needed to toughen up. I learned to defend myself because Luca wouldn't always be there to save me."

"I'm still shocked he would do that for you."

"My brother has a heart," he said with laughter in his tone. "It's just locked inside a steel box buried three hundred feet below the ocean floor."

"We got into a fight last night," I confessed.

"Your life will never be easy. Not with Luca," he said with sadness in his eyes. "But he will take care of you."

"I want him to love me."

"He does," Marcello insisted. "In his way."

Desperate to change the subject, I shifted the conversation

back to his recovery. "You have a long road ahead of you. Pops said it could take months."

"This isn't my first gunshot wound," he said with no emotion in his tone. "It's not as bad as you think."

"Where were you shot before?"

He pointed at a mark on his shoulder, then at another one on his stomach. "It's nothing."

My eyes widened at all of his scars. "Someone shot you, Marcello. That's a big deal."

"Occupational hazard. Bound to happen at some point."

"You took a bullet for me." I cupped his cheek with my hand. "My hero. Thank you."

He snickered. "I'm no hero."

"You saved me."

Marcello turned his head to the side and glanced out the open French doors. "Luca saved you. I took the bullet because I didn't shoot the asshole in the head." A frown pulled at his lips. "I'll never make that mistake again."

"How did it happen?"

"I thought he was dead." His head snapped back to me, and he winced as if the sudden movement was painful. "He grabbed one of our guns from the floor. I tried to dodge the bullet but didn't move fast enough."

"Still, you did it for me." I leaned down to kiss his lips. "Thank you."

He kissed me back. "No need to thank me."

His stomach growled so loud it filled the silence in the room.

"Are you hungry? I can get your breakfast," I offered.

His long, dark eyelashes fanned out against his skin as he looked at me. "Yeah, I can eat."

I hopped off the bed and poked my head into the hallway, looking at Benji. "Can you get Marcello's breakfast?"

He nodded, then removed his cell phone from his pocket.

The house manager knew what everyone liked to eat. This place ran like a well-oiled machine.

Benji's fingers glided across the keypad, and then he said, "I'll bring in Marcello's food when it's ready."

I flashed a smile at him. "Thanks."

After I closed the door, I got back into bed with Marcello. We talked about art and books for ten minutes before Benji knocked on the door. He entered the room without a word, gave Marcello a quick nod, then set the tray on the bed in front of me.

I lifted a plate of egg whites and a fork. "Can you sit up?"

Marcello tapped a button on a remote. The head of the bed rose, but I still shoved a few pillows behind him to prop him up.

As I fed him a forkful of eggs, the door slammed into the wall. I nearly dropped the fork and screamed at the sound. I couldn't handle any more surprises. Every loud noise I now associated with gunshots.

Luca stood in the entryway, dressed in a three-piece suit, arms crossed over his chest, glaring at us. And even though we had done nothing wrong, I felt like I was in trouble.

Chapter Thirty

LUCA

Anger flooded my veins as I stared at them. Alex held a fork in front of my younger brother's mouth. It was happening all over again. He stole my mother from me when we were children. And now, he was doing the same with Alex.

Why the fuck did I agree to share?

I let my hatred for her cloud my judgment back then. Until recently, I still couldn't get over how much I hated her family for the past. I was paying the price for my mistakes every second I had to watch her with Marcello.

He'd stolen all of my mother's love, time, and attention. Her perfect, obedient son didn't enjoy hurting himself and others. I loved my mother more than life itself, and history was repeating with Alex.

She asked me if I could ever love her. Love was such a simple word, yet it held so much meaning to some people. I understood obsession, possession, and the need to claim my beautiful queen. But love? That was such a foreign concept to me. I hadn't felt it in so long that I couldn't remember the feeling.

"Luca," Alex said with a warning tone as she set the fork on the plate. "Why do you look like you're ready to explode?"

Because I am.

My blood felt like it was boiling in my veins. "Why are you in Marcello's bedroom instead of your own?"

Her chest rose and fell as our eyes met. "I'm feeding him."

"My brother can feed himself," I shot back as I crossed the room, moving to her side of the bed.

She slid off the mattress and reached out for me. I recoiled as she tried to touch me. Most of the time, I hated intimacy. Just the thought of someone's hands on my skin made me physically ill. Of course, Alex was the exception to my rules, and I broke them for her. But at the moment, I would have rather stuck my dick in a wood chipper than let her touch me.

"Luca," Alex said in a sweet tone, giving me one of her perfect smiles. "I'm helping Marcello get back on his feet."

"He has nurses who can help him." My mouth twisted into a hateful sneer. "He doesn't need you."

Her nostrils flared. "Watch your mouth. I'm not in the mood for your bullshit. Marcello almost died, and you're acting like you don't care."

I leaned over her, inches from her face. "Marcello is not a little boy. He doesn't need you to take care of him."

"Luca, stop it," Marcello snapped. "Don't talk to Alex like that. You're scaring her."

I glanced over at my brother and pointed my finger at him. "Stay the fuck out of this. We wouldn't be discussing this if it weren't for you."

"No, I think you would," Marcello challenged. "Even if you lived a billion lifetimes, you would never deserve her."

"Shut your fucking mouth before I come over there and shove a tube down your throat."

"Don't you dare," Alex shouted. "He needs to rest, Luca. Marcello doesn't need this stress on his heart."

"Why do you care so much about Marcello?" I caged her against the mattress with my palms on both sides of her head. "Hmm?"

"You're jealous." Alex gave me a taunting smirk. "Wow. This is unbelievable. You have some nerve acting this way. I wanted your time and affection for years, and you gave me nothing. Instead, you made me wait around for the scraps. If you weren't such a shit human being, I would have fallen in love with you. I would have married you. I would have given you everything."

"Sorry, baby," I growled against her lips. "Hate to break it to you, but I am a shit human being. I'm never going to change. So go ahead, make me your villain. I play the role so well."

She slammed her palm into my chest. "Go fuck yourself, Luca. Find someone else to play games with you because I'm fucking tired. This has gone on for too long. You destroy every good thing you touch. And I won't let you steal the good parts of me."

Gripping her shoulders, I lifted her off the bed. She trembled from my touch, terrified of me. Even I was afraid of the darkness inside me. It was always there, trying to claw its way out. Her lip quivered, and I realized I'd gone too far.

"Luca," Marcello warned. "Let her go! You're hurting her."

Marcello looked like he was ready to climb out of bed and rip open his stitches to get me away from her. So I released my hold, knowing I had to let her go. It was the right thing to do.

Alex dropped to the edge of the mattress, her breathing labored. "Get out, Luca. I can't stand to look at you right now. You make me fucking sick."

"No." I crossed my arms over my chest, glancing down at her. "We're talking about this. You can't push me away every time shit gets hard."

"There's nothing to talk about." She sighed. "I can't do this with you anymore. You make my head spin. Why can't you be normal? Why are you so hateful and angry all the time?"

I bent down in front of her, sinking to the floor on one knee. "Do you have any idea what I have done for you? What I've done to protect you for all these years?"

She rolled her eyes. "Do you want a medal?"

My right hand shook uncontrollably. Alex knew how to test my patience and drive me fucking crazy. We were a terrible combination, like gasoline and a box of matches. Marcello was better for her, but I couldn't let her go.

I closed my eyes and took a deep breath, blowing it out before I could look at her again. "I'll fight for you. Always. You're a part of me, Drea. Like I am a part of you. And I'm not letting you go."

Tears welled up in her bottom lids but did not spill. Instead, she was putting on a solid front to push me away. "Why are you like this, Luca? I'm so sick of the games, the lies, the bullshit. You put me through hell. Why can't you just let me be happy?"

"Because you're mine," I confessed. "I need you. We need each other."

Eyes downcast, she played with the seam of her shirt and groaned. "I need some time apart from you."

"How do you suggest we survive a marriage if you can't be around me?"

"We don't."

Her tone had a finality to it.

"You don't have a choice," I reminded her.

"You're the one who doesn't have a choice. I can walk away."

"No, you can't." I reached for her hand, and she pushed me away. "You're mine, baby girl. Forever and always. What binds us will destroy us."

Alex bit the inside of her cheek, looking over my shoulder at the patio. "Those words mean nothing to me."

My teeth hurt from clenching my jaw. And when our eyes met, she looked at me with pure hatred. Marcello and Bastian could give her everything she wanted without a shit ton of baggage attached. They could make her happy. Damian and I were the fucked up ones. We had too many demons to feed and enjoyed exploring the darkness inside our souls.

"I won't let you marry Marcello."

"This isn't about choosing between you and Marcello. Just give me some space to think." Her voice trembled as she spoke. "Please. When you're around, I feel like I can't breathe."

I narrowed my eyes at her. "And when you're with Marcello, how do you feel?"

I didn't want the truth. So why did I bother to ask?

Because you need the pain.

She glanced over at Marcello, and then her eyes landed on me. "Like I can be myself. He doesn't make me feel crazy. It's as easy as breathing when I'm with him."

"And how do you feel about me?"

I was such a masochist.

"Like you're holding my head underwater. I can't think straight when we're together."

I needed to get the fuck away from her before I snapped.

She grabbed my wrist and pulled my gaze back to her. "Let me finish."

"Go ahead. Tell me how much you hate me."

"When I'm with you, I feel out of control. Like I'm standing at the edge of a cliff with you, seconds from falling. You make my skin burn and my insides melt. It's intoxicating and suffocating. So when I say I can't breathe, it's because you are my air. My oxygen. Sometimes, I don't realize how lost I am until I see you. Look into your eyes. Feel your body against mine. And the world disappears because it's you and me and..." Tears streamed down her cheeks by the time she finished her spiel. "But I still need space, okay? Can you give me that?"

She loves me.

When Alex was younger, she wore her emotions on her sleeve. It was so obvious she wanted me. It was one of many reasons I pushed her away.

"I need you as much as you need me," Alex stated. "But I also need your brothers. Deal with it."

I couldn't even look at her. "Guess I don't have a choice."

"Not if you want to keep me in your life."

If I were a decent man, I would have professed my love, gotten down on one knee, and begged her to forgive me. But fuck that. I was not about to grovel at her feet, so I stormed out of the room.

Chapter Thirty-One

ALEX

L ong fingers slid down my arm, and I rolled onto my side, half asleep. I groaned, swatting a man's hand away. He lifted me from the bed despite my protests, enfolding me in his arms. He stroked his fingers through my hair, so loving and gentle.

My mind drifted between sleep and consciousness. Shoes slapped a hard surface. We moved down a set of stairs with my head rested on his chest.

"Where are you taking me?" I slurred.

I tried to open my eyes and peel my head from his chest. But my head buzzed from a migraine, my skull pounding so hard I couldn't see straight. Had someone drugged me? No matter how hard I tried, I couldn't find the strength to fight back.

We walked through a door and into the darkness of the late summer night with nothing more than the moonlight to guide us. A car door opened, and several sets of footsteps followed us. He set me on a leather bench inside an SUV and climbed in beside me. I could smell him, sense him, but I couldn't see my captor.

A few more people hopped into the car with us, and we

drove in complete silence. No music, nothing, only the sound
of the man beside me breathing. As the car rolled forward, he
placed his hand on my back, his fingers tracing slow circles,
which soothed me.

Five minutes passed before someone turned on the radio,
and a rock song I could not place floated through the
speakers.

"What the fuck is this shit?"

A man groaned from the front seat, then switched the song
to rap music. We rode down a hill, the steep decline causing
my heart to race. It felt like I was free-falling, about to roll off
the world's edge, and then muscular arms pulled me back.

We stopped, two men argued in another language, and
then doors opened. Someone grabbed me, rough fingers
poking my sides. The fog slowly cleared from my brain as we
exited the car.

"Wake up, Alex," a man boomed.

I opened my eyes, shocked to see a dark street lined with
shops. Attempting to regain my bearings, I blinked a few times
to adjust to my new surroundings.

"Run," he ordered. "We'll give you five minutes… and
then your pretty ass is ours."

I glanced to my left, then my right. No one was there.

What the fuck?

Am I losing it again?

My fight-or-flight mode kicked into high gear, adrenaline
coursing through my veins. Panicked, I bolted down the street,
desperate to find my way home. Several sets of footsteps
pounded the pavement behind me.

Breathing hard, they followed me into the heart of Beacon
Bay. They were so close I could smell the mixture of their
colognes. Bergamot, sandalwood, citrus, and a woodsy scent
filled the air.

My legs ached when I rounded the corner, flying past the
deserted storefronts. I raced down the sidewalk and blew past

the hair salon, an indie bookstore, and two boutiques. The River Styx was at the end of the block, with its red and black sign dangling from the metal hooks.

Like it was taunting me.

All the Devils are here.

I needed a break, a second to refill my lungs. The men were on my tail, seconds from catching up to me, their footsteps growing louder. A group of drunken men staggered down the street toward me, dressed in dark jeans and short-sleeved T-shirts. One guy smoked a cigarette, took a few drags, then passed it to his friend, who pounded a beer.

"Help me," I yelled. "Help!"

Their eyes flicked to me. Instead of rushing to my aid, they studied me with fascination. Evil smirks turned up the corners of their mouths, so terrifying but beautiful. I ran toward them, but I got a better look at their faces under the lamplight as I approached. Their skin looked like a fucking snake.

The Serpents.

The tallest of the group had golden scales. Another man had yellow scales with white chevrons. The dark-haired man at his side had greenish-yellow skin, and the last one, the black mamba, had dark brown scales.

I attempted to turn and run in the opposite direction, but the men who followed me to The River Styx were only a few feet away. Except, they weren't the men I thought were behind me. The Serpents were on my right, the Salvatore brothers on my left.

I closed my eyes and blinked a few times, but they were still there.

Four Serpents.

Four Salvatores.

Shifting my gaze between them, I sucked in deep breaths to calm down. With each shallow breath I took, my lungs worked too hard, the air draining from them. Five, four, three, two, one... I chanted the words in my head, telling myself it would be over soon.

"This is all your fault," Luca snapped. "You need to face it, Drea. Until you do, you're stuck here with us."

"No," I muttered. "I want to go back."

He shook his head, giving me a sexy grin as he slid his thumb across his bottom lip. "No one is coming to save you, baby girl."

Luca's devilish grin twisted into a pained look that broke my heart. He staggered toward me and pushed up his shirt, revealing his chiseled abdomen. A knife slipped from his grasp and bounced a few times before it landed in front of me.

"Pick it up," Luca ordered.

I noticed the S looked like a snake wrapping around the silver handle as I bent down. The Salvatore crest. Luca carried the knife with him at all times. It was a gift from his grandfather, the last thing he'd given Luca before he passed away.

Hunched down in front of the knife, I glanced up at him. "Why?"

"You know why."

I felt the knife's weight in my hand and turned it over to study the snake handle.

"Look at me," Luca said through clenched teeth. "Look at what you did."

I glanced up at the knife wound over his heart. It stood out against the rest of his scars, fresh blood glistening his skin crimson.

"No," I cried out. "No, I couldn't. I would never hurt you."

His jaw ticked. "But you did."

"You're not real," I whispered.

"I'm real, baby," he growled, hunching down in front of me, sliding his warm fingers beneath my chin. "Do it already. Plunge the knife through my heart."

A sob escaped my throat. "No."

Blood rushed through my veins, going straight to my head. I drew a breath from between my teeth, attempting to still my racing heart. "Are you going to kill me?"

Luca laughed. "No, baby girl. You're the one who's killing me."

My legs wobbled, unable to hold my weight anymore, and I fell sideways onto the pavement. Someone grabbed my elbow, lifted me from the ground, and hooked their arm around me. Luca muttered something, but I couldn't hear him with the ringing in my ears. My pulse pounded with the same ferocity as the beating at the base of my skull.

"I got you," Marcello whispered in my ear.

My eyes shot open, my heart thumping in my chest from the worst nightmare of my life. It was a combination of that awful night with The Serpents five years ago and something much worse. Was I killing Luca by spending so much time with Marcello?

Not like he ever seemed to give a damn about me before. Until recently, we barely even spoke. A surge of emotions ripped into my chest as I stared up at the ceiling of the dark room.

Pressing my palm to the mattress, I pushed myself up and slid off the bed. I clutched my chest, trying to still my rapid heartbeat. It hurt to breathe, the ache so intense it felt like I'd stabbed myself with the knife.

In and out.

Breathe.

Five, four, three, two, one...

My head pounded as if there were a drum beating inside it, working in unison with my heart. The dream felt so real. Too real for my liking. Tears streamed down my face.

It hurt so fucking much that I wanted to carve out the pain with a knife to make it stop. I rushed out of my bedroom, surprised the hallway was empty. Someone was always on duty, even when I slept. Luca made sure his men watched me at all times.

Was he letting me go?

Testing me?

I bolted down the hallway and headed toward the stairwell at the back of the house. There were staircases everywhere in the mansion. It was easy to get lost in this prison on the bay. Taking my time, I used the railing for support and tip-toed down the stairs.

When my bare feet hit the ground floor, a chill rolled down my arms. I should have worn shoes.

Oh, well.

It was too late.

I walked into the Butler's kitchen in the dark and grabbed a water bottle from the refrigerator. A sliver of moonlight shone through the windows. Following the light across the room, I walked toward the main hallway, sipping from the bottle.

I turned left out of the kitchen.

Navigating the house in the daytime was hard enough. They had more rooms than a medieval castle, a never-ending set of doors and mysteries to uncover.

I passed the sitting room, where loud rap music blared from speakers.

I stopped mid-stride and held my breath. Someone was in the room, but I couldn't see shit, and as I turned to walk away, strong arms wrapped around me from behind. Before I could scream, someone put their hand over my mouth and dragged me into the darkness.

Chapter Thirty-Two

LUCA

A lex tried to scream, but no one could hear her over the loud music. With my arm wrapped around her middle, I dragged her to the couch at the center of the room. She wiggled around in my arms, attempting to break free.

Good luck with that, baby girl.

Alex attempted to kick and slap me, though it was no use. I lowered her onto the couch, pinning her to the cushion. The music cranked through the speakers, the beat drowning out her cries.

I used this room for parties. It was ten times the size of an average living room and had enough furniture to accommodate everyone in Devil's Creek. "Venom" by Eminem blared through the speakers in the room's corners. Alex whimpered, and I laughed at her attempts to fight me.

Something fucking snapped inside me after Marcello's shooting. Like I hit the reset button. I didn't hate her anymore, but I was so fucking angry over her love for my brother. She didn't have to say the words aloud. We all knew she was in love with Marcello.

Barefoot and dressed in skimpy pajamas, Alex squirmed beneath me as I caged her against the cushion, my hand still over her mouth. I was over a foot taller than her and had at least sixty more pounds of muscle. She could fight me all she wanted. I was hoping she would because it turned me on. My cock was like a steel rod from all of her whimpering.

"If I release my hand, are you going to scream?"

Alex shook her head, her tears wetting my skin. I dropped my hand, and she released a sob.

"What is wrong with you, Luca?" Alex's chest rose and fell against mine. "Turn on the lights."

"No."

She let out a whine, her fear of the dark taking over.

"I got you, baby." I swiped my finger beneath her eyes, capturing her tears. "Don't cry."

"How could you do that to me?"

I slid off her, resting my arm on the back of the couch. "Quiet, woman. We have to conquer your fears together."

Alex sat up and felt around in the dark, too scared to make a run for it. Her fingers brushed my thigh, then moved to the couch. "I came downstairs to get a drink. Why were none of the guards on my floor?"

"None of them?"

"No," she whispered. "Not a single guard."

I removed my cell phone from my pocket and opened the security app.

"Is something wrong?"

"No," I lied.

Of course, there was something fucking wrong. We had two men posted at each end of her hallway, but none were at their posts. I flipped to the camera in Marcello's temporary bedroom across the hall. Benji sat on the edge of the bed and talked to my brother while cleaning his gun.

I wanted to wring both of their fucking necks for their carelessness. It would only take one wrong move, and we would lose Alex. How could they be so stupid?

"What's going on, Luca?" Alex clutched my wrist. "I don't need to see your face to know you're angry."

I stroked her bare arm with my fingers to put her at ease. "Nothing you need to be concerned about, Drea."

She climbed onto my lap and kissed my neck. The heat from her breath warmed my skin, sending a wave of electricity throughout my body. With Alex, there was always palpable energy. It gave me a high unlike any other.

Until Alex, I'd never felt a connection with a woman and had never even kissed one.

Same for Damian.

Neither of us liked intimacy.

It made my skin crawl, my stomach turn. Alex was the exception to every rule.

She stuck out her tongue and licked my lip. "I'm sorry for ignoring you for the past few weeks. I shouldn't have shut you out, Luca. Marcello is your brother. I should have been comforting you, not the other way around."

She deserved a good spanking—a punishment for being a brat.

"You ignored all of us," I reminded her. "Not just me. Bash and Damian miss you, too, baby."

"I know," she sighed. "I'm sorry. I couldn't handle the thought of losing Marcello. It's all of us or none of us. That's how our relationship works."

"You made that crystal clear."

She brushed her lips against mine and rocked her hips. I opened my mouth and her tongue tangled with mine as I fisted her curls. She tasted like mint toothpaste and smelled like vanilla body wash. And I needed her so fucking bad.

As I slipped my hand into her pajama shorts, she moaned. Her nipples poked through her thin tank top, the tiny buds scratching my chest as I pushed two fingers inside her.

She kissed me harder, moaning into my mouth. "Luca."

Hearing my name awoke the demons inside me. This girl

drove me insane. She turned me into an animal with each scream that slipped from her lips.

I wrapped my fingers around her throat and squeezed hard enough to make her gasp. She loved when I choked her right before she was about to come. Alex craved our rough sex, and she was my greatest addiction.

I nibbled on her earlobe, thrusting my fingers so hard she screamed. "You like this, baby girl?"

"Yes… Don't stop, Luca. I'm going to…"

After she came on my fingers, I shoved her shorts down her thighs. She kicked them onto the floor, and I spread her thighs with my hands.

Fuck, I loved her body.

She wasn't the same bony girl I'd met in high school. Time and space from her parents had helped her heal, and she put some meat on her bones and filled out this beautiful body with delicious curves.

"Take off your shirt," I ordered.

Alex pulled the shirt over her head and flung it onto the floor. Gripping her hip, I moved her on top of me and leaned my head back against the cushion. Her hands shook as she slid my dress shirt over my shoulders. I flicked the button on my pants, and she rolled down the zipper, adjusting her position on my lap to pull them down.

"I missed you," I whispered between kisses and meant it.

My crazy girl made me feel when I was numb. No matter how much I denied my feelings for her, I would always need Alex. She was the angel on my shoulder when the Devil made me sin. And with my girl, I wanted to do a lot of sinning.

Squeezing her ass cheeks, I lifted her just enough to lower her onto my cock. Alex cried out from the sudden pinch. She was so tight as I pushed through her inner walls. So wet and soft I could have died with her in my arms, riding my cock.

"I missed you, too," she breathed against my neck.

"You're always so wet for me, baby girl."

"Yeah," she moaned, then ran her tongue along my neck. "You like that?"

I thrust into her, my fingers digging into her sweet ass. "You know I do. Fuck, baby. You feel so good."

She kissed my neck a few more times, then tilted her head back. Even though we couldn't see each other in the dark, I knew she was looking at me. Searching for me. No matter what, we would always find each other. Fate had brought us together, and only fate could tear us apart.

I leaned forward to suck her nipple into my mouth. Her hand fell to my head, tugging at my short hair. Even over the music, I could hear her moans. She drove me wild, and I pounded into her harder and faster, damn near losing my fucking mind.

"Luca," she whimpered. "Oh, fuck." She tightened her grip on my hair. "Harder. Yes, yes…"

"Fuck, baby girl." I moved my free hand to her throat and pressed my thumb over her windpipe, giving her what she needed. "Keep squeezing my cock. Just like that."

She clutched my wrist, which only tightened my grip on her throat. Rough and relentless, I fucked her hard enough to leave an imprint of my cock. Burn my fingerprints on her skin, mark her for everyone to see.

Her entire body trembled, her skin hot and slick against mine. I tugged her bottom lip with my teeth, stealing another moan from her pretty lips.

"That's it, baby. Let go. Come for me."

My name fell from her mouth, and I loved when she said my name. I loved how she said it with a sweet cadence that sounded like a song lyric slipping from her beautiful lips. Then, as if possessed by the sound of my name, I fucked her even harder. I couldn't get enough of her pussy.

She was my drug, my addiction, and whenever I was with her, I wanted to be high.

My beautiful mess strangled my cock with her pussy,

coming so hard I couldn't hold back. I pumped into her a few more times and kissed her lips before spilling my cum inside her. Then, sweaty and out of breath, she put her hands on my shoulders and dragged her fingers down my chest.

I released my hold on her throat. "You're such a good girl."

Her lips brushed mine in the dark. "I like dreams like this one."

What the fuck?

My heart sank to my stomach, her words gutting me. "This isn't a dream, Drea." My hands glided down her arms, and she shivered from my touch. "Do you feel this?"

She sighed. "Yes."

Still inside her and semi-hard, I arched my back and thrust my hips. "You feel this, right?"

"Yes," she whispered. "You feel so good, Luca."

"Fucking hell, woman." I pulled her lips to mine. "You don't know what you do to me, baby girl."

She yawned after our lips separated, her hot breath fanning across my face.

"Tired, baby?"

Alex nodded against my forehead.

"Okay, pretty girl." I kissed her sexy lips. "Let's get you back to bed."

I set her onto the cushion beside me and pulled up my boxers and pants. She sat there, naked and still panting, like she couldn't control her racing heart. It didn't sound like she was panicking, but it was hard to tell without light.

"Just breathe, baby." I bent forward to grab her pajamas from the floor. "You're okay. Lift your arms for me."

I dressed Alex and then scooped her into my arms and walked out of the sitting room. The music floated down the hallway, following us to the foyer. She rested her head on my chest with her fingers splayed over my heart. I wondered if she could feel what she did to me as I climbed the stairs. My heart never beat this way for anyone else.

By the time I reached her bedroom, she was snoring softly. I kissed her forehead and lowered her to the mattress. She looked so delicate and breakable, so damn beautiful my chest hurt.

But had she changed her mind?

Only time would tell.

Chapter Thirty-Three

ALEX

A wave of nausea smacked me in the face. I clutched the side of Marcello's bed to steady myself, my stomach churning as the taste of bile crept up the back of my throat.

"Are you okay?" Marcello sat up and reached out for me. "Alex, what's wrong?"

I pushed out my hand and shook my head. "No, don't get up. I don't want you to hurt yourself. I'm not feeling good. My stomach has been bothering me for the past few days."

Marcello pushed the covers off his thighs and sat up, groaning as he leaned forward. "What have you been eating?"

"My usual."

I covered my mouth with my hand and ran toward the bathroom. I dropped to my knees in front of the toilet and hurled my dinner into the bowl.

Marcello stood behind me and gathered my hair in his hands. He made slow circular motions on my back with his palm. "It's okay, princess."

It was in his nature to baby me. Marcello enjoyed taking care of me, and he was good at it.

Since the shooting, I had spent most of my time in Marcello's bedroom. Bastian and Damian had been keeping their distance from me. They were busy running Atlantic Airlines and gave me space to take care of Marcello. And, of course, Luca disappeared after the night we had sex in the dark.

It was my fault.

I pushed them away.

After I brushed my teeth, I got back into bed with Marcello. I curled up beside him and laid my head on his chest. "I'm in the mood to read."

He reached for his cell phone on the nightstand. "I can send someone to the library. What do you want to read?"

I rolled my shoulders. "I don't know. What's your favorite book?"

"The Iliad."

"What do you like about it?"

"The themes." Marcello turned his intense gaze on me, searing my skin with one look. "Homer's story focuses on the glory of war, fate, mortality, honor, duty, friendship... and love." His blue eyes held mine as he said the last part. "I can relate to it."

I sighed as thoughts of Luca drifted into my mind. "Me, too. I feel like I've been fighting a war with Luca for years. I'm afraid it will never end."

"It will," he promised. "Luca needs some assurance that you're his."

"But I'm not. I'm yours, too. All four of you."

He licked his lips as he glanced at my mouth. "Until you give in to him, he will continue to act out. When my brother sets his sights on something, he always gets it. You are the biggest challenge he's ever faced. He doesn't realize he needs to come to terms with his feelings if he wants to keep you."

"How do you understand this, and he doesn't?"

Marcello smirked. "My brother is a genius, but he's too fucking stubborn to see what's right in front of his face."

"What's that?"

"You love him," he said with sadness in his tone. "And you would marry him if he'd return your feelings."

Did I love Luca?

Maybe.

I covered my face with my hand and groaned. "I don't know what I want anymore or how I feel about him."

"I'm not normally home this much." He brushed his fingers down my arm, creating tiny bumps on my skin. "You will need to rely on Luca more in the future."

My heart dropped into my stomach.

"What are you saying?"

"I lead a team of mercenaries. They hire us when corrupt men need an army with no affiliation or interest in their conflict. My job takes me around the world. Sometimes, it's for months at a time."

For some sick and twisted reason, it turned me on knowing Marcello was the leader of a badass army.

"Do you steal?"

He gave me a nonchalant shrug. "Whatever the job requires."

"So you're like the anti-Robin Hood." I chuckled. "You steal from the rich and give to the rich?"

A ghost of a smile touched his lips. "Yeah, I guess that's one way of looking at it. But no, it's not that simple."

"What attracted you to that kind of work?"

"Luca's book smart. His mind works in ways mine never will, and my father knew that. So my dad said I had to find my place in the family."

"Yeah, he's an evil genius."

Luca got into Harvard University using none of his family's connections. He was also the valedictorian of his graduating class for his undergrad and MBA degrees.

Marcello bobbed his head in agreement. "I hated school. It was boring and didn't seem to have a point. I wanted to attend York Military Academy, but my dad wouldn't allow it.

So I begged him to let me train with some of his men at Salvatore Global when I was a sophomore in high school. It was basically like ROTC, but more intense."

"If you could do anything, what would it be?"

"People like us don't have choices," he pointed out.

"My parents didn't want me to paint. My mother did everything to destroy my art, and look at how far I've come with my career."

"You don't know my dad." He tucked a few curls behind my ear and frowned. "None of us had a choice."

"Luca doesn't seem to hate it."

He shook his head. "No, Luca is where he wants to be. He's my father's twin. Two megalomaniacs plotting world domination."

"Yeah, I can see that." I readjusted my position so I wasn't putting so much weight on his chest. "When your dad moves, Luca moves with him. I'm surprised they're so close after seeing Luca's back and chest."

He pursed his lips and stared up at the ceiling. "Luca took the brunt of the punishments."

"You're loyal to Luca, even when you shouldn't be. Do you feel you owe him for helping you?"

"Yeah, I guess." His eyes met mine once more. "We were never close as kids, but after my mom died, he would throw himself in front of me and take my dad's punishments. I think he liked it."

"Your brother is a monster."

"No, he's not," he said with a bite to his tone. "Luca cares about you, Alex. I know he has a funny way of showing it, but Luca needs you."

"If that were true, he would have treated me better. He doesn't love me. Most of the time, he hates me."

"He doesn't hate you, not even close. My brother can't process emotions." He raised his arm a few inches and winced, looking away from me, so I couldn't see he was in pain. "When Luca was younger, my parents took him to different doctors. They thought he had alexithymia, but none of the doctors could pinpoint his diagnosis."

"What is alexithymia?"

"It's a disorder that prevents a person from expressing and feeling emotions. They're angry, confused, and disconnected from people, not affectionate. Have a lack of empathy. But Luca doesn't have any underlying medical conditions associated with alexithymia. So the doctors refused to label him. My parents forced Luca to talk to psychologists and psychiatrists. The doctors thought he was making progress, but he's so fucking smart he figured out how to manipulate them. They all fed right into the palm of his hand."

My eyebrows rose at his confession. "Even as a child?"

He nodded. "You don't know how manipulative Luca can be."

"Yes, I do." I snorted with laughter. "Sociopaths don't have feelings."

He tapped his fingers against mine with a stern expression on his face. "You're trying to rationalize your feelings for Luca by adding a title to his bad traits. Unfortunately, it's not that simple with my brother."

"I want to understand why he's like this. You're nothing like him, even though you had the same parents."

"We had different roles to fill within the family. Luca will unravel if he loses you. He's been slowly falling apart since the meeting with your grandfather." Marcello squeezed my hand. "I won't make excuses for Luca, but I will say this. Talk to him. Tell him what you want. And if he tells you no, then you have your answer."

I stared into his eyes for a moment and had the itch to draw him. "I love you, Marcello."

He reached over to grab the back of my head and kissed me. "I've been in love with you for years, princess."

We kissed until it was time for Marcello to take another

dose of pain medication. He didn't need to be on bed rest anymore, but I could tell he still needed the meds.

I loved him.

He loved me.

As we dozed off in each other's arms, I let his words roll around in my head. I was so happy I passed out with a smile on my face.

.

Chapter Thirty-Four

MARCELLO

Alex laid on the bed beside me, tracing her nails up and down my arm. The soft, soothing motion signaled my cock that it was time to wake up. I fixed myself beneath the blanket.

She leaned over me, her sweet scent invading my nostrils. I closed my eyes as my skin pebbled with goosebumps from her delicate touch. Her skin was soft and warm, and she smelled good enough to eat.

As she stared into my eyes, her nails raked down my arm. She woke up at night screaming for her twin brother. It was Aiden or me she called out for in her sleep. I would never forget the promise I made to her brother before he left for his initiation into The Devil's Knights.

Three days after we forced Alex to come back with us to Devil's Creek, I picked Aiden up from the house we rented for him in The Hills. This way, he was still close to Alex without being too close. That was one rule of initiation—no contact with anyone outside the organization for six months.

Aiden had asked for my help to approach The Serpents. My cousins were artists who used their talents for deviant purposes. They knew how to forge everything from bank checks to notable artworks worth millions of dollars. Their unique skills often came in handy with some of our underworld clientele. Because of Aiden's skills, Luca agreed to let him work with The Serpents after completing initiation. He was more suited for their line of work than ours, anyway.

I'd been friends with Aiden since high school. We maintained the illusion we hated each other in front of Alex and my brothers. It was better if they didn't know we spray painted together. Despite how Luca felt about Aiden, he wasn't bad company. I thought one of us should give him a chance since he would eventually be family.

Aiden slid into the passenger seat of my Maserati with his eyes focused on me. "Thanks for doing this. I didn't know who to ask."

I glanced in the rearview mirror and reversed out of the driveway. "No one can know we talk."

"Yeah, yeah," Aiden shot back. "I know. What's with all the secrecy, anyway?"

Luca had plans that involved Aiden, and I wasn't about to reveal them to him. However, Carl Wellington had clarified that Aiden would choose the correct path, regardless of how we had to get him there. If Aiden didn't become a Knight, he could never ascend to The Founders Society. And since he had no interest in joining either of those societies, we had to force his hand.

"Luca doesn't want Alex to know," I said as I flew down the hill that led to Beacon Bay. "Trust me. It's better if she's not involved. There's too much at stake."

Aiden rested his elbow on the armrest and glanced over at me. He looked like fucking hell, his eyes red-rimmed and bloodshot.

"When was the last time you slept?"

"Two days ago," he admitted with a sigh.

"You need to get your shit together. Seeing you like this makes Alex upset. When you come back from initiation, I expect you to be clean and off the drugs."

He ran a hand through his messy curls that were longer than usual and nodded. "You care about my sister, right?"

I clutched the steering wheel and floored the gas down the steep hill as we left Devil's Creek. "She's going to be my queen."

"C'mon, Marcello." He tapped my arm with his fist. "I know you have a thing for Alex. I'm not blind or stupid."

"I don't expect you to understand what our queen means to us."

I'd wanted Alex from the moment I saw her. She was a knockout. What man wouldn't want her? But I knew beforehand that she would marry Luca. No matter how much I liked her, she would never be mine.

So I watched her from a distance. I observed every move she made to ensure her safety. Though, I often checked on her just because I wanted to see her. I needed to know she was happy.

"My sister's involvement with The Devil's Knights is another thing I wanted to talk to you about," he said with a groan. "Alex deserves better than this shit. The whole concept is fucking ridiculous. Why do you need a queen?"

"Your grandfather is the reason we even have a queen. This was his doing."

"I don't care what Pops wants me to do. I will never submit to Luca," he fired back. "I have tried so hard to keep Alex away from him, and no matter what I do, I can't stop her from running back to him. I don't want her to become your queen."

Aiden was aware of what would happen at Legare. The thought sickened him. When we were drinking at The River Styx, he'd expressed his disgust. If he had his way, Alex would have been painting and selling her art halfway around the world. He never wanted this life for his sister, and I couldn't blame him.

"Promise me one thing, Marcello."

I turned onto Beacon Parkway and looked over at him.

"If anything happens to me, promise you'll keep Alex safe. That you won't let her fall apart without me."

"I won't let anything happen to our queen," I assured him.

"I'm not worried about you protecting her from your enemies. But, if this job goes south, Alex will go off the deep end. Her condition is fragile."

"I don't know what you want me to do, Aiden. I'm not a doctor. I don't know how to handle someone with her medical condition."

"Luca doesn't know what she needs," he said with desperation. "He makes Alex the worst version of herself. She could get better if she were with someone else."

I lifted an eyebrow at him. "You think I can do a better job?"

"I know you can."

"Nothing will happen to you," I said to dismiss his fears.

He shook his head, and untamed blond curls fell in front of his clear blue eyes. "What I'm doing for the Knights is dangerous." Aiden sat back against the leather seat. "There's a chance I won't come back from initiation. So I need you to promise you'll help her. She likes you, Marcello. I know she does. And if anyone can bring her back from the dead, it's you."

"I promise," I said and meant it.

As Alex continued running her fingers down my arm, she snapped me out of my memory of the past. I made a promise to her brother, one I intended to keep.

But I also made a promise to Luca.

Marriage was nothing more than a piece of paper, a legal transaction. In the end, she would still be a Salvatore.

I knew what I had to do.

Alex looked into my eyes as if she were searching my soul. "What are you thinking about, Marcello?"

I held her gaze. "You."

Always you.

Chapter Thirty-Five

BASTIAN

I found Alex in Marcello's bed, sound asleep, with her arm across his chest. She was still babying Marcello. Whenever she passed out, Marcello left her with a guard so he could feel normal again.

"She keeps you on lockdown," I joked as I sat in the armchair beside the bed. "When will you tell her you're fine and don't need coddling?"

He ran a hand through his hair and sighed. "I've tried telling Alex a dozen times. She thinks I'm going to die if I leave this room." His fingers glided up and down her arm as he stared down at her. "It makes her happy. And I'm not yet cleared for field work, anyway."

"Wellington said you can go back to work."

"Light work," he corrected. "Basic training and surveillance. None of the shit I want to do."

"You can't leave for any missions with the criminal underworld looking for Alex. The bounty is up to five million dollars now. Desperate people will do desperate things."

"Yeah." He bit the inside of his cheek and looked out the wide-open patio doors. A breeze blew through the room, and along with it, the scent of the bay. "Has Luca heard from Dante? Any new leads from the Five Families?"

I shook my head. "The Russians went underground after we sent back the heads of their higher-ups."

"I can't believe Luca made special boxes to deliver their heads." He laughed. "What an asshole."

"What a waste of money," I shot back. "He spared no expense. Made a real fucking show of it."

I had billions of dollars at my disposal, but I didn't waste money if I couldn't write it off.

Marcello rolled onto his side and lowered his voice. "What are we doing for Luca's birthday?"

She'd been sleeping a lot over the past few weeks—even more than Marcello, who was on pain meds half the time.

"You know Luca. His usual antics." I rose from the chair and smirked. "He's got some game planned for his birthday."

His eyes narrowed at me. "What kind of game?"

I shrugged. "Beats me. He's calling it Capture the Queen. Even sent out invites to the Knights. So I assume it has something to do with Alex."

He nodded. "That would be my guess."

"Luca likes to go big for his birthday."

It was the one day each year he allowed himself a day off from work to drink, get high, and do whatever the fuck he wanted.

One day to lose control.

I walked over to Alex's side of the bed and lifted her in my arms. She stirred when I brushed the hair off her face and kissed her cheek. Our girl was so damn beautiful.

I wouldn't usually wake her this late at night, but I had a surprise. We had spent little time together since the shooting. It hurt like hell to feel like I was losing my grip on her, but I also understood why she'd put an ocean between us. I knew firsthand what it was like to lose someone I loved. Alex was afraid Marcello's heart would stop beating if she left his side.

"I'll bring her back in the morning," I told Marcello and then left his bedroom.

As I walked to my bedroom, she turned on her side and peeked up at me with one eye open. "Bash?" She rubbed the sleep from her eyes. "Where are you taking me?"

"To my bedroom. I want to show you something."

"Where's Marcello?" Her chest rose and fell in panic. "Is he okay?"

"Yeah, baby. He's fine. Sleeping in his bed."

"But..." She squirmed in my arms as we entered my room. "Why are you taking me away from him?"

Her words sliced into my chest.

I sat on the piano bench and put her on my lap. "You're mine, too. But you seem to have forgotten that."

She blinked a few times, still a little sleepy. "I'm sorry, Bash." Her lips brushed mine. "I didn't mean to push you away."

"You've been ignoring all of us because you're mad at Luca."

"No, it wasn't like that. I never meant to make any of you feel that way, not even Luca." She clutched my wrist, her eyes glassy like she was on the verge of crying. "I'm not mad at him. I only asked for some space because he wouldn't stop hovering over me."

I caressed the back of her neck with my fingers. "It's okay, Cherry. I forgive you. But you should kiss and make up with Luca before his birthday."

"I completely forgot." She shook her head, lips pursed. "You're right. I've been so focused on Marcello. I've been neglecting all of you."

"It's okay, baby. You can make it up to Luca on his birthday. He's throwing a big party at the house."

"Another party?" Surprise scrolled across her beautiful face. "Is that smart after those men shot up the house?"

"No need to worry." I turned her to face the piano and

laid her fingers on the keys. "We got it under control. Only about a dozen or two of the Knights will join us for the party. And they won't be leaving the house until the morning."

Sparks of electricity spread up my arms as I moved her fingers across the keys, playing the song I wrote for her. She smiled and even giggled as our fingers moved in unison. The soft, haunting sound floated through the air, and I wondered if Damian was listening from his room. I kept the door open for him when I played because it helped him sleep.

"I can't believe I'm playing the piano," Alex whispered, then she glanced over her shoulder at me. "No matter how many times we do this, it still feels like the first time."

"You're a natural, baby."

I winked, and she laughed.

"Have you named the song yet?"

I stopped playing for a moment and brushed her curls off her shoulder so I could kiss her shoulder. Sliding the thin strap of her top aside, I continued my slow trail of kisses down her arm. She shivered as I made my way up her neck.

I peppered her jaw with soft kisses, sliding my hand beneath her chin to turn her gaze back to me. "For years, you have consumed me. Haunted me." I sucked her earlobe into my mouth. "Bewitched me."

She relaxed into my arms and angled her body to kiss my lips. "Bash, I missed you."

I kissed her back. "I missed you, too, Cherry."

Alex draped her arm across my neck and smiled so wide it reached her clear blue eyes. "The suspense is killing me. What did you name my song?"

"*Ciliegia dolce*," I whispered against the shell of her ear.

"Is that Italian?"

I nodded. "It means sweet cherry."

Her cheeks flushed crimson. "It's perfect."

Then her mouth descended upon mine, parting my lips with

her tongue. She stroked the nape of my neck, slowly sweeping her tongue into my mouth. It wasn't like our usual kisses that were rushed and heated. Instead, this one was slow and sensual.

I wasn't like Luca or Damian. I could be whatever she needed. It didn't matter to me as long as she was mine.

We kissed until I had chapped lips, my cock harder than steel. I gripped Alex's hips and lifted her on the piano, moving between her thighs. I wouldn't disgrace a million-dollar Steinway & Sons piano if she were anyone else. But there was nothing I wanted more than to see my girl writhing beneath me while I fucked her on it.

I draped her leg over my shoulder and kissed her inner thigh. She whimpered the closer I got to her core, and I could smell her desire. Our girl was always wet for us. She was down to play from the first time I touched her, even when she pretended not to want us.

I stripped off her shorts and panties and threw them behind me before I leaned forward and rolled my tongue over her clit.

"Bash," she whimpered, tugging at the ends of my hair. "Oh, my God." Her legs trembled with each flick of my tongue. "Yes, yes, don't stop..." Her words died off at the tip of her tongue, and I could tell she was already on the verge of an orgasm.

I drove into her with my tongue, and when she was about to come, I slid two fingers inside her. Her eyes slammed shut, and she squeezed my fingers, coming so hard she screamed my name as if it were a melody.

She covered her heart with her hand, her chest rising fall with each breath. "Holy shit, Bash. Did I tell you how much I missed you?"

I wiped her juices from my lips with the back of my hand and smirked. "Once or twice."

I unbuttoned my shirt and quickly ditched all of my

clothes. Alex's eyes flicked up and down my body, and she licked her lips when she looked at my cock.

"I know you missed him," I said with laughter in my tone, jerking my shaft. "Didn't you, Cherry?"

"I missed every part of you." Then, licking her lips, she touched me, her soft skin so smooth against mine. "I need to feel you, Bash. Fuck me. Make me come with that big cock."

"Now, when you put it that way." I turned her to the side, away from the keys, so her legs dangled off the piano. I inched inside her, giving her time to adjust to my size. "Damn, baby." Even after taking four big dicks, she was still so tight. I trailed my fingers up and down her right thigh and pushed the rest of the way into her. "My sweet cherry."

She smiled at that, rocking her hips to meet mine. "Oh, my God."

"God can't help you now." I squeezed her ass cheeks, lifting her just enough to change the angle so I could drive into her hard. "Say my name, baby."

"Bash," she cried out, wrapping her arms around my neck, her heel digging into my ass. "Harder."

I gave her exactly what she wanted, fucking her so hard the piano shook. Her big tits bounced in my face, so I took one of her pretty pink nipples into my mouth and bit down. She moved her hand to my head, encouraging me to keep marking her.

Taking turns with her nipples, I drove into her like a feral animal. Hard, fast, and completely out of control. When I was with her, I lost myself. I wanted to bury my cock so deep my brothers could feel me the next time they fucked her.

We fucked until our cum dripped onto the piano. I didn't even care, not one fucking bit. Because the sight of Alex's naked, beautiful body, glistening with sweat and cum, was enough for me to overlook that minor detail.

She massaged her nipples, which had dark marks all over them. "I'm so sore."

"I wish I could say I'm sorry." I knocked her hands out of the way and rubbed my fingers over the swollen buds. "But I love laying my claim to your body." As I touched her, I noticed the slight weight difference in her breasts. "Did your tits get bigger since the last time we fucked?"

She nodded. "They've been sore lately, too."

I bounced them in my hands, noticing the significant growth in such a short time. She'd been sleeping a lot lately. And Marcello said she's been getting sick for the past week.

"You feeling okay now?"

She released a deep breath. "At the moment."

I flattened my hand over her forehead. "You're warmer than usual. Have you taken your temperature?"

"Marcello did before bed." She shoved my hand away. "I'm fine, Bash. Stop worrying about me."

I didn't want to say what I was thinking aloud. But I wondered if Marcello had come to the same conclusion if he was taking her temperature and concerned by her stomach issues. She ate the same food as us. So it wasn't food poisoning or a stomach virus.

"It's our job to worry about you." I clutched her chin and brought her eyes back to mine. "Let us take care of you, my sweet cherry."

"Can you fix me a bath?"

I lifted her off the piano and carried her into the bathroom. She sat on the edge of the garden tub while I filled it with her bath beads and tested the water for the correct temperature. As the tub filled, I got on my knees and rested my hands on her thighs. A grin tugged at her mouth, and then her fingers were in my hair, shoving it off my forehead.

I leaned forward and kissed her stomach. She didn't know what I was thinking, why I was doing this. Every part of me hoped she was sick for a reason. And not because Luca and Marcello needed an heir with a Wellington to maintain their standing with The Founders Society. That would only be a bonus.

I couldn't wait to see our girl with each of our babies in her belly. Marcello wanted the first child. We had all promised him that, yet none of us bothered to pull out. Not like I could have, even if I tried.

I wrapped my arms around her and kissed her lips. With all the drama surrounding us, I was afraid to bring a child into this world. But it also excited me.

"I hope you know I love you." Another peck on her lips. "I love you so fucking much it killed me not to have you in my bed, in my arms, beneath me, on top of me."

She kissed me back. "I love you, too, Bash."

I helped her into the tub and got in behind her. She slid backward into my chest, and I rested my hands on her thighs.

"Just so we're clear." I tucked her hair behind her ears. "You're sleeping with me tonight."

Alex rolled her head to the side and looked up at me. "There's no place I would rather be."

Chapter Thirty-Six

ALEX

A s I fixed my hair and makeup in the mirror, Luca lingered in the doorway to the bathroom. My sexy devil leaned against the doorframe, dressed in his usual black three-piece suit. He wore a white oxford beneath the jacket, paired with a blood-red silk tie and black wingtips.

My red toga-style gown matched Luca's tie and dipped low enough to leave little to the imagination. The fabric swayed around my ankles and had a black rope belt that hugged my waist.

"You look beautiful," Luca said in that deep, sexy voice that rolled down my arms. "Like a Roman goddess."

I dropped the pink lip gloss onto the vanity and smiled at him in the mirror. "Thank you."

"Our guests are arriving." He moved behind me and kissed my shoulder. "Join us downstairs when you're ready."

The halls were empty, save for the guards posted at various positions on the ground floor. An eerie silence hung in the air. Even the lights were dimmer than usual.

Decorated like a palace, the Salvatore Estate had million-dollar paintings hung on the walls and rare collectibles, most of which they had taken by force. When I reached the sitting room, I stopped in the entryway, taking in the scenery.

Damian and Bastian sat on a couch beside Drake. Sonny noticed me first. His adorable green eyes met mine, a smile on his lips. I knew a monster lurked behind his sexy smirks, but at least he tried to hide it.

Sonny brought his fingers to his mouth and whistled. "Well, look at you, gorgeous as ever." His gaze landed on my breasts and stayed there for a moment.

I smiled, even blushed a little. "Thanks."

"I see Luca let you out of your ivory tower," he joked with laughter in his tone. "You ready for a wild night, Little Wellington?"

"How wild are were talking?"

He winked. "Like nothing you've seen before."

I bit my lip as my eyes darted around the room. There were at least two dozen men dressed in suits. Handsome and wealthy, they were the sons of powerful men—members of The Devil's Knights.

I was the only woman.

A sudden rush of fear raced down my spine as they all stopped what they were doing to stare at me. Luca lounged in an oversized leather chair by the fireplace. Cigar hanging out of his gorgeous mouth, he draped his long leg over the arm. He propped his other foot up on the ottoman, looking like a god.

Luca examined my body as I stopped in front of him. Then, he curved his arm around my thighs and pulled me onto his lap.

"Happy birthday, Luca." I brushed my lips against his. "I didn't have time to get you a present."

His forehead pressed against mine. "What I want, you can't buy."

"What do you want?"

Luca sucked my bottom lip into his mouth. "You."

"You have me."

His hands slid over my ass, claiming me with the same hunger I craved. The animal was ready to play.

He kissed my lips. "Lose yourself with us tonight. Let us take care of you. I think you'll like the game we have planned."

"Don't you ever get sick of playing games?"

He laughed as if it was the craziest thing I'd ever said. "Never."

"Why not?"

"Because I can win games."

Luca peppered my jaw with kisses, then he sat up, lifting us off the chair. Tall and imposing, he towered over me. I looked up at him and noted the nefarious glint in his eyes, the devilish smirk touching the corner of his mouth. He looked like he was up to no good, which sent a shiver down my arms.

Luca steered me toward the center of the room with his hand on my back. The sitting room was five times the size of most people's living rooms. It had a vaulted ceiling, high walls, and a ton of furniture. But with the Knights watching us, their eyes traveling up and down my body, it felt much smaller. Like the walls were closing in on me.

Sonny plopped into a chair across from Drake and shoved a glass plate of cocaine in front of him. Two dark-haired men tapped shot glasses, drinking with their eyes on Luca and me. We were the center of attention.

Money exchanged hands.

Why are they betting?

Luca wrapped his arm around me. "I want you to enjoy

yourself tonight. This game will be fun if you relax and learn to conquer your fears."

"What are you talking about?"

Holding me against his chest, he dragged his index finger between my cleavage and whispered in my ear, "See how jealous they are?"

I stared at the men surrounding us.

"Everyone wants a piece of you," he whispered, his deep voice. "They want to take you from me."

"You're paranoid, Luca. I think you drank too much."

"I'm serious, baby." He took another swig, his hand now covering my right breast. "It's only a matter of time before someone steals you away." His hand slipped beneath my top, so his friends could watch him massage my hard nipple. "I have a lot of enemies."

As he cupped my breast, he rolled his thumb over the tiny bud several times. I was so focused on his skin's feel against mine that I almost didn't notice heels clicking on the marble floor in the hallway. The sounds slowly approached the sitting room, and my head snapped toward the room's entrance.

A group of women walked into the room wearing red gowns like mine, except mine was much nicer and probably cost a fortune. Some of them were blonde hair, a few brunettes, and one with auburn hair. But all of them had curly hair like mine, which surprised me.

A man I didn't recognize moved toward the group of women. He had sandy blond hair swept off his forehead, dressed in a navy blue sweater over a white shirt and gray slacks.

"Welcome, ladies." He flashed a cocky smirk. "Now we can get this party started."

I assumed they were high-end escorts or strippers brought here for the occasion. They were not from Devil's Creek.

"It's time," Marcello said from behind me. "Let the game begin."

"What game?"
The lights went out, and my heart sank to my stomach.

Chapter Thirty-Seven

ALEX

I stretched my fingers out in front of me to feel my way in the dark. The panic settled into my bones within seconds, and my heart raced like a speeding train.

It was too dark.

Too quiet.

The old memories came flooding back, washing over me like breaking waves. I closed my eyes and tried to blink a few times, wishing it was all a dream. My body shook uncontrollably as the past collided with my future.

The closet.

The silence.

The never-ending darkness.

My screams.

The dread.

My mom's laughter.

"Luca," I whispered. "What the fuck is going on?"

"Shh," he said against the shell of my ear.

"You know I hate the dark. Turn the fucking lights on. Now!"

He wrapped his strong arms around me and flattened my

back against his chest. "Do you want me to have a happy birthday, baby girl?"

"Yes."

He kissed my cheek. "Then play the game with us."

"What game?" I choked out. "See who can give Alex a panic attack first?"

Luca turned me around so we were facing. However, I couldn't see shit, not even his face. He could have been anyone.

Brushing the hair off my forehead, he whispered against my lips, "It's called Capture the Queen."

My chest tightened, nerves shaking through me. "How do you play?"

"Shh." He tucked my head under his chin. "You don't want the monsters to find you, my queen."

I gasped.

I was the Queen.

They were the Knights.

The women wore similar red gowns, all with curly hair.

"You need serious help," I muttered.

Luca covered my mouth with his hand and led me away from the group. "Shh, no talking. I got you, baby."

"Where's Marcello?"

"Right here," he said in a hushed tone.

"Get lost," Luca hissed. "Do a lap, and then you can look for her."

Marcello groaned. "Even on your birthday, you can't live a little."

"What do you think I'm doing, little brother? I would never have agreed to this game under any other circumstances?"

"I'm so confused," I muttered. "What the fuck are you two talking about?"

Loud rap music blared through the speakers in the room's

corners, drowning out our whispers. At least now I could talk to them without people overhearing our conversation.

I slipped my fingers between Luca's and followed his lead. He knew where he was going. It was his house, after all. Knowing Luca, he'd planned the exact route he would take me beforehand. He wouldn't go through with this silly game without knowing he would win and capture his Queen.

Marcello disappeared a moment later. I assumed this was all part of the game.

Luca slipped his finger beneath the soft fabric over my right shoulder and slid it down my arm. "Take this off. It will make it harder for them to find you."

"Why are you doing this? What happens if someone captures me?"

He dipped his head down and licked my ear. "They get to keep you for the night."

A gasp slipped from my lips.

"Luca, no. I'm not fucking any of the Knights."

"You won't have to," he said with confidence. "This will be fun. I promise."

I saw shadows moving, heard footsteps drawing near, and the sounds of sucking. Moans. Then someone screamed. Skin slapped over the music, the room filling with groans. It sounded like they were having fun like they were getting fucked good.

I released a whimper, doing my best to stifle the wave of anxiety rushing over me. "Luca, I'm serious. This isn't funny. Turn on the lights and end this game."

"Shh, baby." Luca cradled me in his arms. "It will all be over soon."

"Why are you doing this?"

"Because I know the outcome," he said under his breath. "When this is over, we will claim our victory."

That was enough for me.

Luca had this under control.

So I did as he asked, keeping my mouth shut. Speaking would only give away our position, and I wanted to stay off the Knights' radar for as long as possible.

He shoved my dress down, so it bunched around my waist, and then yanked on the belt. The silky fabric dropped to the floor at my feet. I stepped out of the dress and stood before him in the black thong he'd bought for me. A bra didn't go with the low-cut dress. Not like it mattered since he couldn't see me.

His big hands covered my breasts, and he massaged my nipples, continuing his slow appraisal. I moaned as his hands ran down my sides and over my ass. We fell onto a couch, and he pulled me on top of him, so I straddled his thighs.

The darkness fucked with my head and made me see things that were not there. I focused hard and blinked a few times.

"Luca?"

"Yeah, baby?"

I sighed. "Just checking."

Through his pants, Luca's hard cock pressed against my inner thigh. Desperate to feel him inside me, I rocked my hips to create some friction.

"Don't say my name, baby. Don't even speak until the lights turn back on. Not another word. Okay?"

"How long?"

"One hour." His lips crashed into mine, his fingers weaving through my hair. "We don't have long. Just one more kiss, and then you're on your own."

"No," I bit out. "Don't leave me."

He brushed the pad of his thumb across my cheek. "I will find you. Promise. And when I do, your pussy is mine for the rest of the night."

"You can have me all to yourself any night," I whispered. "You didn't need to throw a party to do that."

His mouth closed over my nipple, sucking and biting so

hard I squealed. "My brothers steal too much of your time from me."

"No, they don't. You're just never around, always too busy for me."

"Never." His teeth locked onto my nipple, tearing hard enough at my flesh to leave a bruise. "You got it all wrong. I always watch you, even when I'm not there. Now, be quiet."

He shoved my panties to the side, his finger sliding into my wetness from behind to test my wet slit. I licked his neck and nibbled his skin.

The room filled with groans.

I wondered how many men cared about playing the game.

Would Luca let them win?

Capture the Queen.

We kissed for what felt like hours. My head spun from the mixture of lust, scotch, and his rough hands on my body. I rubbed my pussy against his erection, wishing he would take off his pants and fuck me.

I reached between us, my hand shaking as I grabbed his zipper. But he covered my hand with his. The finality of his actions startled me. I sat back, searched the darkness for his face, and found nothing.

Pitch fucking black.

He could have been anyone beneath me. Fear coiled in my belly, making my stomach churn, terrified of him leaving me alone in the dark. I knew it was coming. My chest heaved as he lifted me and rose from the couch.

This was it.

The moment I feared.

How would I find him in the dark?

He set my feet on the ground, his hands on my hips to steady me. I kicked off my heels, unable to balance myself on shaky legs.

Luca kissed my forehead. "I'll find you." Then he tapped my backside. "Go."

Frozen in disbelief, I stood there, listening to my heart pound in my ears. Feet stuck to the ground. I spun around, stretched my arms out to grab him, and my hands swept through the air.

Luca, I wanted to scream, but he had already disappeared into the room. My anxiety flooded back, and adrenaline rushed through my veins like a shot of heroin. Except, nothing about this game made me feel high or alive.

Feeling in front of me, I moved away from the loudest sounds, hoping they were too busy to hear me. Luca must have known where I was, right? He wouldn't leave me in the hands of his friends. Sure, he trusted the Knights with his life. Even with my life.

But would he let them touch me?

I took a few steps in front of me, hands outstretched, my feet cold against the marble floor. My heels were somewhere near the couch. And with my loss of perception, I didn't know where to start.

Should I hide?

Run?

My head buzzed from the alcohol. I needed my bearings in a room filled with over two dozen horny men. If I couldn't get to Luca, I needed to find one of his brothers using my senses. The night I lost my virginity, I couldn't tell them apart in the dark, not with their scents blending, my brain on over-drive from the excitement, alcohol, and lust.

Someone with thick arms pulled me back against a hard surface. Vodka mixed with cranberries assaulted my senses.

Not Luca...

Or his brothers.

I peeled his fingers off my breast and pushed him away as I took off, unable to see a foot in front of me. Another hand grabbed me, fingers skated down my arm, and a hand cupped my ass. Unlike the last man, he smelled like bourbon. His hands roamed over my body, taking in my curves. Maybe if I let them touch me, I could run away without getting pinned to the couch.

Without getting captured.

I'd only made it a few feet before two men grabbed me, caging me between them. Sucking in a deep breath, I tried to still my racing heart. Hands slid down my bare arms. Another pair of hands cradled my ass. Electricity sparked down my arms and thighs.

I moved toward the left side of the room, closer to what I thought was the entrance. Women moaned, and men grunted. The sounds of skin slapping broke through the noise. It smelled like a den of iniquity, the stench of sex and liquor hitting the air like smoke in the wind.

Everywhere I walked, their scents and sounds followed me. Liquid heat pooled between my thighs with each moan, soaking my panties. My skin burned with desire, like an itch I needed to scratch.

I had to find my men.

Someone hugged me from behind, stealing a scream from my lips. His hand covered my mouth, and he spun me around me, his scent filling my nostrils—cigars and scotch with a hint of the saltiness of the sea.

I relaxed in his arms.

His hand slid up my stomach, between my cleavage, and straight to my throat. He tightened his grip, his free hand sliding down my stomach, between my thighs. Right over my soaked panties, he plunged two fingers inside me.

The fabric scraped my inner walls, ripping a moan from my lips. It felt so fucking good I never wanted him to stop. I arched my hips and met each of his thrusts. A guttural groan escaped his throat right before he sank his teeth into my neck and finger-fucked me without mercy. My gums went numb from the sheer intensity of the orgasm building. Maybe it was the suspense of not knowing if I would find my handsome devils. But now that I had one of them, I wasn't letting him go.

He slid his fingers out of me, put his hand on my shoulder, and pinned me down on the couch. My skin pebbled with tiny bumps. The leather was cold against my skin, sending a shiver down my arms. We had some distance from the others, their moans far away.

Luca never cared about privacy. None of them did. They would have fucked me in front of their friends to see the jealousy on their faces as they claimed me.

Rough and unforgiving, fingers etched into my skin, burrowing into my hip. He took what he wanted and claimed my body like a land he wanted to conquer. I climbed onto his lap, my tits bouncing in his face. Licking my skin, he tasted me, rolling his tongue over my painfully sore nipple. My hand fell to the back of his head, and his teeth closed over the tiny bud.

His big cock rubbed my clit over my panties, making me even wetter. I grabbed his tie and brought his lips to mine. He tasted like scotch and smelled of cigars, a familiar scent in the Salvatore household.

I unbuttoned his dress shirt, and with his help, I stripped off his suit jacket and shirt, then worked on his pants. He gripped the waistband after I unzipped him and slid his boxers and pants down to his knees. Then his long shaft pressed against my entrance.

I wrapped my hand around his big cock. He groaned as I stroked him. Then, chest rising and falling, I clutched his shoulder for support and lifted my hips. I was so damn wet my panties clung to my skin. They were the only barrier between us, but I didn't want to break the connection to remove them. So I shoved them aside.

He fisted his cock and lifted my ass just enough to fill me in one quick thrust. A whimper escaped my mouth from the sheer force of his cock buried so deep inside me. My arms around his neck, I fell forward, panting against his lips.

He had one hand on my hip, the other on my throat, and fucked me like he wanted to kill me. His fingers cut off my air as I rode him hard and fast, my nails digging into the flesh on his back. I licked his neck and tasted the saltiness on his sweat-slick skin. Losing myself in him, I rocked my hips to meet his thrusts, swept away in a cloud of pleasure that consumed me.

Both of his hands moved to my ass cheeks. He lifted me higher and higher, bouncing me so hard on his cock my pussy was already sore. Heat rushed down my chest and arms like wildfire as an earth-shattering orgasm stirred inside me. My inner walls clenched around him, holding his thick cock in a vise.

He held me tight with our bodies joined, trembling in each other's arms. It felt so good to forget about everything and lose myself. Let him take care of all my dark desires. I came twice on his cock, so damn hard my orgasms shook through me one after the other.

He tilted my head to the side, bit my earlobe, and sucked on it as he rocked me to the core. His cock pulsed inside me, and I felt so full by the time he finished.

He parted my lips with his tongue, his cock still hard and inside me.

Then the lights turned on.

Chapter Thirty-Eight

ALEX

Marcello won the game, not his sick and twisted older brother. It was not like it mattered who won when all four had already claimed a piece of my heart. I looked around the room, and all eyes were on me. My breasts were on full display, Marcello's big cock still inside me.

I hopped off him, fixed my panties back into place, and sat on the couch beside him. He didn't bother to pull up his boxers or hide his cock that was wet with our cum.

Among the group, I spotted Luca.

I could always find him.

Just not in the dark.

Luca stood in the center of the room with a bottle of scotch in his hand. Drake bobbed a dark-haired girl's head up and down on his cock until he came in her mouth. Another guy, one I didn't know, bent a girl over a chair and fucked her from behind. He smacked her ass and went to town.

Naked and holding his hard cock, Sonny sat on a couch across the room. A pretty brunette with barrel curls and huge tits sat naked beside him. His eyes flicked from me to Marcello, and then he gave him a nod that said, Well done.

Marcello got similar looks from the Knights, except for Luca. He gritted his teeth, his demon eyes focused on us.

Damian and Bastian stood a few feet away from Luca, fully clothed. They both looked annoyed that Marcello had won the game. But where were they when I was looking for them in the dark? Were they the two men who caged me between them?

"Marcello won fair and square," Luca said, his tone dripping with anger. "She's yours for the night, brother."

Marcello rose from the couch, pulled up his boxers, and zipped his pants. I spent half of my nights in his bed, anyway. So why didn't Luca try harder to keep me all to himself?

Luca's jaw ticked like he wanted to say something. He looked like a demon had possessed him. Then he took a deep breath and flung his hand out. "Go ahead. Take her."

Without a care that I was topless, I walked toward him. "You never play games you can't win. So why didn't you find me?"

Luca looked as if he weren't breathing, his expression unreadable, like he'd gone somewhere else mentally. "I played by the rules, Drea. You disappeared on me."

Marcello stepped behind me and put his hands on my hips.

"What was the point of this game?"

Luca's eyes flicked up and down my body, then he licked his lips. "To have fun. It's my birthday."

"You said you wanted me for your birthday." Annoyed with him, I shook my head. "You had me and let me walk away. What if the other Knights had captured me? What if it wasn't Marcello fucking me when the lights turned on?"

He rolled his shoulders, unaffected. "They wouldn't have touched you."

I glanced around the room at the men who stared at me like a piece of meat they wanted to devour. "Are you sure about that?"

"Yes," he said without hesitation.

Marcello squeezed my bicep, and I glanced up at him. He looked like he wanted to continue what we started. I slid my lip between my teeth. A guttural groan fell from his beautiful lips.

"Let's go, Marcello. Time to claim your prize."

Marcello led me out of the sitting room with his hand on my shoulder. Luca didn't protest since that was part of the rules. No one followed us. Not even Bastian and Damian attempted to join.

Marcello had a mural of a man from the Greek underworld with a snake wrapped around his arm on his bedroom wall. He was so talented I couldn't wait to have him paint me. To reveal how he saw me.

He was alone on the top floor, his father at the far end of the hall. I didn't think when I walked out of the sitting room topless. Marcello at least had the sense to pull up his pants. Thankfully, we hadn't run into Arlo. That would have been awkward as fuck.

The room had high ceilings, tall windows with dark curtains, and a balcony overlooking the bay. He had the same room as Luca but one floor above him. I stood at the center of the room and noted every detail which spanned two walls.

"I knew it was you," he whispered. "I will always find you, princess."

"Luca's mad about losing the game. But he could have won." I bit my lip as I looked up at him. "Why did he let you win?"

"He's been drinking since this morning. Very unusual for my brother. It's rare to see him out of control."

"Why is he drinking so much?"

"He allows himself this one day each year. That's it. Nothing more, nothing less." Marcello gripped my hips and pulled me toward him. "I won. And I want to claim my prize."

He ran his hand up and down my right side. His thumb brushed my nipple, and a whimper slipped past my lips.

Before we could take things further, the door slammed into the wall. My breath caught in my throat. Luca stood in the doorway, a bottle of Macallan in his hand, a blood-red tie hanging loosely around his neck. He wore a black suit, the jacket open, his white shirt wrinkled, looking like he'd been to hell and back again.

Marcello narrowed his eyes at his brother. "What the fuck are you doing up here?"

Luca leaned against the doorframe, so drunk he could barely stand. "She's mine, Marcello." Luca plopped into an oversized armchair across from the bed, his thighs spread as he drank from the bottle. "It's my birthday. She will be my wife." He extended his hand. "Get over here, Drea."

"Not tonight," Marcello challenged. "You could have won, Luca. Get lost."

"Her pussy is so tight, don't you think?" He sat in the chair by the bed and took a swig of scotch. "She was worth the wait. We waited close to six years to bend her over and make her scream."

Marcello grunted in agreement.

Luca's eyes moved to me. "Tell my brother you'd rather have me. You like it when I embarrass you, hurt you. Spank your ass. Pull your hair. Tear your pussy up. Isn't that right, baby girl?"

I stared at him, unblinking.

"Tell my brother." Another sip of scotch. "You like getting punished. Don't you?"

"Is that what you want, Luca? You want Marcello to punish me with his cock?"

His lips parted with the sexiest look in his eyes. "Get on your knees," Luca ordered. "Bend over. Show Marcello your pretty pussy."

Luca fisted the bottle in one hand and then whipped out

his enormous cock. He took sips of scotch as he jerked his cock, looking like a demon had possessed his body. His eyes were blank like he was physically in his body but not mentally present.

I glanced over at Marcello, then got on my knees on the mattress with my back to him. The bed shifted beneath his weight, and his hands fell to my hips. He shoved his knee between my thighs and kicked them open wider. After he ripped off my thong, his finger traced the length of my wet slit, and I moaned from his touch.

Luca drank from the bottle, one eye open. "Feel good, baby girl?"

"Yes. Your brother feels so good."

Luca stroked his cock harder. "Keep going. Choke her with your tie."

"Luca," Marcello groaned. "I know how to fuck a woman. Get out. I'm not taking orders from you."

"If you want to be the Grand Master of the Knights, put a bullet in my skull. Until then..." He tipped his head at me. "Make my girl come. Look at her, begging for your cock. She wants it."

My eyes found Luca's blue ones that were bloodshot. I licked my lips when he jerked his shaft the way he fucked me. Hard and relentless.

Marcello undressed and then pressed his cock against my slick entrance. Rubbed the tip up and down my slit. He hooked his tie around my neck and tightened it just enough for my eyes to close. It wasn't as hard as when Damian choked me.

"Wait." Luca shot up from the chair, his cock hanging out of his pants. He moved to the other side of the bed. "Fuck her. Hard."

Marcello dug his fingers into my hips and slammed his monster cock inside me. One quick thrust. Not even a warning before he filled me up.

This was what Luca wanted.

What we all wanted.

He rocked his hips, gripping my hair from behind. Marcello broke through my inner walls, pulling back, so he could slam into me again. I glanced over at Luca. He watched me with those hunter's eyes, enjoying the show.

Marcello tugged my hair harder and smacked my ass with his other hand.

"Harder," Luca commanded. "Our queen has been a bad girl. Isn't that right, baby?"

"I'm a bad girl," I moaned.

"Yes, you are." Marcello yanked on the tie, the fabric molding to my throat. He pulled tighter. "Come on my cock, bad girl."

A shiver rolled down my arms. Fuck. Between the two of them, I wasn't sure who was dirtier. And I loved it.

Our moans filled the silence. The room smelled like sex and alcohol. A soft breeze blew in from the bay, bringing with it the saltiness of the sea. I love that scent.

A wave of pleasure rolled down my arms, spreading down my chest. My skin seared from Marcello's rough hands, his big cock thrusting inside me. He took what he wanted, the same as his older brother.

My Devils.

As I rode out my orgasm, Marcello spanked my ass again.

"Harder," I screamed, pushing my ass into his cock and meeting his thrusts.

His hand landed on my other cheek. And by the time he hit me again, my legs shook, my pussy clenching around his cock.

I knew he could feel it.

So close, I was about to come.

"You're such a dirty girl." Luca moved beside the bed, still drinking and jerking his shaft. "You gonna come for my brother like a good little slut?"

I loved when he talked to me like that. It was such a fucking turn-on. He didn't try to be sweet or whisper sexy things into my ear. Luca was nothing like his brother, and I wouldn't have had him any other way.

"Uh-huh," I groaned.

"You gonna come for me, too?"

"Yes," I whimpered.

Luca put the bottle on the floor and dropped his hand from his dick. I stared up at him, licking my lips. He bent down and smacked my tits, one at a time. A taunting look crossed his handsome face. Then he pinched my nipple, damn near tearing it off my body.

"You like the pain, baby?"

"Yes," I bit out.

He grabbed Marcello's tie that moved between my bouncing tits and yanked so hard I would have fallen over if Marcello wasn't holding my hips in a vise. He gripped both of my ass cheeks, burrowing his fingerprints into my skin. I would have bruises in the morning, but I didn't care.

It felt too good.

Luca wrapped the fabric around his hand, crushing my windpipe with the tie. But I didn't bother to stop him. Another orgasm brewed inside me, building like a storm. Slow and steady and then in delicious succession, crashed over me like breaking waves. Hit me so hard my arms and legs shook.

When I came, every nerve ending in my body lit on fire. Heat coursed over me, my heart racing out of control. My chest heaved as I moaned, "Marcello, Luca."

Luca gripped my bicep while Marcello drove into me, holding me in place. Luca sat on the bed beside me as I came down from my high. He rubbed his big cock, each pump matching Marcello's pace.

Luca shoved his fingers into my mouth, slid them down my throat, and choked me until saliva dripped from the corners of my mouth.

Luca smiled.

A real one, for once.

But this one was sadistic.

Psycho.

Marcello's arms trembled, his thrusts quickening as his cock pulsed inside me. He hugged me from behind with one arm. The sweat from his chest coated my back. We were a tangle of limbs, so fucking spent.

He pulled out of me, ran his hand over my ass, then slid his finger down my wet slit. I felt his cum drip out of me. Marcello dropped to the bed beside me with a satisfied groan.

"Don't move, baby." Luca stood at the edge of the bed, his cock in front of my face. "Give me that sexy mouth."

Already on my hands and knees, I moved closer to him.

He fisted my hair with one hand, cock in the other. "Good girl."

My scalp hurt when he grunted curses, whispering my name as he rode out his orgasm.

"Open up," he ordered, his warm cum coating my tongue. His aim wasn't bad for being so drunk, but some of it got on my chin. He swiped his thumb across my bottom lip. "Swallow all of my cum, baby."

After I swallowed, I opened my mouth for him. He licked his lips, then bent down to kiss me. Just a peck so he could taste himself on me.

I sat back on my heels, my hands on my thighs, and looked up at him. He clutched my chin and kissed my lips.

"You fucked up tonight. Don't do that to me ever again."

His thumb grazed my lip, his eyes burning into mine. "I'm trying to prepare you for Legare." Luca stepped back, studying me before turning his gaze on his brother. "Marcello, make sure our queen gets a bath and then off to bed."

He shoved his cock back into his pants and fixed himself. Then he swiped the bottle of Macallan from the floor, took a swig, and then he left the room.

The door slammed behind him.

I glanced over at Marcello, still trying to catch my bearings. "What the fuck just happened?"

He shrugged, unaffected by the unusual turn of events. "That was Luca being Luca." Marcello tipped his head toward the door. "You heard him." His long legs dangled off the side of the bed, his feet hitting the floor. "Let's go. Bath and then bed."

Chapter Thirty-Nine

ALEX

My eyes shot open, and panic flooded my chest. Struggling for air, I sucked in deep breaths as his hand covered my mouth. The other wrapped around my throat as he caged me against the mattress with his muscular body.

I attempted to scream, and he tightened his grip on my throat, crushing my windpipe with his hand. Even in the dark, I could see the evil smirk pulling at the corner of his mouth. I kicked and squirmed, desperate to break free from his death grip. But, he was too strong, his body hard as steel and pressing down on my chest.

I gasped for air and pawed at his fingers. "What are you doing, Luca? Get off me."

He slid his hand up and down my throat, massaging the skin while maintaining a firm grip. "Are you going to play nice, baby girl?"

His words were cold and silky, his usual calm before the storm. Luca never yelled, which always struck me as odd for someone with so much rage inside him. I shook my head, and his nostrils flared, matching the intensity that brewed in his eyes.

"Then my hand stays over your mouth," he snapped.

I groaned, my words muffled as I attempted to scream.

"So, what's it gonna be?" Luca stuck out his tongue and licked the length of my cheek, stopping right below my eye. "You ready to act like a good girl?"

Using every bit of my power, I shoved my palms into his chest, but it was like trying to move a car with my bare hands, pointless and not worth the energy. He would only make it hurt worse, dragging out the pain because he got off on it.

"Now," he said, his voice like gravel. "Are you going to scream if I move my hand?"

"No," I muttered.

He uncovered my mouth. "I just want to talk, baby."

"Get out of my room, psycho." I turned to my side, where his brother had fallen asleep beside me. "Where is Marcello?"

Luca's lip trembled from the wave of anger shaking through him. "He's dealing with an issue for Salvatore Global. Don't worry about him."

"There are other ways to talk to a person." I squirmed beneath him. "You don't have to hold me down like an animal."

"You're going to choose him over me. I know it."

I was so angry with his intrusion that I wanted to hit him where it would hurt most. "Are you afraid no one will ever be dumb enough to love you?"

His laughter shook through me. "You think I want your love?" Luca shook his head. "Nah, baby girl. I want to hear you scream, feel your body tremble beneath mine."

"There's something wrong with you. You have no heart, no soul. You're empty. That's exactly why I will choose Marcello over you."

He glared at me, his mouth inches from mine. "After everything I have done for you… might as well spit in my fucking face."

I closed my eyes and breathed through my nose. "I didn't ask for this."

"You never had a choice." His lips hovered above mine, his breath heating my skin. "You will be my queen. Stop fighting this."

I squirmed beneath him. His cock was hard and rubbed against me through his pants. Why did I like the feel of his body on top of me?

"Then tell me something real, Luca. I feel like I know nothing about you. I can't marry someone who doesn't care about me, who hasn't taken the time to get to know me. You only want to fuck me."

"That's a lie, and you know it. If I only wanted to fuck you, I would have taken you over that sink in the bathroom years ago." He rolled his thumb over my lip. "You're a part of me, my Queen D."

"You need me," I bit out. "More than I will ever need you."

He clutched my chin, forcing me to look into his eyes. "We need each other."

I hated he was right.

Luca brought down my walls, one at a time, until I bared myself to him. He peppered my jaw with aggressive kisses, his fingers sliding down my throat. I widened my legs for him, tilting my head back against the pillow so he could suck and bite my neck. Heat rushed between my thighs, and I arched my hips to create some friction.

"I need to know one thing."

He caged me against the mattress and covered my mouth with his. "Anything."

"Why do you call me Drea? Not Alexandrea or Alex. Not even a nickname like your brothers."

I'd never asked him that.

He stiffened on top of me. "Why? You don't like that name?"

"It's not that. I always wondered if you called me Drea to disrespect me."

His hard body crushed mine as he shifted his weight. "I wanted you to have a name no one else would use. Not my brothers, your family. No one."

"Why?"

"Because I knew you were mine the second I laid eyes on you. Even though I hated you, I knew." He brushed my cheek with his thumb. "Mine. The first time I saw you, I said your name, and it didn't sound right. Alexandrea is a beautiful name. But you look like a Drea to me."

"We still haven't talked about the past. It's what shaped our future. I think we should at least…"

He pressed his fingers over my mouth. "No, baby. We don't need to talk about it. It took me a long time to realize you're not your mother. That you had nothing to do with my mother's death."

"And how long did it take you to see that? Because until recently, I felt your hatred every time you walked into a room."

"The truth?"

I nodded.

"When your grandfather told you."

I frowned at his response. "Luca, I'm nothing like her."

"I know, baby. I saw the pain on your face. The hurt in your eyes. You look like your mother, which has made it harder for me to separate the two of you. So when I saw you for the first time, I wanted to wring your neck. I didn't see you. I saw your bitch mother."

"So you pushed me away. It made me feel like shit every day for a year straight." My chest ached as I thought about the past, all the shit I had endured because of my mother. "You forced me to watch you with other girls."

"I got off to you, not them. Did you ever see me look at them?"

I shook my head. "No, you always looked at me in the mirror."

"Because I pretend I was fucking you. I couldn't even come if you weren't there."

"That's not the point, Luca. You could have had me instead. I wanted you. You knew it and let this secret between us ruin my life."

"Bash and Damian begged me not to kill you," he confessed, breathing scotch in my face. "They obsessed over you from the first day of school. I guess I did, too. Just not in the same way as them. I couldn't bear the thought of touching you. To do so would have been a betrayal to my mom. So I told Bash and Damian everything I wanted to do to you, and they did it for me."

"Is that why all four of you agreed to share me?"

"Yes."

Sucking his bottom lip into my mouth, I rocked my hips, and Luca groaned, threading his fingers through my curls. "Luca, I need you to kiss me."

His right eyebrow lifted in question. "You need, or you want?"

"Does it matter?"

"Yes, Drea. The words have two entirely different meanings."

"I want you to kiss me."

He smirked. "That's better, baby."

He always kissed me like he wanted to devour me, but he tried to conquer me tonight. Claim me. Brand me with his searing hot kisses. Our kiss didn't last long, and as our lips separated, I pulled my shirt over my head and flung it across the room. He dipped his head down, stuck out his tongue, and rolled it over my nipples.

"Luca," I panted. "Please don't wake me up with your hand over my mouth ever again."

He grinned with a glimmer of mischief in his eyes. "I promise, but under one condition."

"And what is that?"

"Marry me."

"How about you make me come first, and then I'll decide."

His eyes traveled up and down the length of my naked body. "Fuck, woman. You're going to be the death of me."

Luca moved my thighs apart with his hand, teasing my wet slit with his long finger, and I cried out as he pushed his finger inside me. "You're always so wet for me." He added another finger and raised my left leg over his shoulder. "So tight."

His tongue rolled over my aching clit. Every part of my body came alive as my skin pricked with tiny bumps. Luca spread me open, making love to my pussy, consuming me with each flick of his tongue. One moan after another escaped my lips, and my eyes slammed shut, lost in the moment.

He whispered, "Be a good girl and come for me, Drea."

His tongue moved inside me, giving me long, aggressive licks. My legs shook as my orgasm rocked through me, and he held me down as his tongue darted in and out of me. I exploded on Luca's tongue, coming so hard my entire body felt numb when I stopped trembling.

He dropped my leg on the bed and licked his lips. Luca stripped off his shirt, and my hands found his scarred chest. I leaned forward to kiss his skin, tasting every inch of him. He growled when my tongue flicked his nipple.

I inched my way down his chest and licked right below his black Dolce & Gabbana boxer briefs. I rolled down his zipper, and he kicked off the rest of his clothes. Kneeling between my thighs, he ran his fingers through my hair as I licked the pre-cum from the head of his cock.

"My Queen D." Luca fisted my curls in his hand and grunted. "Suck my cock into your pretty mouth."

I wrapped my hand around his thick shaft and looked up at him.

"Fuck, baby," he hissed. "Suck the tip."

Holding his cock in front of my mouth, I rolled my tongue across his soft skin. He palmed the back of my head, forcing me to take more.

"That's it. Keep going."

His hand fell on top of mine as he helped me stroke his shaft. I jerked his cock, my movements in sync with his. And he groaned as he hit the back of my throat.

He was so big I felt him everywhere. My cheeks puffed out, tears streaming down my cheeks. I had to slap his hand to loosen his firm grip, and he gave a little slack so I didn't choke on his massive cock.

When I felt him pulse in my mouth, he pulled back, staring down at me with an intensity in his eyes. Luca pushed me back on the mattress and slid the pad of his thumb across my lip. "I want you to come on my cock. Let me feel you, Drea."

Kissing me hard and fast, he lifted my leg and hooked it around his back, making my head spin from pleasure. His hand moved between us, guiding his cock to my entrance.

"Relax, baby."

My chest heaved as I felt the first pinch. "I am."

Luca ran his fingers down my thigh, massaging my skin as he inched inside me. "No, you're not." He rubbed my nipple with the pad of his thumb, his gentle touch helping to ease the tension in my body.

"It's just you and me," he whispered against my lips. "You don't have to be afraid."

Sometimes I feared the man on top of me. But deep down, I always knew Luca cared about me. Maybe it wasn't loving, but our bond was much more profound.

His eyes found mine as he stretched me out, careful not to move too fast. An intense wave of pain shot through my body as he thrust his hips, my eyes slamming shut from the sheer force.

His long fingers grazed my cheek. "Baby, look at me."

I whimpered his name as he trailed his fingers up and down my thigh, my body melting into his. After a while, I relaxed, no longer worried about the pain, because with it came intense pleasure. His skilled hands and cock felt so damn good, and with each moan, he covered my mouth to silence my screams.

I unraveled beneath him, losing myself to the man who'd haunted my dirty dreams and nightmares. He sucked my lip into his mouth and tugged on my flesh. A carnal hunger flared in his pretty blue eyes, and then his legs trembled, shaking through me as he spilled his cum inside me.

Out of breath, he muttered a few curses and kissed my forehead and lips. Then, he rolled off me, drenched in sweat, and propped himself up on his elbow.

"How come you went easy on me?"

He parted my lips with his tongue, kissing me with a crazed hunger. "Because I'm trying to give you what you want."

I curled up on my side, resting my head on his chest. "What do you want?"

"You." He stroked his fingers through my messy curls. "Always you, Queen D."

Since he was forthcoming for once, I had to ask the one question I needed him to answer. I knew how I felt about all four of them, but I wasn't so sure Luca would let me have his brothers after we married. And I wasn't about to let go of them.

"What about your brothers?"

His head snapped to me. "What about them?"

"It's all five of us."

Luca nodded. "Don't worry, baby girl. After you marry me, you'll still get to have your cake and eat it, too."

He hooked his arm around me. My eyelids grew heavier, and exhaustion won out. It was one of the best nights until I rolled over the following day, alone and naked. No matter how much I wanted Luca to change, for me to be the one who changed him, I had to come to terms with one fact.

Men like Luca would never change.

He would always be an asshole.

But at least he would be mine.

Chapter Forty

ALEX

I t had been a while since the five of us had eaten breakfast together in the formal dining room. Marcello was feeling better and no longer needed me to mother him. He only agreed to stay in bed because he knew it made me happy.

I sat on Luca's lap, the dining room spinning around me as the kitchen staff set plates on the table. The smell of eggs made my stomach churn. Just one whiff and I had to grip Luca's arms to steady myself. A nasty taste filled my mouth, forcing me to swallow hard to get rid of it.

Luca clutched my wrist. "You okay, baby?"

"I don't know." I slid my arm across his neck and rested my head on his shoulder. "My stomach hasn't been right for a while."

"It's probably your nerves." Luca sipped from his mug and inspected my face. "We're still dealing with the Russians. Until all of them are dead, you won't feel safe."

"It's not that." I kissed his lips. "But I know you will protect me from them."

Luca drank from his cup, eyeing me up like I was his meal. Even the scent of coffee, which I loved, spun the contents of my stomach. I hadn't eaten since dinner the night before. Maybe it was food poisoning, or I was getting sick. Or perhaps he was right, and my nerves got the best of me.

"Yeah." I shrugged. "I'm sure it's my nerves."

His lips touched mine. "If I didn't have a meeting in a few minutes, I would devour you on this table."

"Later," I whispered, trying to fight the wave of nausea. "Come find me after your meeting."

Luca's hand inched up my thigh, his fingers dangerously close to the seam of my panties. His skin felt amazing pressed against mine, but another wave of sickness washed over me, stealing the air from my lungs.

"I think I'm going to be sick."

He hooked his arm around me and brushed his thumb across my cheek. "Your color isn't good. I'll call the doctor and have him stop by today to look at you."

I clutched my stomach and jumped off his lap right before I vomited on the floor. It wasn't pretty. Chunks of food and bile splashed across the marble floor and hit Luca and Bastian's dress shoes. I tried to aim better, but I only had seconds to react.

Bastian got out of his chair and was at my side in seconds. He rubbed his hand in circles over my back. "Get it all out. It's okay, baby."

Luca groaned and then tapped a few buttons on the phone. "I'm calling the fucking doctor."

"The floor," I choked out.

"Don't worry about it." Luca snapped his fingers for one of the staff to clean up after me.

I didn't grow up with live-in staff, so I wasn't used to this, not even after all these years of being a Wellington.

"I'm sorry," I said to the brown-haired woman who kneeled on the floor in front of me and wiped up my vomit with a rag.

As Luca spoke to the concierge doctor, Bastian grabbed a

cloth napkin from the table and wiped my mouth. Damian and Marcello were also out of their chairs and at my side.

Marcello gave me a wary look as he studied my face. "You've been feeling sick a lot lately, princess."

"I'm sure it's nothing." I stepped backward to move out of the vomit path and then looked at Bastian's expensive shoes and sighed. "Sorry about your shoes, Bash. I thought I could…"

He held up his finger in front of my mouth. "Shh, baby. No more apologies. I can get another pair of shoes." Bastian wrapped his arms around me, molding his body to mine. "I only care about getting you better." He flattened his hand and held it over my forehead. "You feel warm."

"She's not sick," Marcello said with certainty in his deep voice. He raised the phone in his hand and scrolled through a few screens before glancing up again. "Alex has been living with us for close to three months. She hasn't had her period since she moved into the house."

"Fuck," Damian hissed, clawing at the back of his neck as he turned his head away from me.

Bastian ran a hand through his hair and breathed through his nose. "I think he's right, Cherry."

"The doctor will be here in two hours." Luca dropped his phone on the table. Then he hooked his arm around my waist and pulled me out of Bastian's arms, pushing me down on his lap. "We'll find out for sure today."

Marcello looked thrilled by the idea and even smiled. Bastian bit his lip, his gaze shifting to Damian, who had his hands stuffed into his pockets, staring at the floor. Luca, of course, gave nothing away, tapping his fingers on my thigh.

"Okay, so how does this work?" I asked them. "If I'm pregnant, one of you is the father. So how do we do this?"

"You have the baby," Luca said, which was obvious.

I turned on his lap so I could look at him. "But what if the baby is Damian's? Am I supposed to have his child and marry you? Don't you need an heir to satisfy The Founders Society deal?"

"The marriage is the first step," Luca told me. "They expect it will take time for us to produce an heir."

I looked at my guys. "Are all of you okay with pretending the baby is Luca's?"

Marcello nodded. "Optics are important in our world. You will be Luca's wife. The media would tear you apart if the baby isn't his."

"I still haven't accepted his proposal."

Luca kissed my neck, his tongue branding my hot flesh. "You will."

"None of you care, one way or the other?"

Bastian shook his head. "Nope."

Marcello nodded in agreement.

"I wouldn't be a good father," Damian said in a hushed tone. "You're better off with one of my brothers being your baby daddy."

I reached out for him, and he hesitantly slipped his fingers between mine. "Damian, you could be the father of my child. I want you to be part of their life."

"I'll be here." He shifted his stance, his movements strange as if he were nervous. "But I won't be good at it."

"Stop talking like that. You always put yourself down whenever it comes to normal life stuff. You're capable of so much more than you realize."

"The child would grow to hate me."

I shook my head and squeezed his fingers. "Not true. You made me love you."

His green eyes widened, lips parted in surprise.

Bastian gasped.

"I love you, Damian." I slid off Luca's lap and inched my hands up Damian's chest, slowly making my way to his neck. "I still love you, even after you tried to kill me, you crazy ass motherfucker."

He laughed, and then his hands were on my ass, lifting me off the ground. I wrapped my legs around his back and kissed him before he could change his mind. His back hit the wall as his tongue swept into my mouth. After drinking my blood, I assumed nothing bothered him. Like the fact, I could taste the vomit on my tongue long after our lips separated.

"I don't expect you to say it back," I said, out of breath from our kiss. "In your way, I know you care about me."

"I do." He sucked my bottom lip into his mouth. "You're my obsession, Pet."

I smiled. "That's good enough for me... for now."

His eyebrows rose. "For now?"

"You can love, Damian. Look at your relationship with Bash. Whether you realize it, you love him."

He bit the inside of his cheek, unable to meet my gaze. Our conversion ended with him setting me on the ground. And then Marcello stole me from his arms.

He snaked one arm around me and pressed a soft kiss to his cheek. "I hope it's mine."

"We don't even know if she's pregnant," Luca said harshly. "All of you are getting way ahead of yourselves."

"The timeline makes sense," Marcello told his brother. "I know everything about Alex. It's my job to know every detail about her life."

"He's right," I interjected. "I haven't had my period. And this doesn't feel like the flu or a cold."

Luca shoved up the sleeve of his suit jacket and checked his watch. "I have a meeting." He got up from his chair and kissed my cheek. "We'll know for sure in a few hours, baby girl. Take a shower and get ready for the doctor. I'll see you when he gets here."

Two hours later, the doctor arrived and drew my blood. Dr. Carpenter left us with three different brands of home pregnancy tests. Luca had insisted we have an instant response since the blood would take more time to process through the lab. We all had been on edge since Marcello blurted out the P-word at breakfast.

I headed into the bathroom, unboxed three different pregnancy tests, and peed on them. Then I washed my hands and looked in the mirror. My cheeks flushed from the nerves spreading through my chest.

Over the past two weeks, even Bastian had noticed my boobs were bigger. In addition, my nipples often felt sore and sensitive. And then my stomach wreaked havoc on me.

I opened the door and gestured for Marcello to step inside. He clutched my shoulder with his big hand, standing beside me in silence as we waited for the results. It didn't even take the full two minutes for all three tests to change color. One had a blue plus sign, the second test had two pink lines, and the final one said positive.

My heart dropped to my stomach as I studied each of the tests. "The timing could not be worse. Men are still trying to kidnap me and add me to their stupid fucking auction."

"We have allies committed to destroying the Bratva. They won't get to you inside the walls of our estate."

"They almost got me once. And you paid the price for it. You barely survived the gunshot wound."

He rolled his broad shoulders. "Look at it this way, princess. I stared into the depths of Hell and somehow lived to tell about it. For you, I climbed through the fiery pits and battled the demons that tried to keep us apart. No one will touch you." He rubbed his hand over my stomach. "Or this baby."

I stepped out of the bathroom with Marcello in tow. Luca sat in the armchair by the window in my bedroom with his shoe propped up on his knee. Damian sat on the other side of the table while Bastian had his shoes off and laid across the mattress on his stomach, staring at me.

Luca dropped his foot to the floor and leaned forward, elbows on his thighs, as his blue eyes seared a hole through me. "So? What did the tests say?"

I smiled. "I'm pregnant."

Luca got on his knees in front of me so fast I didn't even have time to comprehend what he was doing. He moved both of his hands to my hips, kissed my stomach, and then rested his head there. I held the back of his head and looked at each of my guys. They didn't seem surprised by this rare display of affection.

Bastian got up from the bed and dropped to the floor beside Luca. Then Marcello took a knee on my right, Damian on my left. I reached out and shoved my fingers through each of their hair, needing to touch them.

Luca lifted his head and reached into his pocket, producing the same velvet box from The Mansion. His mother's engagement ring. He cracked open the box and held up the massive diamond.

"Drea, baby, I didn't do this the right way last time." He clutched my left wrist and brought my hand to his mouth to kiss my skin. "All five of us." His eyes moved to each of his brothers before landing on me again. "We're in this together."

Marcello grabbed my other hand. "Marry me, princess."

Bastian stole my hand away, dipping his head down to lick my skin. "Marry me, Cherry."

Then Damian took my other hand from Luca's grasp and sucked my fingers into his mouth. "Marry me, Pet."

Of course, Luca saved himself for last. He took both of my hands and kissed each of them. "Marry me, Drea."

Tears streamed down my cheeks, dripping onto my shirt. Maybe it was the pregnancy hormones, or perhaps it was the fact all four of them had asked me to marry them.

"Just to be clear," I said to break the silence in the room. "I can only legally marry one of you, right? You didn't bribe a congressman to change the marriage laws?"

Bastian laughed.

Damian smirked.

Marcello shook his head with an evil glint in his eyes. "No, but if it's that important to you."

It wasn't.

Luca removed the ring from the box, now holding my left hand. "You can only marry one of us on paper, but you'll still be Mrs. Salvatore."

"What about the wedding?"

"You will marry all four of us, legal or not."

"We don't care about that kind of shit," Bastian said to reassure me. "You'll still be our wife."

"Did you ask my grandfather for his permission?"

"We don't need it." Damian snickered. "He owes us too much to say no. And it's not like you're going anywhere, Pet."

My eyes shifted to Luca. "I'm guessing I will be married to you on paper."

He nodded. "So what do you say, baby girl?" Luca licked his lips as he looked up at me. "Will you marry us?"

A rainfall of tears soaked my cheeks and shirt as I got on my knees in front of them and let Luca slip the ring onto my finger. "Yes."

Chapter Forty-One

LUCA

Alex said yes. *Finally.* I had always known she would be my wife, but she was stubborn.

So before the doctor arrived at the house, I met with my brothers. I told them about my plan to ask Alex to marry me.

Bastian laughed and said she would say no. Damian didn't have an opinion. He was too sick with worry over possibly being a father. Not like he didn't know the risk each time he came inside her.

It was Marcello who had suggested we propose as a group. He knew her best of all and was right. She wanted to hear the words from each of our mouths.

After dinner, we changed out of our suits and into khaki shorts and polo shirts. We wanted to take Alex on a date, but we couldn't risk someone grabbing her in town.

Alex sat cross-legged in the middle of the mattress, dressed in a low-cut pink tank top with no bra and black spandex shorts. Her nipples poked through the thin fabric, the hardened points begging me to notice. She looked up when we entered her bedroom, smiling at us as she patted the space beside her on the bed.

I placed a black satin box in front of her. She peeked up at me, eyes wide with wonder, a smile in place as she glanced at the box.

"What's this?"

I slid the box across the duvet until it tapped her fingers. "Open it and find out."

She flipped the lid, unable to contain her excitement, beaming with delight at the sight of the diamond and sapphire necklace worth as much as a luxury car.

Only the best for our girl.

Alex lifted the necklace from the box. "My birthstone? But my birthday isn't until September. What's the occasion?"

I took it from her hand and draped the gems around her neck. "This necklace belonged to my mother. She would have loved for you to wear it."

Her lips parted in surprise. "Thank you, Luca. It's beautiful."

"And from all of us," I told her.

She hugged Marcello next, then Damian and Bastian.

I extended my hand to her. "We want to show you something. It's important you keep this secret and only use it in an emergency."

Her eyebrows knitted together. "Like life or death important?"

I nodded. "If it comes to that, we need to prepare you."

She dug her teeth into her bottom lip. "Luca, you're scaring me."

"Don't be afraid, Cherry." Bastian stroked her cheek with his fingers, and she leaned into his touch. "We'll protect you from the monsters."

Alex tugged on her top. "You said to get comfortable. Is what I'm wearing okay?"

"I'll get your jacket," Marcello said as he walked toward the closet. "It gets cold on the beach at night."

He came out of the closet and slipped a light jacket over her shoulders, and slid jeweled sandals on her feet. My brother always babied her. But that was what she expected from him. She wanted something different from each of us, which was why this worked so well.

We left her bedroom and climbed the stairs to the third-floor library. Alex shot a curious look in my direction. I held open one door, and Marcello grabbed the other. Bastian tapped her on the ass and ushered Alex inside the room.

The house was full of secret passageways and hidden laundry chutes. We had a lot of secrets and plenty of ways to escape our palace on the sea. My grandfather had the sense to build the house with various exit strategies. He was slightly paranoid, and with his Mafia business deals, it was necessary.

I wanted Alex to know about one passage in particular in case shit went south again. We had the Knights working around the clock to help eliminate threats. My cousins were also working with their Mafia counterparts to deal with the Russians.

But with the bounty now five million dollars, everyone in the criminal underworld wanted a piece of our girl. The owners of Il Circo had issued an order to bring Alex to the next auction at the end of the month. We had no way of knowing who would try to come for her next. Too many people wanted the reward for her head.

Alex's eyes traveled up and down the two-story library in awe. "I thought we were going to the beach."

"Shortcut." I led her to the front of the large, open room with vaulted ceilings and endless cases of books. "My grandfather had built this house during Prohibition. My family used the secret passages to move illegal alcohol and evade the cops."

"Nothing has changed," she quipped.

Pressing my hand to the center of the bookcase on the exterior wall, I reached for a book a few shelves above my head and pulled it down.

"The Count of Monte Cristo?" Alex laughed. "What an

appropriate choice, given the situation. Are we digging our way out of this prison?"

"Nah, my ancestors already did that for us."

I pushed on the shelf, and it swung inward, revealing a stone encasement and a narrow spiral staircase. Lights built into the walls illuminated the cramped area.

Alex poked her head inside, her eyes wide as she looked at me. "Why are you showing me this?"

"In case you need an exit strategy."

"If that happens, all of you better be at my side." She hugged her middle, biting her lip. "You're talking like you're going to die."

"You can't kill the Devil, baby."

She shook her head and frowned. "No one is invincible, not even you."

"You let me do the worrying." I held out my hand and tipped my head toward the passage. "After you."

She took one hesitant step forward. "It looks dark down there."

Bastian cupped her shoulders and moved behind her. "There's enough light to guide the way. Trust us, Cherry. We wouldn't do anything to hurt you." His hand moved over her stomach in a circular motion. "Or our baby."

She smiled at his last statement.

"If you feared for your life, you wouldn't think twice about running down those stairs if it meant freedom."

Alex peeked up at him. "Why don't you go first?"

I tapped his shoulder. "Go ahead, Bash. I have to seal the door behind us."

He moved in front of her and headed down the stairs which led to the catacombs.

She took a step forward and then glanced at me. "Can we come back this way?"

I nodded.

She crept down the stairs without further complaint,

pressing her hand to the wall for support. Marcello went down behind her, then Damian. I closed the door and pulled up the lever before I followed. As we moved through the catacombs, the air became denser. My nostrils tingled at the earthy smell pouring through the cracks in the old stone walls.

Alex sneezed a few times. "Damn allergies," she groaned with her hand over her mouth.

Once we reached the bottom, I grabbed Alex's shoulders and steered her toward my father's favorite place in Devil's Creek—his precious wine cellar. It was bulletproof, theft-proof, and temperature-controlled. I stopped in front of a glass wall and pressed my palm to the hand scanner.

Once the device accepted my handprint, the glass door slid to the right. Stone walls with oak accents gave the space a rustic vibe. Wine racks built into the walls reached the ceiling on three sides. A high-top wooden table sat in the center of the room with a dozen chairs surrounding it. Empty decanters and glasses were on top of the table, turned over.

"I feel like I'm in a Bond movie," Alex said in disbelief.

I smacked her ass. "You'd make a good Bond girl."

She squealed as she entered the room. "As long as I don't get a name like Pussy Galore, I'd be down with playing side-kick to a hot secret agent."

I grabbed two Dom Perignon Brut Rose bottles and handed them to Damian. Then, after the door sealed behind us, we walked toward another hidden door at the back of the house.

"This place freaks me out," Alex whispered. "It's so fucking creepy."

"Don't worry." I hooked my arm around her, pressing her back into my chest. "I'll keep you safe, Pussy Galore."

She tilted her head back and chuckled. "If I were a Bond Girl, I'd go with Betty Boner."

"Speaking of boners," I whispered, rubbing her ass on my semi-hard cock.

Bastian flipped the bolts on the steel door, and Damian helped him slide the door to the left. The saltiness of the sea rolled through the cramped space. Alex gave me a worried look, then bent down, inching her way through the narrow channel.

My brothers went before me so I could lock the door behind us. Only the other four founding families of Devil's Creek knew about this entrance to our house. The catacombs linked my estate to Wellington Manor, Fort Marshall, the Cormac Compound, and the Battle Fortress. We only used the catacombs to reach each other's homes in emergencies.

The tunnel dumped us on the beach at the dead center of my property. Some nights, I stood out here to gain some clarity. Other nights, I washed the blood of my enemies into the bay.

The wind whipped through Alex's hair and blew it in her face. She groaned as she pulled the curls out of her mouth and shoved them behind her ears. Marcello shook out a blanket for her to sit on the sand. She plopped down between my brothers and patted the spot in front of her. My gaze flicked between Alex and the water.

"You look less serious when you're not wearing a suit," Alex commented. "But still ridiculously handsome. Get down here so we can get this party started."

"I'm not a man who takes orders."

She rolled her eyes and tapped the blanket with her palm. "Tonight, you do."

Because she had me under her fucking spell, I dropped to one knee in front of her. Damian passed a bottle of champagne to Marcello. They popped the corks, and Alex squealed at the popping sounds, still traumatized from the shooting.

We passed the bottles around, and I remembered Alex couldn't drink. So I downed half of it in one gulp and moved her between my legs.

"This is nice." Alex looked up at me. "I'm not used to this side of you."

"You said it best with your paintings." I drank from the bottle and placed it in the sand. "The Devil has many faces."

"I like this side to all of you." She smiled. "I'm getting ideas for more Devil-themed paintings."

"You can't deny how you feel about me. It's clear in your paintings."

"I called the first one The Devil I Hate." She rubbed her glossy lips together as she looked up at me. "That was the truth back then."

"And now?"

She shook her head. "I don't hate you."

"How about me?" Damian inched his hand up her thigh. "Do you still fear me?"

"No. But art tells the truth…"

"Even when people lie," Marcello finished for her, a direct quote from my mother and one of her most famous paintings.

"I'd like to start my work at the Franco Foundation. I scheduled a meeting with Madeline Laveau, and then Marcello got shot."

I sucked her earlobe into my mouth. "Consider it done. I'll summon her to the house. We can't risk letting you off the property to meet with her."

I threw the empty champagne bottle on the sand, then rubbed her shoulders.

Alex closed her eyes and moaned. "You have your moments, Luca. This is one of them."

After we finished the second bottle of champagne, Bastian laid down on the blanket and pulled Alex on top of him. I lifted my shirt over my head and dropped it onto the sand. Alex's eyes flicked up and down my chest, her tongue darting out to slide across her bottom lip.

"See something you like, baby girl?"

Alex laughed. "Who says I like you?"

"You've always run from me, but you can never hide. I know you inside and out."

She traced her fingers over the scars on my chest. Alex was the only woman I ever let touch me or my scars. Much like her, they were a part of me. A part I would never hide from her.

Her fingers glided over my shoulders, trailing down my back to the worst ones. When I was younger and displeased him, my father made me kneel in front of him with his belt wrapped around his fist. Sometimes he hit me to show me his power, his strength. To remind me that I belonged to him.

We all bore different scars, various reminders of the man who taught us the value of cruelty. How to wield it, how to use it as a weapon. I understood pain, punishment, and torture. Without those lessons, I would have become a different man.

Bastian gripped her hips and rubbed her pussy against his cock. "Fuck, Cherry. Just knowing there's a possibility you're having my baby is making me so fucking hard."

Her head tipped back, eyes closed as she moaned. "Bash," she whispered. "Mmm, don't tease me."

His laughter filled the air. "I'm only a tease if I don't let you ride my cock."

She giggled. "I guess this means I'll get to call one of you Daddy."

Bastian always brought out the playful side of her. With him, she looked so comfortable, like they had been dating for years. The same with Marcello. They had the most natural ease with her.

Bastian squeezed her ass. "You can call me whatever you want as long as you come on my cock."

She pushed up Bastian's shirt and planted kisses across his stomach, right above the waistband of his shorts.

"I prefer master." Damian moved behind her and pulled her tank top over her head. He bit her neck and cupped her big tits from behind. "Don't call me Daddy."

She turned to look at him and raised an eyebrow. "Master?"

"You're my pet." He left teeth marks down her neck and played with her nipples. "Are you not? Every pet has a master."

"Oh, God, Damian."

Damian's hand wrapped around her throat. He pinched her perfect pink nipples with his other hand, and she whimpered from his roughness. My brother was different with Alex. He was too afraid of scaring her away to show her all the darkness in his soul.

"Master," he corrected, then his teeth trailed down her neck again. "Say it, Pet."

Her big tits bounced as she moved on top of Bastian, who had his cock out of his shorts, grazing her wet slit. "Yes, Master."

He lifted her by her hips and shoved her onto Bastian's cock in one quick thrust. "Good girl."

She fucked my brother like she'd never get to ride his cock again. Damian teased her asshole with his finger as he bit her shoulder.

Alex screamed with each forceful thrust from Bastian, holding onto him as she would fall off his cock. He was like an animal tonight. It was as if a switch had flipped inside all of us after finding out she was pregnant. That completely changed the game.

Marcello still had to heal and wasn't as aggressive as usual. He watched our brothers dominate Alex. Kneeling on the blanket, he shoved his shorts down to his knees and stroked his cock.

I rose from the sand and stepped out of my shorts. Alex fisted the base of my cock and licked the tip. Damian straddled Bastian's legs and slapped her ass as she fucked our brother. Since we didn't have any lube, they took turns slamming their cocks into her tight pussy. If she were any other woman, they would have destroyed her.

That was what we all did.

We ruined things and broke them until they were useless and unrecognizable. Years ago, we tried to do it to Alex. Except she was more formidable than any of us had expected and so addicting.

That was the best word to describe how we all felt about her. We obsessed over her, addicted to her smell, her taste, even the sound of her voice. She consumed each of us in different ways.

Bastian came inside her first, cursing and grunting her name. She sucked on Damian's fingers as he slammed into her, the two of them molded to Bastian's chest. Her screams of pleasure filled the air like a sweet melody, and then Damian was right behind her, chasing his high.

After Damian pulled out of her, I bent down and offered her my hand. "Come on, baby girl. Let's get you cleaned up."

I'd wanted to take her into the bay. That was the plan before Bastian had to whip out his cock. He was like a teenage boy around Alex. No fucking self-control.

She slipped her fingers between mine, and I helped her up from the blanket. I glanced over at Marcello and tipped my head toward the bay. He stripped off his shorts and joined us by the shore. We stood there for a moment, the water splashing our ankles, and just looked at the moonlight. We had the best view of Devil's Creek, right at the center of the town.

Alex took my hand and reached over for Marcello. The sand and shells crunched beneath our feet as we waded through the waist-deep water. It was high tide, so it was not the best time to swim. But I didn't plan to take her far, just enough to wash my brother's cum off her.

I lifted her in my arms, and she squeezed her legs around my back. Marcello brushed her frizzy curls off her shoulder and kissed her neck, right over the bite marks from Damian. She rubbed her clit on the tip of my cock and moaned.

"You have no self-control, woman. Haven't I taught you anything?"

"I want to feel every inch of you inside me." Her lips brushed mine. "Fuck me, Luca. Make me come."

I swept the pad of my thumb across her lips. "I'm a patient man and have learned to control my desires."

"Well, I'm not patient." She dug her nails into my neck and sucked my lip into her mouth. "I want you."

I gripped her hips and lowered her onto my cock, filling her in one quick thrust. She let out a moan that matched the groan that escaped my throat. I ripped even more sounds from her beautiful lips as I bounced her up and down on my cock.

"Scream for me, baby," I said against her lips as we found the perfect rhythm.

Her tongue swept into my mouth, tangling with mine, and a wave of emotions rocked through me. That happened with her every time.

She humanized me.

Alex scratched her fingernails down my back, etching herself into my skin. She looked beautiful and uninhibited, free in my arms. I was an evil man who did terrible things, but she trusted me. She knew I would never hurt her. This was her safe place, where she could relax and lower her guard.

Her orgasm shook through me, hitting her hard and fast. Out of breath, she pressed her lips to mine. She felt so damn good that I thrust into her a few more times before I came inside her. I kissed her jaw and neck, leaving no part of her untouched.

Her gaze swept over to Marcello, who had been so quiet, so patient for his turn with our queen. That was his strength. Marcello was level-headed, controlled, and not one to make waves.

I slid her off me and handed her to Marcello. She

wrapped herself around him like a koala hanging on its mother. He made no move to fuck her, wincing in pain as he shifted her weight.

Was he still too weak after the shooting to resume his normal activities? He hadn't asked to return to work and didn't fight Alex when she insisted he stay in bed.

Built like a tank, Marcello was durable, strong, and reliable. But he must have still been in a lot of pain. I hadn't asked him about his progress because I was mad at him and Alex for a while afterward. I hadn't even bothered to visit him.

I took her from his arms and carried her back to the beach. Marcello sat on the blanket next to Bastian and Damian. They were still naked and staring at our queen like fresh meat introduced at the slaughter. I lowered Alex on top of Marcello so he didn't have to hold her up, and then I moved behind her.

I sucked on her earlobe and gave her ass a light spanking. "Sit on my brother's cock, baby girl."

She did as I instructed and lifted her hips to push Marcello inside her pussy. I gripped her thighs from behind, taking a second to appreciate each of her delicious curves.

"Play with your pussy," I ordered.

She rubbed her thumb over her clit like a good girl, moaning as Marcello filled her to the hilt. As I licked and nipped at her neck, she moaned our names.

"Fuck, princess." Marcello gripped her hips and slammed into her, taking her with force. "You feel so good."

Each time he raised his hips to meet hers, he closed his eyes, but Alex didn't notice. She was too busy tilting her head up to the sky and singing his praise.

I slid my fingers across her lips, and she sucked them into her mouth. Her body tightened around Marcello's cock, her thighs trembling as he fucked her. After they both came, she collapsed on top of Marcello and attempted to catch her breath.

"Damn, princess." He shoved his hands through her messy hair, his cock still inside her. "I came so fucking hard I can't see straight."

After Alex slid off him, she flipped onto her back. Damian rolled onto his side next to Bastian. I made room for myself between her spread legs and massaged her clit. She moaned as our cum dripped out of her and onto the blanket.

I couldn't wait to find out which of us was the father of her child. Even though I wasn't so sure I was ready for parenthood, I wanted it to be mine.

"I know you keep secrets from me because you think you're protecting me." Her eyes flicked between us. "Just tell me one thing. Is this the calm before the storm?"

I kissed her inner thigh and lifted her leg over my shoulder. "Yeah, baby. Don't get too comfortable. Hell is about to rain down on us."

Chapter Forty-Two

ALEX

W e stayed on the beach for hours, well past midnight, breaking Bastian and Damian's rules. However, they made an exception for tonight since it was a special occasion.

How often do you find out you're pregnant and have four men propose to you?

Marcello held my hand from the beach to the dark tunnel that led to the steel door hidden beneath the estate. This house was so bizarre. Secret passages and catacombs connected to each of the mansions owned by the founding families of Devil's Creek. My grandfather hadn't shared this secret with me. All the other founders' children knew except for me.

No matter where the Salvatores went, they always seemed to have an escape route. A master plan.

My life had been in danger from the moment I stepped foot onto this estate. What kind of future would a child have with me for a mother and four dangerous men as their father?

Luca opened the steel door with a key, and then Marcello tapped my backside to move me into the dimly lit space. He seemed a little off tonight like he was doing his best to act normal in front of us. But, of course, Luca noticed and took the lead.

I thought it was strange that he was doing things for Marcello. Like lifting me on top of him, helping me fuck his brother. Not that it was entirely out of the ordinary. Luca was always in charge of every situation.

Still, I hoped Marcello was okay and that he wasn't putting on a brave face for me. I didn't want him rushing his recovery.

"I have to stop by the vault," Luca announced as he led the pack down the long, narrow channel lit by sconces built into the wall. "Marcello, come with me. Bash, Damian, take Alex upstairs."

I moved beside him, even though we barely had enough space. "What's in the vault?"

"Lots of things." He flashed a devious grin. "Stolen artwork, jewels, money… If it has any value to my family, it's in the vault."

"What are you getting out of it?"

His blue eyes met mine for a moment. "Something for you. And before you ask, it's a surprise."

He stopped a few feet from the staircase that led to the library and gripped my hip, pulling me closer. "I'll be up soon, baby girl." Luca kissed my lips, a peck that left me wanting more. "Go take a bath and get ready for bed."

Bastian's hand wrapped around my bicep. "C'mon, Cherry. It's past your bedtime."

Before he pulled me upstairs, I stood on my tippy toes and kissed Marcello. It was quick but still left me breathless.

"Come to my room when you're finished."

He nodded, a smile stretching the corners of his mouth before he followed Luca toward the vault. Damian took the stairs to my right and halted a few steps before the top landing. I crashed into his back and nearly fell backward. If

Bastian hadn't been there to scoop me into his arms, I would have fallen on my ass.

"What the fuck, D?" Bastian growled. "Are you trying to kill her?"

"The door is open." Damian angled his body to look down at Bastian. "I thought Luca locked it."

"He usually does." Worry furrowed his brows as he fished his cell phone from his pocket. "Go ahead. I'm calling Luca."

Proceeding with caution, Damian pushed open the door that was ajar. I was positive Luca locked the door behind him. He was so meticulous and planned everything down to the smallest detail.

"They don't get cell service in the vault," Bastian groaned.

He reached for the gun tucked into his back pocket. Damian stepped into the library, and that was when I noticed he also had a gun in his hand. Nerves stirred in my belly, tearing up my insides. My heart raced so fast that it felt like it would explode.

"Clear," Damian said.

I let out a sigh of relief.

Bastian ushered me into the library with his hand on my shoulder. Satisfied there wasn't a threat, he released his hold on me. His eyes roamed around the space, and I did the same. The room was beautiful, unlike any library I had ever seen.

I walked around the room, entranced by the sheer volume of books that reached the ceiling. This place was a dream, like something from a movie. I stopped in front of the bookcase closest to the windows that overlooked the backyard.

Waves crashed against the shore, the moonlight illuminating the beach. It was peaceful, perfect in every way. This place was so enchanting. I often forgot about the beauty of Devil's Creek with all the bad memories that surrounded this place. For a long time, it was my worst nightmare. But over the past few months, I fell in love with this town and my men.

The floorboards creaked behind me.

"What the…?" Damian's words cut off before he could finish his thought.

I spun around as he hit the floor with a thud. It all happened so quickly that my brain couldn't process anything. Frozen in place, I watched Bastian raise his gun in the air. Someone knocked it out of his hand from behind, and then he was thrown backward, his head hitting the floor.

I screamed. And then something stabbed the right side of my neck.

In the corner of the room, someone stepped out of the shadows. A familiar face burned into my brain so vividly that I would never forget it. My vision blurred from the drug working its way through my bloodstream. Maybe it was an illusion, a trick of the mind.

"Hello, darling." She twirled her finger around her long, blonde curl and smiled, her lips tinted with the same shade of red she'd worn for most of my life. "Did you miss me?"

"How?" I muttered, blinking in disbelief at the last person on earth I expected to see in this town.

"It's not how you should be asking." She grinned so widely it touched her blue eyes. "It's why."

My legs wobbled, and as I was about to hit the ground, everything went black.

The Frost Society

You have been chosen to join an elite secret society for readers who love dark romance books.

When you join The Frost Society, you will get instant access to all of my novels, bonus scenes, and digital content like new-release eBooks and serialized stories. You can also get discounts for my book and merch shop, exclusive book boxes, and so much more.

Join the Society

The Frost Society

Welcome to The Frost Society!

You have been chosen to join an elite secret society for readers who love dark romance books.

When you join The Frost Society, you will get instant access to all of my novels, bonus scenes, and digital content like new-release eBooks and serialized stories. You can also get discounts for my book and merch shop, exclusive book boxes, and so much more.

Learn more at JillianFrost.com

Also by Jillian Frost

Princes of Devil's Creek

Cruel Princes

Vicious Queen

Savage Knights

Battle King

Read the series

Boardwalk Mafia

Boardwalk Kings

Boardwalk Queen

Boardwalk Reign

Read the series

Devil's Creek Standalone Novels

The Darkest Prince

Wicked Union

Read the books

For a complete list of books, visit JillianFrost.com.

About the Author

Jillian Frost is a dark romance author who believes even the villain deserves a happily ever after. When she's not plotting all the ways to disrupt the lives of her characters, you can usually find Jillian by the pool, soaking up the Florida sunshine.

Learn more about Jillian's books at JillianFrost.com